D1236726

The Art
OF KEEPING SECRETS

**Center Point
Large Print**

**This Large Print Book carries the
Seal of Approval of N.A.V.H.**

The Art
OF KEEPING SECRETS

PATTI CALLAHAN HENRY

CENTER POINT PUBLISHING
THORNDIKE, MAINE

This Center Point Large Print edition
is published in the year 2008 by arrangement with
New American Library, a member of Penguin Group (USA) Inc.

The text of this Large Print edition is unabridged. In other
aspects, this book may vary from the original edition.
Printed in the United States of America.
Set in 16-point Times New Roman type.

ISBN: 978-1-60285-258-7 ✔

Library of Congress Cataloging-in-Publication Data

Henry, Patti Callahan.
    The art of keeping secrets / Patti Callahan Henry.--Center Point large print ed.
    p. cm.
    ISBN: 978-1-60285-258-7 (lib. bdg. : alk. paper)
    1. Large type books. I. Title.

PS3608.E578A89 2008b
813'.6--dc22

2008013098

To Anna Henry,
in celebration of her courage and love of life

ACKNOWLEDGMENTS

I am astounded that I'm writing the acknowledgment pages for my fifth novel. Although some names appear in each book, my gratitude to these people continues to increase immeasurably. The relationships that surround and nurture me make it possible for me to continue to write. My heart is full of thanks for the following people:

—To my husband, Patrick T. Henry, who loves me even when I emerge bleary-eyed from my writing office, having forgotten to cook dinner.

—To my children, Meagan, Thomas and Rusk, who open my heart to the beauty of life.

—To my agent, Kimberly Whalen, who was integral in the plotting of and motivation for this novel. I am more grateful for her entry into my life than I can say.

—To my editor, Ellen Edwards, who created a cleaner and more lucid story than I actually wrote. Her patience and eye for detail are unsurpassed. And many thanks to Becky Vinter for her invaluable assistance.

—To the extraordinary people at New American Library—especially Kara Welsh and Claire Zion—who work so hard to get my work out to the readers.

To the sales force on the road, who make sure the booksellers know about us. To the art department, who labor to find the perfect cover for each novel.

—To all of my family for living with and loving me even when I'm under deadline and forget to call you back; for going to more book events than anyone should ever be forced to attend—George and Bonnie Callahan, Barbi and Dan Burris, Jeannie and Mike Cunnion, Chuck and Gwen Henry, Kirk and Anna Henry, and Mike and Serena Henry. I love you all.

—To Andrew Read, Associate Professor and Rachel Carson Chair of Marine Conservation Biology at the Duke University Marine Laboratory in Beaufort, North Carolina, who conducts groundbreaking research in the conservation of marine life. For more information go to www.marineconservation.duke.edu. I thank him for allowing me to interrogate him about dolphin and whale research in the Outer Banks. His work, and that of others in his field, will save hundreds of thousands of marine mammals.

—To the booksellers who welcomed me with open arms during book tours. You made every city worth the trip. To the booksellers who spread the news about my novels—I can never find adequate words to thank you. Your love of books is an inspiration.

—To the readers and book clubs who e-mail me, show

up at book events, talk about the books and make the extra effort to visit me on the road.

—To my tribe of writing friends, who enrich not only my writing, but also my life. You remind me why I write, and why story is powerful. You hold me up when I'm falling and you make me continue when I want to quit.

—To Anne Rivers Siddons, for her rare and extraordinary gift of storytelling and her generous heart. Unbeknownst to Anne, her stories have carried me through many hard times, and now her words about my writing fill me with humility and gratitude.

—To Marjory Wentworth, South Carolina poet laureate, whose poetry inspires me to become a better writer. I'm honored to have your work in my last novel; I'm honored to call you friend.

—To my dearest friends—you know who you are—who listen to me, hang out with me, buy me wine, watch my kids, send me words of encouragement and make me laugh. I love you deeply.

—In the beginning, there was the Word (John 1:1). My eternal thanks to God for offering the gift of writing, story and the Word.

To the dolphin alone nature has given that which the best philosophers seek: friendship for no advantage.

—Plutarch

ONE

ANNABELLE MURPHY

*T*he horizon became Annabelle Murphy's touchstone, her confirmation of love and her memorial to joy. When her husband, Knox, had first died, she'd wished she could disappear into that place of marked beauty. Later, she'd believed she could find comfort and meaning where the earth met the sky, where she imagined Knox's plane had vanished.

Knox had been gone for two years now, but as the sailboat sliced through twilight-tinted water, she found herself once again staring into the horizon, his name unspoken on her lips. Blessedly, she was surrounded by the best kind of friends, those she'd loved the longest, with whom she'd shared the most tender moments of loss and joy: Cooper and Christine, who had been married since the year they graduated from college; Mae and Frank, who had been together since he'd moved to Marsh Cove in tenth grade; and Shawn, whose sailboat this was.

There had once been eight of them, but Shawn had lost his wife, Maria, to divorce and Annabelle had lost Knox to death. When the thirty-foot sloop moved through the water, Annabelle felt Knox as surely as if he were poking his head around the mast and asking her if she'd like another glass of wine. Death had taken the man, but never her love for him.

As the boat reached the mouth of the harbor, Shawn at the wheel hollered across to Cooper, "Why don't you throw out the anchor and we'll hang here until sunset?"

Annabelle stepped back from the railing to allow Cooper to grab the anchor. She reached into the cooler, pulled a beer from the ice and threw it to Shawn. He caught the can and mouthed, *Thank you.* Annabelle often marveled at the fact that of them all Shawn was the least changed in appearance, yet the most transformed in his approach to life. He had been the wild one, the winner of the most detentions and voted most athletic all four years of high school. Now he worked for an insurance company, although he did keep his sailboat and escaped as often as possible to the water he loved.

Only Shawn's blond curls remained as unruly as his behavior had once been. He'd been Knox's very best friend, but hers first. He'd defended her on the playground, told her lunch was stuck between her teeth; he'd treated her like a regular person even though she was a girl. When Knox had moved to Marsh Cove, he'd stolen Shawn from Annabelle. She'd threatened to beat up Knox under the monkey bars, but Shawn had diplomatically assured them that they could all be friends, and he'd been right.

This group had remained woven together with the threads of childhood, adolescence, marriage, parenthood, divorce and death. Now they kept the fabric strong with once-a-month dinner parties in one another's homes. When it was Shawn's turn, he always offered a sunset cruise and a cookout at the dock upon return. Annabelle would never let slip that this was her favorite way to get together. She wouldn't want to hurt Mae's or Christine's feelings, as they always made a large production of the parties.

Cooper startled Annabelle as he came up behind her, pressed his hand to her back. "You okay? You look a million miles away."

"I'm great. Look at this night—it's magic."

"Yes," he said, "it is."

Annabelle tore her vision from the horizon to look at Cooper. "I swear, on nights like this, I think he's going to pop up from below deck with a tray of his famous crab cakes and tell us all a very bad joke."

Cooper leaned down and kissed the top of Annabelle's head, and she reached up to grab Cooper's hand.

Mae's laughter rang out, abrupt and crisp; Cooper and Annabelle turned to see her try to drag Frank back as he walked toward the bow and spread his arms. "No way," Mae hollered. "Old man, get away from the front of the boat."

Frank lifted his wineglass. "Who you calling an old man?"

Annabelle jumped back when Frank went up on the bow, handed Mae his wineglass.

"Go ahead," Shawn hollered. "You don't have it in you anymore, do you?"

Annabelle laughed. This was a regular and dogged

fight—who would resume the night swims of their youth? Now that they were all in their forties, there was much threatening, but no one had jumped in years.

A Knox-shaped emptiness overcame Annabelle, an intense longing followed by the impulse to be in the water, nearer the horizon. She stepped past Cooper, tapped Frank on the shoulder and motioned for him to move aside. He laughed. "You're kidding, right?"

"Out of my way," she said with a grin. "Girls first." She climbed over the railing to the tip of the boat. She spread her arms wide as she'd done in their younger days, when the eight of them ate, drank and loved one another without the memory of loss. Why had they stopped diving into the water? Why had Knox died? Why had Maria left Shawn? Why did life move on without the permission of those it carried in its current?

Annabelle stood on her tiptoes and felt her pale blue skirt billow upward as she executed a sleek dive, and entered the water with a splash. Silken warmth surrounded her as she closed her eyes and let herself sink. She remained still for a brief moment before opening her eyes under the water, where the setting sun no longer sent light. Pure darkness surrounded her, yet the laughter above reached her ears.

She rose above the surface, smoothed back her hair. Shawn leaned over the railing. "You are insane, Annabelle Murphy."

"You don't have it in you anymore, do you?" She pushed her palm against the sea to send a spray of water toward Shawn. She treaded water in a memory of her stronger swimming days. Her skirt tangled around her legs and she grabbed the anchor line; her white linen shirt clung to her skin and her hair curled around her face.

"Who you talking to?" Shawn laughed, yanked off his shirt and jumped over the railing in his khaki shorts. The water remained dark and warm around Annabelle. Shawn rose beside her as Cooper, too, jumped in, and Frank did a lopsided flip from the bow. In the encroaching night, their laughter traveled across the water, across time and space, until Annabelle half-believed Knox was with them.

Christine dropped the ladder over the side of the boat, shone a flashlight toward the four of them. "There is absolutely no way I am jumping into that dark water. There is something wrong with all of you. Now get out of there. I'm starving and the crabs are going bad back at the dock."

Mae joined Christine, sat down and dangled her legs over the side. "If I hadn't just paid for these brand-new capris . . ."

Annabelle bunched her skirt into her left hand and swam toward the ladder, inhaled with long, deep breaths and remembered a time, long ago, when she and Knox took his Sunfish out into the bay and accidentally tipped it over. They'd held on to the upside down boat, enjoying the touch of their legs floating in the water below them, brushing up against each other. She doubted she would ever find a moment that didn't bring Knox to mind and heart. Even now she could barely swim five feet without thinking of him. No matter how or where she redirected her attention, Knox was there.

They clambered back aboard, raised anchor and passed towels around. They laughed, held up wine-glasses and toasted to friendship. Shawn navigated toward the dock as they asked for updates on one another's children and jobs. They teased Mae and Frank about having named their only child Thornton, the most "country club" name possible, and now he was off in Africa doing mission work.

They agreed with Cooper and Christine that having kids in high school involved a constant battle of wills. Shawn stood at the wheel and laughed at their stories without contributing his own, since he'd never had children. His wife had left him in their second year of marriage, and he'd never remarried, despite his best friends' many efforts to set him up. "How's Jake doing at UNC?" he asked Annabelle. "Is he hanging in there?"

She nodded. "He seems to be doing great. I miss him insanely. The house echoes like an empty cave without him and his music. But he calls every day. He doesn't like his roommate, but he has so many friends I don't think it matters. Classes are kicking his butt. I think he wishes he'd backed off on the advanced courses."

Cooper shuffled his feet. "If he needs . . . anything, you know I can help."

"We all can," Shawn said.

"He's fine," Annabelle said. "Really fine. Keeley is the one who's killing me right now, with her cocky attitude and newly acquired driver's license."

"There's no worse combination," Christine agreed. "It's like that 'hunch punch' y'all made in college—remember? You guys threw anything you could think of in a trash can and then added grain alcohol."

A collective groan came from everyone.

Christine laughed. "The same dangerous combination as a sixteen-year-old girl going through adolescence and driving a car. We just pray they don't do anything truly stupid."

Shawn adjusted the direction of the boat. "Wow, you're really making me wish I had teenagers." He smiled, and then hollered at Cooper, "Grab the bowline, will you?"

Once they'd piled out of the boat and settled onto the dock for fresh crab, the familiar motions, words and feelings of friendship surrounded Annabelle. Shawn stepped up behind her. "I'm glad you came. For a while there I thought you'd never come back out on the boat."

"Me, too," Annabelle said, touched Shawn's arm. She spent the rest of the evening grateful for what remained constant: her love for her friends and her children.

Spring had settled quietly into the Lowcountry, bringing soft breezes and a green haze. A shower had passed through earlier that morning, but now sunlight sifted between the leaves and fell onto a lawn sparkling with raindrops, onto pavement varnished by rainwater. From the front porch of Annabelle's home—her and Knox's home—on Main Street, Marsh Cove, South Carolina, she could see across the street to the park that bordered Marsh Cove Bay, running wild and full as the tide rushed in.

A large magnolia tree stood in the side yard, its thick roots pushing up the earth in all directions and sprouting offshoots that had long since merged with the original tree. Annabelle suspected that by now the smaller trees actually supported the main, ancient trunk, that without them the entire tree would topple.

Annabelle's son, Jake, who loved myths and legends, had once told her about Tristan and Isolde, ill-fated Irish lovers from whose graves, side by side, there rose two willows that over the years grew together as one. The story made Annabelle think of her own family, her and Knox, their son, Jake, and their daughter, Keeley, all entwined. When the tree expert came and told her that the main tree was being strangled and would need to be cut down, Belle told him to take his chainsaw and his expert advice and climb right back into his dented truck and go home. She knew the magnolia tree and its offshoots would support each other until they all fell together.

Even now, with Knox gone, Annabelle still believed that.

She balanced her laptop on her knees, her feet propped up on the wicker ottoman. She fingered the keys, lifted her face to a shaft of sunlight and closed her eyes, allowing the warmth to wash over her. She needed to find an answer to the bridesmaid question in her advice column, "Southern Belle Says."

Dear Southern Belle,

I have been in thirteen weddings and now I'm getting married. Do I need to ask all thirteen of these girls to be in my wedding? I only want two of them, but don't want to lose friends and make them all mad at me.

Confused in Corinth

Annabelle wanted to tell Confused in Corinth that it really didn't matter who was in the wedding—all that mattered was whom she was marrying and if she loved him. But that wasn't what old Mrs. Thurgood, the *Marsh Cove Gazette* publisher, wanted for this column—no, Annabelle needed to give the precisely correct etiquette.

The Emily Post book lay on the wicker table at her side, but Annabelle liked to answer the question before comparing it to her ultimate source. In the past year or so, her advice hadn't differed once.

Dear Confused in Corinth,

Click, click, her tongue went on the top of her mouth while she thought. She watched the leftover rain clouds move from left to right, clearing the way for a long-distance view of a sailboat headed south, only its sail visible against the pale blue sky. She smiled at the memory of the previous night and her swim with old friends.

A movement at the corner of the house caught Annabelle's eye, and she turned to see a man standing near the bottom step of the porch. His hands were in his pockets, and he leaned back on his heels, watching her. She stood so quickly she almost dropped her laptop, but she grabbed it in time, snapped it shut, placed it on the side table.

"May I help you?" she asked. Often tourists thought her home was on the historical tour, and she had to tell them it was a private residence. Then she smiled: the man was Wade Gunther, the local sheriff. Just as abruptly her smile faded with a razor-edged thought, *Not Jake . . .*

"Hey, Annabelle," he said, took one step onto the stairs.

"Is something wrong?" she asked, digging around in her mind for a reason, any reason, why Wade would visit her. Nausea rose as she attempted with no success to force down the memory of the last time she had said those words to a man in uniform.

He cleared his throat. "I need to talk to you, and I thought it would be best in person." He pinched his lips together, and Annabelle knew this was not a facial expression one made when delivering good news. He continued. "Some mountain climbers in western Colorado were lost for a few days . . . freak snowstorm. Anyway, they were experienced outdoorsmen and survived just fine. . . ."

Thank God it had nothing to do with Jake, but Annabelle couldn't wrap her mind around any other cause; Keeley was in the house doing her homework. . . . "And?"

"They stumbled across the wreckage of a plane . . . a small plane that had been consumed by fire. . . ."

Annabelle's knees gave way beneath her, and she sat in a childlike cross-legged pose on the white-painted floorboards, looked up at Wade and attempted to speak. Nothing came out.

He took three steps up onto the porch and squatted next to her. "The FAA—the Federal Aviation Administration—contacted me and asked me to come talk to you. I know this must be a shock. I'm sorry to tell you so bluntly. I just never know how else to say it."

"It's him," Annabelle said. "Knox, right?" And some seed of hope she hadn't known existed sprouted anew; maybe, just maybe he was alive. Maybe.

"Yes, we found his body . . . and whomever he was traveling with," Wade said.

"Oh, oh, then it's not him." Annabelle stood and Wade rose with her. "He was traveling alone to go hunting."

Wade looked up at the porch ceiling, as if the sight could help him. "There was . . . another person inside the burned-out plane. As you'd guess, there's not much left after a gutting fire and two years in the woods. But it is Knox's plane."

Her question rose of its own accord, like a shoot of grass through a cracked sidewalk. "Man or woman?" she asked, believing she knew the answer before it came.

"A woman." He paced the porch. "The FAA is hoping you can tell them who it is. . . ."

A tempest of warring emotions battled inside Annabelle, and stunning to her, embarrassment won. Not grief or anger, but shame. Her dead husband caught with another woman. For the briefest moment she imagined she could hear the gossip and speculation.

Annabelle bit her lower lip and spoke in a stuttered sentence. "I don't know." Simple words. "I thought he was alone." Embarrassing words.

Wade turned away.

Annabelle sat down on a wicker divan and pointed to the chair across from her. "Please, sit. I don't want us to go inside—I don't want Keeley to hear any of this."

"I understand," he said, and sat.

"Now," she said, "what will you need from me?"

"We have to discuss where to send his remains. . . . The FAA will need to know." His voice droned on and Annabelle pretended to listen, but her mind spun. She pictured her thoughts like cotton candy whirling around inside the machine, waiting to be gathered around a single cardboard cone.

She remembered the day they'd come to tell her about the crash—how even then they'd known there was no chance of survival. That time after Knox's death rushed in again all the way to her core; the places she had thought healed after years of therapy and grieving were now open. She remembered how she couldn't feel things, as if the world had lost all sensory meaning in the weeks and even months after the news. Now, as she stared at Wade, she saw her spirit broken, grief coming again in a way she'd hoped it never would.

And she understood: you can never completely heal. You can ignore, cover up, scar over, but never heal, because if she had been cured of this grief, it wouldn't return now with its grappling need to take her to that dark place again, that space where she wanted to disappear into the horizon and meet Knox.

She often imagined that the horizon was the last thing he saw on that plane. She saw him trying to restrain the fuselage, wrestling with the knobs and buttons, fighting to right the nose, then losing control.

Now her imaginings of his last minutes changed completely, from solo to two. Not a huge difference, but one that was as wide and deep as infinity—a number too large to count.

"Belle?" Wade said, leaned forward.

"Yes?" Annabelle asked.

"Did you hear any of what I just said?"

"I think so," she answered, trying to focus on his face, on the lines around his mouth, on the blue of his eyes, anything but his words.

"Well . . ." He stood, looked down at her. "I am very

sorry for your loss. We'll be in touch about . . . the remains, and if you . . ."

Annabelle squinted up at him. "If I what?"

"If you know who was on the plane, call me. For now, they will just have to search the missing-person files, and eventually try to match dental records and DNA. So, if you have any more information about who it was, it would help tremendously."

Annabelle felt the familiar blanket of hopelessness spread over her as it had when they'd asked her a million questions after the initial accident. She smiled up at him. "Well, I'll certainly ask around to see if anyone knows whom my husband might have snuck away with on that particular weekend."

He stared at her, and then looked away. "Thank you."

Then he was gone down the stairs. Annabelle watched him until he rounded the corner to the public parking lot next to Marsh Cove Bay. She sat down.

Wade couldn't have been on her porch for more than ten minutes. Fifteen at the most. And yet everything, absolutely everything had been altered. The air shifted, lifted the hanging ferns and swirled leaves across the bottom porch steps. She understood that at that moment she couldn't comprehend or absorb all that was different.

A thought came in a dull throb like a headache: *Isn't that curious? A woman in Knox's plane.*

Annabelle had never wanted to contemplate the facts of Knox's plane crash again. She had spent too many nights going over and over every *What if?*, searching for the impossible: a way to change the end of the story.

Now her mind raced through the details one more time: he had filed a flight plan to stop in Newboro, North Carolina, refueled and flown straight toward Durango, Colorado. Fifty miles from Durango he called in a mayday message that his engine was on fire. An explosion was heard on the radio. The story made national news for a full twenty-four hours as they searched for the plane and its sole occupant, Knox Murphy, the lawyer from South Carolina who often traveled to do pro bono work for underprivileged clients in small Carolina towns. Annabelle had watched the news with the detachment of a numb observer. And then the story had disappeared from the national news. But not from their lives.

People from the U.S. Air Force Rescue Coordination Center explained that there were well over 150 missing planes in that remote and inaccessible area of the country. They often found planes years later while searching for something or someone else. They kept a registry of wreck sites and would add Knox's. But the plane hadn't been found . . . until now.

She'd answered so many questions at that time. Did he help a client in Newboro? No, she'd told them. He always told her when he was doing work on the way to another location. Had he taken any explosives with him? No, only his guns, which he never brought loaded inside a plane.

Annabelle stood on the porch and dropped her forehead onto the closed screen door. "Oh, Knox. No, please, no." She wasn't sure what she was begging for, but she understood, the same way she had understood she was pregnant before the test showed positive, that something new had just been born with this discovery brought to her on a quiet afternoon.

She stepped back, knocked her hip against the Emily Post book, lifted it and tossed it onto the chair. What was the proper etiquette here? What would Emily Post say now? Maybe in that book of perfect behavior, there were answers to cheating husbands, but what did one do when the culprits were found together long after the fact—dead and gone? Irrational laughter at the situation—that she made a profession of giving advice and now had none for herself—began low in her belly and died before it reached her mouth. She dropped into the chair.

Nothing, at that moment and for a long time afterward, seemed as important as finding out who this woman was and why she was with Knox Murphy when he died.

Two

ANNABELLE MURPHY

*A*nnabelle paced the porch. A list, she needed to make a list of the things to do next, and then next, and then next. If she was going to keep this life intact, keep her world from spinning completely and utterly out of orbit, she needed to pull her mind together. There were so many people to tell about the discovery of the plane and . . . the woman. The need for action in the face of numbing grief was a nightmare returned. She'd once made numerous calls about Knox and his death: to her mother, his parents in Florida, Aunt Barbara, the cousins . . . and now she would have to do it again. Thank God her father, who had passed away years ago, had never had to hear about Knox's death.

The overwhelming need to hide returned to Annabelle as it had two years ago. Back then, she'd drawn on the strength of her family, on her love for Knox and his for her. What did she have to draw on now?

Names came to mind, one by one.

Keeley.

She was inside doing a school science project with Laura—Annabelle would have to wait until Laura left to talk to Keeley.

Jake.

Annabelle grabbed her cell phone from the side

table, and punched in her son's phone number. The double beep let her know he was on the other line.

Shawn.

He answered on the first ring. "Hey, Belle."

She didn't answer, coughed on a suppressed sob.

"You all right?" His voice came quickly over the line.

"No," she said.

"You sick?" he asked.

"No . . ."

"I'll be there in a minute. . . ."

"No, that's not why I called. . . ."

He'd already hung up. Shawn's office was around the corner, and she knew he'd be on her doorstep, as he'd been for every crisis since Knox had died, in less than ten minutes. She dropped into a chair and waited.

His car pulled up in front of the house. Shawn took the porch stairs two at a time and sat down next to Annabelle. He reached over, tucked her hair behind her ear, a movement of such familiarity and kindness that tears rose in her eyes. He'd known her since she was four years old. They had fought over toys in the sandbox, then over whose turn it was to drive, then over boys he thought were wrong for her.

"What is it, Belle?"

"It's Knox," she mumbled, and then looked at him. "If there was ever anytime in my life when I'd needed you to tell me the truth, it would be right now."

"I've never lied to you, Belle."

"Just be completely honest," she said.

"Damn, what is it?"

"Was Knox cheating on me?" She leaned back so she could see his face.

He furrowed his brow. "Hell, no. What are you talking about? What's gotten into your head?"

Annabelle dropped her face into her hands. "They found him, Shawn. They found his plane."

"Oh, Belle. Oh . . ."

"I'm not done," she said.

"What do you mean?"

She peeked at him through her fingers. "He was with a woman."

He lifted her chin, stared at her, put his hands on either side of her cheeks. "No, he was going hunting alone."

Annabelle shook her head to free his hands. "No, Wade came today—they found his plane and there was a woman on it. They don't know who she was, and both bodies were burned so badly they can't identify anything at all."

"Who found the plane?"

"Some hiking expedition got lost in a freak snowstorm. Isn't that kind of . . . weird? Someone else had to get lost for him to be found?"

Shawn nodded. "It does sound ironic."

"Well, whatever it is, they found him, his plane, all burned. And a woman."

"They're sure?"

"Shawn . . . I think they'd be sure of another body."

"I can't imagine who it could possibly be."

Annabelle leaned closer to see his face, and she glimpsed the same confusion and hurt she herself felt.

"I believe you," she said. "But that leaves me with questions. Who the hell was she? Why was she there?"

"For now . . . just for now, let's not say anything. Let's try and figure this out."

"But I have to ask our friends. I just do. What if one of them knows?"

"If you don't know, and I don't know—they definitely don't."

"Shawn, on any other day, at any other time, I would agree with you. But when Wade Gunther walked up on my porch this afternoon and informed me that my husband was found dead with another woman—all of my assumptions were shattered. All of them. Someone knows who she was. And it's not me. And it's not you. Who says it's not one of them?"

"You say 'one of them' like they're strangers. We've known those people our entire lives. They wouldn't, they couldn't hide something like this."

"I have no idea what anyone is capable of anymore."

"We never do," he said, sat back in his chair.

Keeley opened the front door, poked her head out. "I thought I heard your voice," she said to Shawn. She stood in the doorway and leaned against the frame. Her dark curls fell past her shoulders in a poignant reminder of the way her dad's dark hair had fallen across his forehead. Annabelle's stomach rolled, threatened to rise, then settled again, but left her with numb hands, tingling arms.

"Hey, Keeley," Shawn said as he stood and hugged her.

Annabelle wiped at her face as if to remove remnants of emotion her daughter might see and take into herself. Keeley stood in front of Annabelle and Shawn. "I called Jake to make sure he was okay. . . . I saw Sheriff Gunther here and I thought maybe something was wrong . . . with Jake," she said.

Annabelle looked up at her daughter. "Oh, that was you on the other line. . . ."

"What?" Keeley's eyebrows dropped into a V of confusion.

"I tried to call him . . . ," Annabelle said. She stood and grabbed her cell phone, touched Shawn's shoulder. "I didn't mean to make you leave work. I'll call you later. . . ."

He threw his keys in the air, and Keeley stuck her palm above his and grabbed them. Her laughter momentarily lifted Annabelle's heart.

Keeley dangled the keys from her fingers. "I now have the convertible's keys."

Shawn laughed. "Still not letting you drive it, Keeley. You've got six more months to prove you can drive that Volvo without a single dent, a single ticket. . . . Then you'll get your chance."

"Come on, Mr. Shawn. One time?"

"Nope." He tousled her hair. "What kind of friend would I be if I went back on my word?" Shawn glanced at Annabelle. "Call me later. . . ."

Annabelle nodded, touched Keeley's arm. "Where's

Laura? Are y'all done with your science project?"

"She left about a half hour ago—when you were talking to Sheriff Gunther."

Shawn had reached his car; Annabelle waved goodbye and then turned to her daughter. "Sit down, Keeley."

They both sat down. "Sheriff Gunther was here to tell me some news. They've found Dad's plane."

"They found Dad?"

"They found his body, Keeley."

Keeley's eyes filled immediately; tears overflowed onto her cheeks. Annabelle saw that this news killed any nearly impossible wish in Keeley that her dad was still alive. "So, he's really dead." Keeley wiped furiously at the tears. "Dead."

"Oh, Keeley." Annabelle held out her arms. "There's more. I don't want you to hear it on the news, or from other people, but there was another person on the plane with Dad."

Keeley threw her hands in front of herself like a shield. "Who was it?"

Annabelle cringed, closed her eyes and leaned back in her chair as the world seemed to rotate in the opposite direction. She dully thought that it was weird to finally feel the movements of the earth, which she had always taken for granted.

Keeley's words came sharp and clear through the dizziness. "Who was with him?" she asked again.

Annabelle didn't want to open her eyes—to this question, to more grief—yet she did open them because this was her daughter, whom she loved.

"You don't know, do you?" Keeley said.

The fierce words sliced through Annabelle's pain and disorientation. She dropped her hands on Keeley's shoulders. "No, I don't know who was with him."

Keeley collapsed into her mother's arms, and together they sat silent and still, both afraid to enter this new world in which Keeley's father and Annabelle's husband might not have been the man they thought he was.

"Oh, Keeley, I love you. I'm so sorry we have to go through this . . . ," Annabelle whispered.

Keeley released her mother, sat back and lifted her chin. "Do we have to have another funeral?"

"God, no." Annabelle wouldn't let go of Keeley's hand. She gripped it tighter.

"Okay . . . I can't talk about this with you. . . ." Keeley pried her hand free. She bit her lower lip, stood, then turned and entered the house without another word.

Annabelle stared at the closed door. Where had her sweet little girl gone? The one who made signs that said, *You're the best mom ever* and slipped them under the bedroom door. The girl who called from a sleep-over at a friend's house and asked to come home because she missed her mom too much.

That Keeley seemed to have died along with Knox, and for one moment that loss seemed more monstrous than all the others combined. A dull fatigue that Annabelle recognized as her response to grief over-came her—a sadness that melded into confusion and anger in a mangled mess that would follow her all day and into the night. She didn't want to talk to a single person—she ached for rest. Yet she had so many phone calls to make, so much to do.

The sun burst from behind a cloud, shone directly on Annabelle's face. She lifted a hand, shielded her eyes and felt as though someone had just thrown a thousand-pound weight over her body. Questions began to take shape and hammer her with each unknown. Why would he have lied about going hunting? Had he always lied about where he was going? What about those deer heads he brought home—had he bought them off some real hunters? She strode across the porch, back and forth, as though she were trying to take bites out of it with her footsteps. Had he taken her every time? Had she always been on these trips, or had he just met her? Why would he have done that?

Her cell phone rang; she jumped, answered it when she saw Jake's number flash on the screen. "Hey, buddy," she said, forcing normalcy into her shaking voice.

"You okay, Mom?"

"Why?" Annabelle asked, rubbed her forehead.

"Keeley just called. . . . She told me, Mom. She told me about Dad and the plane and the woman inside."

"Yes," Annabelle said to her son with a swift and desperate need to see his face. "I tried to call you a minute ago. . . ."

"How did they find him?"

"A hiking expedition," she said.

"Oh . . ."

Annabelle sat in silence with her son on the line and marveled how Jake or Knox could leave—to college or death—but her love for them never left; it remained planted in her heart.

"Mom?"

"I'm here," she said. "I'm fine. It's crazy for him—them—to be found like this . . . but I'm fine."

"This doesn't change anything, Mom."

Annabelle felt the tears come now. Who was Jake kidding? Knox was the cornerstone upon which all else in her life had been built. Didn't Jake see that once that stone was removed, everything else cracked and shifted? Of course this woman's presence on the plane changed everything.

If Annabelle was wrong about Knox and who he was, his integrity and love, then what else was she wrong about? If her assumptions about his commitment, his ethics and where his heart had lain were wrong, maybe the sun did rotate around the earth; maybe the earth was flat and one could fall off the horizon.

Who this woman was mattered as much as anything had ever mattered. Her presence shattered Annabelle's faith in a life and love already lived.

She took a deep breath—she would not pass her darkness onto the light and beauty that was her son.

"Jake, I'm sorry you heard it from Keeley before me. As soon as I know more, I'll call you."

"Can you tell me the details?"

Annabelle rattled off all she could remember of what Wade Gunther had told her.

"Do you need me to come home?"

Annabelle wanted to scream *yes*, tell her son to come permeate the house with the assurance of their beautiful life, but she knew she could not ask that of him. It was she who needed to replace the doubt inside her children with faith and love.

"Jake, please don't leave school. As soon as I know more, I'll call. I love you."

"You, too, Mom. I love you, too."

Annabelle hung up feeling as if her body had been emptied out, hollowed, all that remained of her faith scooped out and handed to her son.

The *Marsh Cove Gazette* offices offered a chaos Annabelle loved. The bustle, the deadlines, the hollering and the ringing phones allowed little time for contemplation and grief. She entered the back room, knocked on Mrs. Thurgood's office door.

"Come in." Her voice was rough from the cigarettes she pretended to have quit at the start of each new year.

"Hello, ma'am." Annabelle entered her office, dropped papers on the desk. "Here is this week's advice column."

Mrs. Thurgood's gray hair stuck out in odd directions, as though she'd come to work on a boat instead of in the black Cadillac she drove all over town. "All you had to do was put it in the in-box or e-mail it. Why are you bothering me?"

Annabelle smiled at Mrs. Thurgood. "There's a news story coming in . . . and I wanted to ask you a personal favor."

"The story about your husband's plane?"

Annabelle tried to smile, but was unsuccessful. "Yes, that one. I was sure Wade had told y'all by now. I'm hoping that you'll wait at least a day before printing it to let me notify friends . . . and family."

Mrs. Thurgood raised one eyebrow. "So they found a woman in the plane? And no one knows who it is? How can I hold a news story like that, Belle?"

She held up her hand. "This is not a story. It's my life." She had the panicked feeling that this news had opened a door she had never even seen. "And maybe you can help me. You seem to know everything there is to know about this town anyway."

"Everyone loved Knox. He was involved in the community, did pro bono work for the underprivileged, helped fix up downtown—everyone will want to know about the recovery of his plane. That's my job, to get the news to the people."

"But . . . they also found a woman." Annabelle was already tired of saying it.

"Don't you know that releasing information is the only way to gain information?"

"I don't want this to be a story at all, much less a national one. It's embarrassing."

"You don't know that . . . yet. There are a million different reasons—"

"What is it you always tell me?" Annabelle leaned forward, tapped the desk. "The simplest explanation is usually the right one."

"And I thought you didn't listen to me." Mrs. Thurgood laughed at her own joke, then patted down her wild hair as though she'd just seen herself in the mirror. "Seriously, Annabelle, did you notice you used the word 'usually' in that sentence? Just usually. Not always. Let's not go jumping to conclusions, okay?"

"Conclusions?" The word tasted foreign and bitter in Annabelle's mouth, like a food she'd never tried before. "I had so many of them. Conclusions and assumptions—lots of both of those. Until now, that is."

Mrs. Thurgood closed her eyes. "We all travel with them, and frequently they are like poorly packed luggage—falling apart and needing to be redone as we journey through life. You aren't any different than any other woman. We take our conclusions and our assumptions and set them aside until we pick up new ones, and then we set them aside until we realize we shouldn't ever carry either."

"Then," Annabelle said on an exhaled breath, "what do we carry?"

"Faith," Mrs. Thurgood said.

"In what?"

"That, my dear, is for you to decide. But you should have faith that we will find out who was on that plane. Okay?"

"What if . . . ?" A question traveled from a long way off and crash-landed directly on Annabelle's heart, right in the center of her body, where she had always trusted Knox.

"What if . . . what?" Mrs. Thurgood asked.

"What if none of it is true?"

"None of what?" Mrs. Thurgood came out from behind her desk, which she rarely did because it meant grabbing her cane.

"Everything I've ever believed about my life." Annabelle bent forward with the words, which must have been forming since Wade left her porch. "What if everything I've ever believed about my marriage, my life, was a lie? What if all I trusted and relied on wasn't true?" Her hands shook when they landed on the desk to steady herself.

Mrs. Thurgood touched her elbow. "Oh, Belle. That is, of course, a dreadful thought."

"Can you at least wait to publish the story until I've had time to call family, friends . . . ?"

Mrs. Thurgood nodded. "You'll have the rest of the day—it won't be in the paper until the evening edition."

Annabelle dropped her head. "I've got to go. . . ." She retreated from the office without saying more.

Light and shadow danced across Cooper and Christine's porch in an afternoon choreography. Annabelle held her hand in midair before the door, wanting to find the perfect words to ask her friends about Knox's woman. She didn't want to emotionally spew the news and questions as she just had in Mrs. Thurgood's office.

Christine opened the door and smiled before Annabelle could knock. "Hey, Annabelle." Christine hugged her. "I swear I cannot mix white wine and boat rides. I'm getting too old. . . . I have a horrid headache today. How are you?"

"I'm good. . . . I was hoping I caught y'all at a good time. I was wondering if I could talk to both of you for a second. Or is Cooper traveling today?"

"He's leaving in about an hour for a plane to Phoenix. Let me see if he's done packing."

Annabelle pictured the newspaper headlines, the gossip that would surely flow, the phones ringing across town. "I just need five minutes to talk to y'all . . . if you don't mind."

"I don't mind at all. Let me get Cooper." Christine motioned for Annabelle to follow, then shot a teasing look over her shoulder and laughed. "I can't believe you jumped in last night."

"God, that already seems a million years ago," Annabelle said.

"What do you mean?"

"I got some news today. . . . Get Cooper so I don't have to keep saying it. . . ."

"Okay." Christine walked down the hall to the bed-room. She'd met Cooper in college and had set her sights on marrying him after their second date. Christine was from Florida—a place, she said, that was in the South, but wasn't Southern. She fell in love first with the Lowcountry and then with Cooper, as though he were a piece of the land broken off and given to her as a gift.

Annabelle remembered a long-ago New Year's Eve party when Christine had told her that she knew Cooper loved her because he'd stayed with her when he'd had the chance to reunite with an old girlfriend who had once broken his heart.

When Christine had told Annabelle this story—following too many glasses of champagne, after both of them had been married for years—Annabelle experienced a rare moment of doubt about Knox. Would he have left her if he'd *really* had the chance? She'd watched Knox across the room talking to Shawn, and laughing. Then he'd glanced around until he found her, met her eyes and smiled. So many years they'd been married by then—ten—that she knew he was looking for her, seeking a point of comfort in the crowded room. But, she wondered, was she merely that for him: a source of comfort and familiarity?

Now standing in Christine's foyer, Knox dead and gone, Annabelle remembered Knox's smile for her as if she had just received it.

Cooper came from the back bedroom, hair wet and buttoning his shirt. "Hey, Belle, what's up?" He kissed her on the cheek.

"Can I talk to y'all for a few minutes?" Annabelle asked.

"You sound so formal—you don't have to ask to talk to us. What is it? You don't look so . . . well."

"Thanks, Cooper," Annabelle said, punched the side of his arm.

He waved toward the kitchen. "Come on, let's get coffee."

Annabelle followed him into the kitchen—newly remodeled to look antique. An oxymoron: Christine's new old kitchen. It had heart-of-pine floors, granite counters honed to look ancient, a black Viking stove with a false patina of age and custom-built mahogany cabinetry.

Cooper poured coffee beans into the grinder, Annabelle seated herself on a bar stool at the counter and Christine paced the kitchen as though she were looking for one more thing to put in its proper place.

The grinder noise kept them silent for a moment, and then Cooper tapped the coffee into the brewer and turned to Annabelle. "Shoot, girl. What's up?"

Christine sat, too, now, across from Annabelle at the discreet family desk with the roll-down top that hid the bills and paraphernalia of family life.

"Sheriff Gunther came to visit me this afternoon. It seems they've found Knox's plane, his body," Annabelle said.

Cooper came around the counter, hugged Annabelle. The simple fragrance of soap and toothpaste clung to him. He didn't say anything at all, and for this, she was grateful.

When he stepped away, she added, "There was another person with him. A woman." She thought she might as well get to the point quickly. "I'm really hoping you can tell me who she is. . . ."

Cooper leaned down to look her in the eye. "You're kidding, right?"

In that single moment, she understood that he had no idea who was on that plane. "No, I'm not kidding."

Christine abruptly stood up on the other side of the room, walked toward them. "Damn, Cooper, of course she's not kidding."

Annabelle faced Christine. "Do you know something, anything about who this woman was?"

Christine held up her hands as though Annabelle had thrown her empty coffee mug at her. "No, I just meant that no one would joke about such a horrible thing."

Annabelle turned back to Cooper. "God, who was it?"

"Let's retrace here," Cooper said. "Knox said he was going hunting in Colorado. Alone. He did it . . . how often—once a year, every other year?"

"Yeah, no real pattern." Annabelle twirled her empty mug on the counter. "No exact dates every year."

Cooper walked over to the coffeepot, filled three mugs.

Annabelle blew on her coffee. "Listen, I know you have a plane to catch, but if you think of anything, even one thing that would help me know who she was, please tell me. Now, more than any other time in my life, is not when you should spare my feelings—you have to tell me everything. The FAA is trying to identify the body—it will end up in the papers."

Cooper shook his head. "I have absolutely no idea whatsoever who this woman was. I thought I knew everyone Knox knew. If he lied to you about this— then he lied to me, too."

"I'm not sure what he did or didn't lie about. I'm just sure that . . . Actually I'm not sure about a damn thing." Annabelle took a swig of coffee.

Cooper sat down next to her. "Don't let this make you doubt what you knew about Knox. There is probably a very logical explanation."

Annabelle stared out the window, across Cooper and Christine's yard to the creek running behind it; a yellow chickadee sat on top of an iron bench. "Can you think of even one explanation that doesn't involve deceit or betrayal?" Annabelle asked. "Because I can't. Every explanation I come up with includes one of those two things," Annabelle held her palms up as if weighing something, and then dipped her right hand downward. "Deceit"—she dipped her left hand— "betrayal." She dropped both hands. "I'm not particularly fond of either option."

"Didn't he stop somewhere on the way to Colorado? Refuel or something?" Cooper asked.

Annabelle sat up straight. "Yes, he did. Newboro, North Carolina. He stopped there. . . ."

"See? Maybe there's a perfectly reasonable explanation. . . . Don't get yourself all worked up about things you don't yet know."

"Okay, I grant you—it doesn't make sense," Annabelle said. "I'll try to believe it still might make sense at some point." Annabelle closed her eyes, dropped her forehead on the counter. "Please let there be a good explanation."

"We're here if you need us." Cooper placed his palm on top of her head.

Christine came to his side and sat next to Annabelle. "Please let us know if we can do anything."

Annabelle lifted her head and forced a smile. "Thanks, y'all." As she stood to leave, she wondered about the next logical step in this unchoreographed dance. A dance whose steps she didn't know.

Back home, Annabelle made all the phone calls she had been dreading: to her mother, her in-laws, cousins and aunts. Each time she repeated the story in a false upbeat voice, she felt as if she were taking apart her life, removing building blocks from the foundation of her marriage.

Afterward, she needed to hear that Jake was okay, that this news was not piercing him as it was Keeley. She dialed his number and got his voice mail. "Hey, Jake, it's Mom checking in. Call me. I love you," she said, and hung up.

Schoolwork kept him busy. He'd been the only one in his high school class accepted to the University of North Carolina's political science school. His grades and activities, his father's reputation and Jake's own amiable personality had won him a spot in the prestigious program. Jake had once wavered about his college major—until upon his father's death he firmly resolved to continue his father's work of bringing justice to those who'd been denied it.

Annabelle sat on the living room couch and closed her eyes. Her own strength dissipated, she wished for something, anything to help her in her unbelief. Yet even as she formed the thought, doubt began its long, circuitous journey into her soul.

THREE

SOFIE MILSTEAD

The waters off Newboro, North Carolina, changed personality with every movement of cloud, every shift of wind, every pull of the moon. The rich sea bound Sofie Milstead to this place where the dolphins had become her hope and balm in a world of human misunderstanding and loss.

She'd spent the day on a commercial fishing trawler recording dolphin calls. The water was rough and her gear rattled against the metal hull. Overhead video cameras were positioned to record the dolphins' behavior around gill nets—the huge weighted nets used to capture species-specific fish. Sofie desperately desired to prevent the deaths of the hundreds of thousands of dolphins that were caught in the fishing nets every year. The goal of her research project was to gather enough information about dolphin behavior around the boats to support new legislation that would save the lives of these mythical creatures.

The boat captain, John Morris, hollered at her across the deck. "Hey, Sofie, there's a pod starboard."

"Thanks, John. It's the Delphin pod. I already have so many of their recordings—now I can make some comparisons." She smiled at him and pulled her rain-coat closer, adjusted the controls on the passive acoustic monitoring system. She yanked a logbook and camera from her bag, placed them on the seat. John and several of the other commercial fishermen were kind enough to allow the researchers on their daily fishing trips; this was Sofie's favorite boat.

"Why do you call it the Delphin pod?" John asked.

Sofie looked up at him. "I named the lead dolphin after one from a Greek myth—a love story."

"Ah," he said. "I've been meaning to ask. You think he likes your name for him?"

She shrugged. "Probably not. I didn't like his name in the catalog—Spike, after his torn dorsal fin—but, hey, I might not like the name he's given me either." She laughed and ducked her head against the wind as she flipped the switch on the machine.

She became lost in her work as she photographed the identifying dorsal fin of each dolphin, then logged their movements around and behind the boat. She carefully noted the exact times so that the visual and sound records would coincide. She could never tell how many hours had passed when she worked like this—usually John had to call to her that the boat was ready to dock. Time collapsed in on itself, disappearing like morning mist without warning.

Water burst over the side of the boat as the crew pulled up the fishing nets. Sofie looked up from her logbook and realized that the sky had darkened. As John came to her side, another splash of cold water across the bow hit Sofie full in the face. She backed up, wiped her eyes and stared down at Delphin, who had clearly just sprayed her. "Not funny," she said.

The sleek gray dolphin's fluke shot out of the water, which meant he was going deep for food—probably for the bycatch of the nets. Sofie sighed. Swimming so close to the nets was how the dolphins became entangled and injured in them, was probably how Delphin had lost that chunk out of his dorsal fin. The pods were becoming accustomed to eating the bycatch off the fishing boats. If she only knew their language, knew how to tell them to steer clear of the nets.

The water began to churn, and the dolphin pod shot from the water and swam in a quick group toward the mouth of the sound, riding one another's currents and calling out. Each dolphin had a signature whistle, which she matched to a prerecording so she could be certain who was calling and who was initiating the movements of the pod. Years ago she'd learned that the hearing part of the dolphin brain had twice the number of nerves as the human. Maybe that was why she believed the dolphins understood her soft, whispered words.

How she wanted to speak their language, call their names.

Her own name had changed three times since birth,

although only she knew this fact. The thought that the most beautiful creatures on earth had names they kept all their lives was a comfort to her. The loss of loneliness began with the naming.

She was blessed to have this job, to be able to be on the water with her dolphins almost every day. The Marine Conservation Technology Lab had chosen Sofie to work on this project for her summer research. She'd worked with the center since she was fifteen years old, always willing to do whatever was needed. She'd cleaned tanks, swept floors, filed and entered data, until this year when she'd been hired as an intern to record the movements, behavior and vocalizations of the dolphins around commercial fishing boats. The head of the lab, Andrew Martin, said her meticulous record keeping made her one of the best interns they'd ever had. There was already a thorough catalog of identified dolphins from New Jersey to Florida, so after identifying each dolphin, Sofie could spend her time recording and listening to the mammals. What Andrew didn't know was that the acoustic records were contributing to her own private investigation into whether dolphins called each other by name.

She didn't understand her deep-seated need to prove that the dolphins loved one another enough to give names. And maybe they named the humans they also loved. She'd once read an essay by Loren Eisley in which he called the human need to bridge the gap between human and animal "The Long Loneliness." It was an apt description of her own belief that if she could call a dolphin by name and also understand his name for her, the abyss between them would be crossed.

A single flash shot across the sky and water—lightning. John grabbed her arm. "Get under cover in the cockpit, Sofie." Rain fell in a sudden, sharp downpour as though gravity were pushing the rain into her face harder than necessary.

She felt the ache of isolation. After the dolphins left her, she often felt even more alone than before, as though they opened that empty space inside her. They seemed, she thought, to lower her emotional barriers so that when they were gone she was more aware of her own needs.

Being with the dolphins was the only time when she thought: *This, now, this is what I was made for.*

John poked his head down into the cubby of the boat. "We're getting ready to drop you off at the research center."

"Got it," she said.

"Come on up. We're pulling up to the dock."

Sofie went up on deck, sat on the wet bench in the back, lifting her face to the rain and shivering. The Marine Research Center was situated on a massive outcropping of rock that edged into the bay like a floating fortress. John tied the boat to the cleats while Sofie unloaded her gear and recording equipment.

Sofie liked John and felt comfortable with him, but often she grew uneasy when men paid her too much attention. Her mother had taught her, long ago and early, not to trust men, to avoid eye contact at all costs, and to confide in only the few men they already knew. Sofie's deeply ingrained lessons were hard won and firmly entrenched.

She grabbed her overstuffed bag and headed back toward the research center. "Thanks, John. See you tomorrow."

"Yeah, yeah," he called after her.

She crossed the parking lot, pushed open the door with her foot and entered the center, where moist, artificially cooled air caused her breath to catch. She made her way to the locker room, showered and changed before sitting down at her computer. She needed to transfer the recordings to a hard drive and enter the statistics she'd logged.

Now that she was back at her desk, she felt safe from emotions she didn't want to admit.

The phone rang; she grabbed it and Bedford greeted her with his warm voice. "Hey, darling, just making sure you weren't out on the water in this weather."

"Nope, here at my desk," Sofie told him, clicked open a document.

"I'll come get you around six o'clock for dinner, okay? I need to talk to you about something. I thought we'd go to Benittos."

"What do you need to talk about?" Sofie's fingers paused over the keyboard. Had she done something wrong?

"Nothing big, baby. I'll see you soon."

Sofie hung up the phone, and closed her eyes. She

loved Bedford; he made her feel secure, cared for. The few times she became overwhelmed by his demands, she reminded herself of the utter and total panic she felt when she imagined leaving him, or when he threatened to leave her. She still hadn't told him many things about her life, and maybe if she confided in him, she could cross that bridge of lonesomeness she often felt when she was with him.

Bedford Whitmore was forty; she was twenty. She'd first noticed him two years ago when he strode onto the dock of the research center; he'd looked like a safe harbor. He'd smiled at her and she'd gone to him without hesitation. He'd asked her name, then asked her out to dinner. She'd practically moved in with him less than a month later.

Everyone at the research center told her not to get involved with him—he was too old for her, a wanderer; he never stayed in Newboro for more than six months at a time. He was a marine biologist who specialized in environmental chemistry. He taught as a guest lecturer at numerous universities, yet was in Newboro often to consult with the research center on environmental problems in both the natural habitat and in the tanks housing the wounded marine life.

He'd stayed with Sofie for the past two years. He hadn't moved on except for the few weeks he traveled to various universities for his lecture series, which allowed him more freedom than full-time teaching would have. This month he would be in Raleigh.

Bedford loved her; he told her so every morning and

every night when she lay in his king-sized bed under the white down comforter. She felt guilty sometimes, knowing that she kept so many things from him—her family history and her love of mystery—intangibles that could not be measured on charts and proven with experiments.

He was proud of Sofie's research, of the work she was doing for dolphin conservation, which he thought would bring her both academic distinction and publication in scientific magazines. She basked in his admiration.

The rest of the day flew by as she transferred numbers onto databases and graphs. Although Bedford would also proof her work, she felt the need to get everything as perfect as possible before his red pen hit the paper. She'd made a deal with herself—if she finished this section, she could work on her private research.

She wanted to prove that dolphins communicated with one another, named each other. It would be a landmark paper. But more, Sofie felt instinctively that her theory was true. Providing empirical evidence would elevate the mammals to a higher place in the animal kingdom, and thus, she hoped, help protect them.

Then she wanted to write a children's chapter book in which a child learned how special every dolphin was, since each had a name. If there really were a way to combine "truth" and "story," Sofie thought, life would make some sort of sense, shift into a definable paradigm. But she would tell no one of her work or why it mattered so much to her. She had made a bar-gain with God—*I'll only have one* real *dream and not ask for anything more.* She wasn't quite sure if God was in on the bargain or not, and she was being a bit dishonest since she also wanted to prove that dolphins not only named each other, but also had names for the humans they loved.

When she looked up at the clock, the day was gone and she hadn't been able to switch to her own work. She pushed her hair out of her eyes, stood and was stretching when Bedford walked into the room.

She smiled at him. "Hey."

"You look tired, baby." He walked toward her, touched her face and kissed her lips.

"I am. Can we just go back to your place and grill some shrimp?"

"I don't have any food at home."

She grabbed her rain slicker off the chair. "We could stop by the market."

"I thought we could sit and really talk if we weren't rushing around the kitchen cooking."

"Oh," she said, as usual unable to find an argument against his irrefutable logic.

He held out his hand. "Let's go."

She took his hand, felt the warmth of him and leaned into him.

Philip, the maître d', welcomed Bedford and Sofie, led them to their favorite table at the far end of the restaurant and left them alone.

"Okay, what is it, Bedford?"

"I know you don't like to talk about your mother, but I thought you should see this."

"What is it?"

Bedford reached down, pulled a newspaper from his briefcase and held it out to her. "Read page one of the arts section."

Sofie took the Raleigh newspaper and read the article while her feet and hands went numb, while her heart slowed to an erratic pace as if she'd dived too far down following a dolphin.

The article told of an art historian, Michael Harley, who was traveling along coastal Carolina communities looking for Ariadne—the painter whose art was characterized by broad brushstrokes and translucent paint; who employed innovative methods to integrate background and foreground images on metal, wood and other surfaces. Her work had been dispersed throughout the country by tourists who had bought pieces while on vacation in the Carolinas, yet no one knew who the artist really was, not her full name or where she lived. No new work had shown up in years.

Harley had started to collect Ariadne's work. He was researching her for an article, and he was intent on finding her—or him.

The article explained that in Greek mythology Ariadne was the daughter of King Midas. She married Dionysus, god of the sea, after escaping from the island of Crete. The historian's theory was that the artist was a strong woman who wished to hide her identity behind a goddess who represented an escape from patriarchal society.

Sofie faked a smile, looked up. "None of this makes sense. Greek myth? Art technique? Fake names?"

Bedford touched the top of her hand, stroked her wrist with a featherlight touch. "Sofie, that is the name of the artist whose canvases are sold in the Newboro Art Studio. The article says Newboro has the largest collection of Ariadne's work. Your mother owned the art studio. I know you know about this. . . ."

Sofie felt her bones soften, collapse into her flesh as though she might disappear. She dropped the newspaper onto the table, closed her eyes and felt the room spin; nausea rose and she stood, ran for the bathroom.

The door safely shut, she leaned over the toilet and retched. Panic ran through her body in a familiar pattern, and then Bedford's voice echoed through the bathroom. "Sofie, Sofie, are you okay?"

She stood, walked to the sink to wash her face. "I'll be right out," she called to the closed door.

She pinched her cheeks, smoothed her stick-straight blond hair back into its ponytail and walked out to face Bedford. "I think the oyster sandwich I had for lunch was bad."

"Tell me what's going on." He hugged her. "I know when you're hurting. I hate bringing up the subject of your mother, but you have to talk about her death someday. This man"—Bedford held up the paper—"is coming to Newboro to ask questions. You can't pretend your mother is coming home in two days." He said this in the quiet voice of a father—or what Sofie imagined a father would say, since she'd never had one.

They walked back to the table. She sat across from him, and he reached his hand out to her; she took it. "Just talk to me. . . . Did your mother know this artist?"

Sofie released the long-rehearsed words she'd prepared for this moment. "Bedford, she's gone. I can't ask her if she knew Ariadne. I have no idea who Ariadne is. It was Mother's studio—not mine."

He ran his fingers across her palm, over her forearm. She shivered with the familiar desire that rose up in her when he touched her. "I'm really not that hungry. Can we just go now?" she asked.

"I'm starving," he said, smiled.

The waiter approached and took their order. When the wine bottle arrived, Sofie nodded yes to a glass. She spooned her clam chowder, but didn't take a bite. Bedford cut into his steak, stared at her. "Why don't you eat? You're going to float away soon."

Sofie was thin—she always had been. She could eat a lot or a little, and her frail frame neither gained nor lost weight. Bedford circled his fingers around her wrist. "Eat."

She sipped her soup, looked up at him and realized he had no idea, whatsoever, of the fear that lived and moved inside her when she thought of the consequences of telling the truth. Each time she contemplated the possibility of speaking the facts of her mother's life, anxiety folded over her in a suffocating blanket of silence.

"Well." Bedford sat back. "You know he's going to come try and talk to you."

"Let him. What do I care? I'll tell him the same thing I'm telling you. I don't know anything about the artists whose work Mother hung in her studio, where she found them or where they went. I was a child. I didn't pay any attention."

Bedford ran a hand through his hair, a familiar and irritating gesture that Sofie often thought feminine. He dropped his hand and lightened his furrowed expression. "So," he said, "tell me about your trip out with John. How did it go?"

For a minute or two she forgot about her mother, Michael Harley and Bedford's questions as she talked about her work, content to be discussing the subject she loved best. She told Bedford about her day, or at least the part of her day that would make him smile. She wanted to love him as much as he did her, as much as she had once loved another man.

Yes, there was a time when she'd loved someone else. Of course she'd never told Bedford about him: Christian Marcus, who'd worked with her at the Marine Research Center. When she thought of Christian, sorrow came in a wave of regret. He was the loss she bore because of her inability to tell the truth. He was the debt she paid for keeping secrets.

She had believed Christian would love her despite the things she couldn't tell him, regardless of the past life she refused to speak about. When he had informed her that he was taking a research job in Alaska, he claimed his heart was broken, but he could not love someone who did not love him in return. No matter how hard Sofie tried to convince him that she cared for him beyond words and without measure, he felt the wall around her heart, and so he left.

Although she was young and her mother told her she could not truly love yet, Sofie had blamed her mother for this great bereavement and didn't speak to her for a month after Christian moved away. Sofie then vowed never again to feel the hopeless and frantic need she'd often seen in her mother: the reckless desire to make a man love you back when his heart and commitment obviously resided elsewhere.

Sofie reached out and took Bedford's hand, stroked his palm. "I do love you," she said, a magic incantation to prevent more loss.

FOUR

ANNABELLE MURPHY

The phone rang in the far end of Annabelle's house, four times, five times, before the answering machine clicked on. She walked to the kitchen to listen to the messages. Mrs. Thurgood wanted to know why the advice column wasn't on her desk. It was only two hours before deadline and she refused to print a repeat.

Annabelle put her hands over her ears. Every single phone call over the past four hours had been a reminder of something else she hadn't done since Wade Gunther had walked up on her veranda: attend the fund-raiser committee meeting for the new women's room at the church; drop off the bulbs at Ann-Marie's before the neighborhood gardening club's planting party; work tomorrow's shift at the food pantry; and now write her column.

In not one of these calls had anyone inquired about her well-being or provided the only news she wanted to hear: who was with Knox on that plane.

Annabelle stood, stretched and walked to the computer in her small office at the front of the house. The question Mrs. Thurgood wanted Annabelle to answer in the "Southern Belle Says" column would be in her e-mail in-box.

"I can do this." Annabelle spoke out loud to the empty room. "I've been through worse—I will not let this take me down." She rubbed a hand across her face.

The old computer whirred and hummed, threatening to quit at any minute. Now might be a good time. Her in-box scrolled full. She scanned for the e-mail from the newspaper and clicked on NEW QUESTION.

Dear Southern Belle,

I have a secret I have kept from my best friend for over five years. I can't hold it in anymore. But I don't know how to tell her now; it is too late to change what happened or the consequences that have followed. My guilt is eating away at me. Is five years too long to wait to tell the truth? What is the proper etiquette? Is there a time limit like with wedding or baby presents?

Guilt-ridden and Confused in Charleston

"Moron," Annabelle said to the screen. "A time limit like with wedding presents?" She slammed her hand on the keyboard; random letters and symbols appeared on the screen.

"Mom?"

Annabelle glanced over her shoulder at Keeley leaning against the doorframe. "Hey, darling."

"You talking to yourself?"

"No, I'm talking to the person who asked this stupid question for my column."

"I thought you said there are no stupid questions."

"This one is." Annabelle tapped the screen. "Hey, what are you doing home?" She glanced up at the wall clock. "It's only two."

"I hate math."

"What?" Annabelle went to her daughter. "What do you mean? Are you telling me you left school in the middle of the day because you hate math?" Her voice rose.

"Chill, Mom. Geez. It's not the middle of the day. There was only one class left. And I don't feel good. I'm going to lie down."

"Oh, Keeley, did you go to the nurse or check out at the office?"

Keeley rolled her eyes. "Whatever."

"That is not an answer. If you're really sick, go to bed."

Keeley held up her hands. "I am."

Annabelle watched her daughter walk down the hall, drop her backpack in the middle of the foyer and take the stairs two at a time to her bedroom upstairs. She should tell Keeley to come back and pick up her backpack, holler at her for leaving it in the middle of the hall, but Annabelle had only enough energy for the task at hand—the advice column.

The computer blinked and Annabelle sat down to answer the question.

Dear Guilt-ridden and Confused,

This is the stupidest question I have been asked in the nine years I have been writing this column. A time limit as with a gift? What kind of upbringing did you have that you believe there is a time limit on the truth? Of course you should tell your best friend the truth. If you claim to have a best friend, if you are living as if she is your best friend, then you are living a lie. Deceit and betrayal cannot exist between two people who care about each other.

Sincerely,
The Southern Belle

Annabelle clicked SEND to Mrs. Thurgood and leaned back in her chair. A slow laugh began below her chest and rose until she sat giggling at her computer. There was *no way* Mrs. Thurgood would let an abrasive and rude column through her "Southern Belle" filter.

Annabelle began to type her real answer.

Dear Guilt-ridden,

This is a complicated question, just as relationships are complicated and multifaceted.

Annabelle leaned back on her office chair, rubbed her fingers on her temples and thought about what to say next. She was staring at the ceiling when the *ding* of incoming mail made her look back down at another e-mail from Mrs. Thurgood:

Thank you for the quick reply on the column. See next e-mail for article on Knox's plane. Please let me know if you have any input.

Annabelle took in a sharp breath. Mrs. Thurgood must not have read the advice column—she had sent it straight to print. Yet what really knocked the air out of her lungs was the new attachment that scrolled across her screen:

KNOX MURPHY'S PLANE FOUND

Annabelle slowly read the facts she already knew

from the sheriff. But here they were, about to appear in the evening and then morning papers for all of Marsh Cove and South Carolina to see, for Internet readers and the Associated Press to find.

Annabelle dropped her head into her hands. "Oh, Knox. Sweet, sweet Knox, what were you doing?"

The room seemed to spin and Annabelle closed her eyes until footsteps entered the room. "Mom?"

Annabelle lifted her head. "Yes?" Keeley stood before her with a coat in one hand, car keys in her other.

"I'm headed out."

"No, you're not."

Keeley laughed and Annabelle marveled at the unknown child before her. "Yes, I am," Keeley said.

Annabelle stood, took four steps toward her daughter and grabbed the car keys from her hand. "You cannot skip school and then take the car. What is wrong with you?"

"Nothing is wrong with *me*. But there is definitely something wrong with this family—Dad was running off with some woman."

Annabelle dropped her hands, gripped them behind her back. "Is that what you think?"

"Isn't it what *you* think, Mom? Come on, really."

"No, that is not what I think."

"Please." Keeley rolled her eyes. "Don't be a fool. He didn't want any of us, and he was running away with some woman."

Annabelle shook her head at hearing her worst fear

coming out of her daughter's mouth. "We've been through this together before, Keeley. Your dad did not willfully leave us. He did not choose to leave us. His plane crashed and he died."

Keeley backed a step away from her. "Yeah, I finally believed all that shit you and the counselor told me. Now I see he really was running away. He might not have meant to die, but he did mean to leave. Lucky Jake, away at college. I wish I was gone and didn't have to see and hear all this."

"Do not curse. And no, he wasn't leaving us. Just because we don't know why he was on that plane with that woman doesn't mean there isn't a good reason."

"Mother, do you hear yourself? Quoting the same old stupid thing my whole life: 'Just because we don't know the reason doesn't mean there isn't one.' I am so out of here." Keeley tried to grab the car keys back from Annabelle, then dropped her face into her hands and attempted, unsuccessfully, to stem the flow of her tears.

Keeley's words threatened to open a drain at the bottom of Annabelle's soul. She wrapped her arms around her daughter. "Oh, Keeley."

The mystery overwhelmed Annabelle—how giving herself away in love filled her up with more to give. To love her child was to offer part of her heart while hers grew larger. Sometimes, in the middle of the night, she swore she could feel Keeley breathing, or hear her heartbeat.

The phone rang behind them and Keeley released

her mother, wiped the tears from her face. "I'm going to . . . my room."

"I'll make us a nice dinner . . . and . . ." The phone rang again.

Keeley ran up the stairs and Annabelle grabbed the receiver.

"Hi, Annabelle dear. This is Lila. We're all sitting here at Bible study, wondering where you are. You were in charge of the food today."

"I was, wasn't I?" Annabelle stared across the room, wondering what she might have in the kitchen cupboard that would suffice for a snack for ten women: stale muffins, brown grapes.

"Yes, and Reverend Preston is our guest speaker today. Remember?" Lila trilled into the phone.

"Yes, but I just can't make it today."

"You should have called someone to take your duties . . . or at least dropped food off for us."

"Yes, I should have, shouldn't I?"

Lila's irritated exhale traveled through the receiver. "I guess we'll just continue without food."

"Sorry. I can drop some off, if you'd like," Annabelle said as she went to the kitchen with the intention of finding something, anything to pack in a Tupperware container. She acted on autopilot—obligation moving her forward, commitment thrusting her into action as it had the day after the news of Knox's death, when she'd stood in the laundry room and folded clothes into neat little piles while family and friends crowded the living room and kitchen.

"Too late," Lila said.

"I really am sorry." Annabelle's hand rested on the refrigerator door in defeat. She hung up and sank onto a bar stool. She was making a mess of things—a complete and utter chaotic jumble. Pretending to go through the regular motions of life was not working. All she could think about was who had been on that plane with her husband and how someone had to know something. She mentally ticked through the list of people she needed to call and talk to before the newspaper landed on their doorstep that evening.

Who might know about this woman? If not Shawn, if not Cooper, then who? She believed both of them. They'd all grown up together, kept one another's secrets and hidden their mishaps. Even so, in such a close-knit group, there might be unknowns. Maybe the years had spread far and wide enough to weaken the bonds that held them together, pushing the joints and junctures where they were connected.

The only person left to ask in their original group of five—Cooper, Shawn, Annabelle, Mae and Knox—was Mae.

Annabelle grabbed her car keys, left Keeley a quick note that she'd run to the store and instead headed out to the county road that led to Mae's horse farm.

The asphalt unwound as her mind reeled backward—to the day Knox had left on his hunting trip. Nothing had seemed amiss. She'd kissed him goodbye. They'd said, "I love you." He'd pulled out of the driveway and waved out the driver's-side window. This was her last memory of him; she'd gone over it a million times and knew it to be true: he'd smiled and waved, a shadow from the magnolia tree crossing his forehead.

The memory was as palpable as a person sitting in the passenger seat while Annabelle drove toward Mae's house. Mae had been the last to know about her and Knox's wedding. Their joy had been subdued in the aftermath of Hurricane Hugo, which had just blown up the coast. They'd gone from one friend to the next and informed them of their decision to marry.

The simple ceremony had been held in the pasture of Knox's family farm. Annabelle wore a white dress borrowed from Aunt Barbara in Atlanta, and Knox slipped his grandmother's wedding ring onto her finger. She'd been twenty years old. They'd moved into the guest house at the far end of the Murphy property and started their life together. Every time anxiety had overcome Annabelle, Knox had said, "Trust me." And she had.

Now Annabelle parked in Mae's driveway and heard his words again. *Trust me.*

"I'm trying. I'm really trying," Annabelle said out loud in the car. She tried to remember the peace she'd felt when she'd relied on Knox before—*Trust me*—and how those words had comforted her during the tortuous days when she couldn't find him during Hurricane Hugo. His "trust me" had always been enough.

But now the words she'd said to Mrs. Thurgood echoed in her head, stronger and louder than Knox's.

What if everything I've ever believed about my life was a lie? What if all I trusted and relied on wasn't true?

She jogged up to the front door. Mae answered her knock with a cup of tea in one hand. "Well, hello, Belle." She hugged Annabelle with her free arm, held her mug out to the side. "You okay?"

Still in the foyer, Annabelle plopped into a side chair, which was probably meant just for show.

Mae pulled up another chair, sat and faced her. "What's happened?"

And for the third time that day, Annabelle repeated the story. "No," Mae said when Annabelle finished.

"Yes."

"Men are so stupid. They have everything they've ever wanted right in front of their faces, and they still think they need to go find it somewhere else. But, just damn, I never thought it would be Knox."

"So, you think it was an affair?" Annabelle leaned forward, touched Mae's knee.

"Isn't that what you just said?"

"No, I said they found a woman—I didn't say I knew who she was or why she was there."

"Oh, I just assumed. I'm sorry."

"Yeah, that's the problem. I just assume, too. But now I don't know. There could be . . . other reasons; through all the trials, you've always been a dear friend. But you've also been Knox's friend, and if you've kept a secret *for* him or kept something *from* me, I need to know now. It will come out in the papers, and the police are looking for the woman's identity. . . . If you know, please tell me."

Mae shook her head. "I have no idea. I really don't. I never, ever saw Knox with anyone but you. Ever. He never talked of anyone else. You knew everyone he knew that I know."

Annabelle looked at Mae's face, stared hard and long; she was telling the truth. Annabelle leaned back in the chair. "I've been going over our lives, and I can't find the moment when he would've lied or known someone else or left with someone else. I mean . . . maybe on a business trip or another hunting trip."

"I guess there could be a million explanations. . . ."

"Yeah, I guess so. But there's only one true one. . . . I just don't know what it is."

Mae rubbed her face. "Did you have any reason, whatsoever, not to trust him? Was anything weird going on?"

"No, I always trusted him." And this was true.

"Then don't stop now."

"I'm trying not to." Annabelle stood up. "Can you think of anyone else I should ask? Do you think Frank would know anything?"

Mae gently shook her head. "No, I don't think Frank would have a clue. But I'll ask him. Who else have you asked?"

"Shawn, Cooper and Christine."

Mae shrugged. "If we don't know, I don't know who else would."

"Someone has to know. I mean someone has to

know she's gone or missing. People don't just not come home without someone being affected."

"I'm sure the police will figure it out."

"Yes," Annabelle said, "but I'd like to know first."

Mae hugged her. "Call me if there's anything I can do."

"If you think of something else . . . someone else, please tell me."

"Of course. It doesn't change anything, you know."

"Of course it does," Annabelle said. "It changes everything." She opened the front door, turned back to Mae. "Thanks."

Annabelle got into her car and shoved the key into the ignition a little harder than necessary. She drove home through the familiar streets of Marsh Cove, every corner and curve filled with reminders of Knox and of their life together.

FIVE

ANNABELLE MURPHY

The mirror fogged over with steam from the hot shower Annabelle had just taken, clouding her face, softening the lines and puffiness. She'd made such a mess of the day, forgetting all her obligations. They'd never ask her back to Bible study, nor would her book club, the volunteer organizations, the library and school.

She wrapped the tie around her bathrobe and walked

through the hall to the kitchen. A slight thump echoed from the front door: the evening paper landing on her porch. Keeley's footsteps clicked on the hall stairs and Annabelle bolted for the front door in her dripping hair, not wanting Keeley to see the headline before Annabelle had a chance to read it first, to figure out how to discuss the situation with her daughter.

Her stocking feet skidded across the hardwood floors when she ran around the corner. She grasped the handle, threw open the front door and reached for the paper lying on top of the WELCOME TO OUR HOME mat. She shut the door, leaned against the bead-board wall and slid down to the floor to rip off the plastic and open to the front page.

Her eyes blurred with tears at Knox's photo filling the entire left column. Annabelle began to reread the article she'd already received from Mrs. Thurgood.

Keeley's voice startled her into looking up at her daughter standing at the foot of the stairs. "Oh, my God, you're insane now, aren't you?"

"What?"

"You're reading the paper half-nude. Should I call nine-one-one?"

Annabelle pulled her bathrobe closed where it had slipped to reveal her chest. "I am not insane." Annabelle pinched her daughter's foot in a teasing gesture. "I was in the shower. . . ."

"No, you're insane." Keeley laughed, then her gaze went to the floor, to the scattered paper. "Dad." She mentioned her father as simply as if he had just walked in the door after another day at work.

Annabelle fumbled with the newspaper, closed it on the article. "I wanted to read it before you. . . . This is hard."

Keeley sat down next to her, took the front page and read the entire article. Annabelle watched her daughter with a tightening of her chest. She wanted to protect this young woman from pain as much as she had the newborn and toddler Keeley once was. Even as her children changed, the need to guard them from the arrows of life remained the same. Anger rose at Knox for shooting this near-fatal arrow at their family, at their daughter.

Keeley finished the article, handed the paper back. A single tear dangled at the edge of her right eye, and then fell. She stood and ran up the stairs, and the foyer chandelier shook with her slammed door. Annabelle swallowed around the lump in her throat and took the newspaper to the kitchen, poured herself a generous amount of Hendricks' Gin, tossed a splash of white cranberry juice over it, cut a cucumber and placed a thin slice in the glass. She took long sips until it was gone, then made herself another.

This had been their favorite drink on Friday afternoons—hers and Knox's. They'd make a batch in a small glass pitcher, place thin slices of cucumber on top and take glasses to the porch to talk about their week. As she poured her second drink, she realized that she hadn't pulled out this bottle of gin in two years.

The bar stool wobbled where, years ago, their dog at the time had chewed on the back left leg, and Annabelle stabilized herself by bracing her thigh against the underside of the counter. Then she reread the full article.

The printed words had more impact than they had had in an e-mail. It had always been this way with her: someone could tell her a sad story, but if she read it on paper, the story made more of an impression. The written word held a power she almost revered: to be able to write so as to influence the hearts and minds of other readers seemed nothing short of a miracle.

She folded the paper into a neat pile, took another sip of her drink, tasted the cold liquid at the back of her mouth and ached for Knox in every part of her body, for his touch and his talk, for his brown eyes softening in understanding while she told him about her day.

The deepest loneliness came from not knowing whom to call to share the mundane details of her life. With habitual motions, she opened the paper to her column before she remembered her smart-ass answer to Confused in Charleston.

Annabelle held her breath as she read exactly what she'd written in her fury, thinking no one but Mrs. Thurgood would see it. She groaned just as the phone rang. She flicked open the front cover of the cell phone, and heard Mrs. Thurgood chastising her in rapid and formal words of rebuke.

"Mrs. Thurgood . . . ma'am . . . ," Annabelle said. "I can't understand a single word you're saying."

"What in the bloody hell were you thinking? Have you lost your ever-loving mind?"

"Okay, okay. I know it was rash, but I thought only you would read it, then tell me no way were you going to publish it—it was a joke. I meant it as a sarcastic joke. I was in the middle of typing another, nicer answer when I got your e-mail about Knox's article and I just . . . forgot."

"Belle, I haven't felt the need to check your articles in over two years. I read them in the paper just like everyone else."

"Oh." Annabelle bit her lower lip. "I didn't know that."

"Damn, we are going to get so much flak about this."

"Maybe it was what Confused in Charleston needed to hear."

"It's not about what the readers *need* to hear. It's about what they *want* to hear, my dear. You know that."

"Hmmm . . . maybe that's just half the problem—everyone is always telling everyone what they want to hear and not what they need to hear."

"Love makes the world go round, baby." Mrs. Thurgood laughed her deep, husky laugh. "Listen, Annabelle, I can't have you ruining the reputation of this column or my paper, so why don't you take a week or two off, and we'll figure this out later, okay?"

"What am I going to do with a week or two? Wander aimlessly through South Carolina and ask everyone if they knew who the hell my husband took a trip with two years ago?"

"Newspaper articles seem to bring out answers. . . . Someone will call. Someone knows."

"Yeah," Annabelle said. "And it's not me."

"No, it's not, is it?"

Annabelle hung up the phone, poured herself another drink and walked to the living room, sat on the couch and stared out the window. Keeley ran the upstairs shower. A complete sense of uselessness took over, and Annabelle lay down, closed her eyes. It didn't matter how hard she attempted to hold their family together. It was now coming apart at the weakened and ill-stitched seams.

When a pounding on the front door wouldn't stop, Annabelle roused herself. It was dark outside, the front porch light spilling into the room. The aftertaste of gin had soured in her mouth. She had no idea what time it was.

The clock on the far wall hid in shadow, her watch was somewhere in the kitchen and she was still in her bathrobe. She stood, hollered to whoever was at the front door, "Hold on."

She ran to her room, threw on a pair of jeans and a beige tunic, clasped her half-wet hair behind her head and hurried back to the front door without ever looking in the mirror. Shawn stood on the other side of the door.

"Hey," he said, smiled. "Were you asleep?"

Annabelle opened the door. "Can't fool you, can I? Come in. I'm sure you're here to check on me, find out if I'm okay after that article. Well, I'm just fine."

"Yeah, fine and drunk."

"I'm not drunk." Shawn wavered in front of her eyes.

"Oh, okay . . ." He took her hand and they walked to the living room, sat down. "So this really sucks."

"Well, yes, Shawn, that is a very adult description." Annabelle rested her head on the back of the chenille couch.

"*I* sound juvenile?" he teased.

"I have screwed up so many things. I am falling apart. I have got to let this go—drop it. You know?"

"Why?"

"Okay, I'll list the multiple reasons. I will soon be kicked out of every volunteer organization in Marsh Cove; I will lose my job; the church will have a sign on the front door that says 'Annabelle, Go Home'; Keeley will run away and join some cult."

He laughed at the last comment. "Okay, I think you're overreacting now, don't you?"

"No, I don't. Shawn." She stood and motioned for him to follow her into the kitchen, where she put her glass in the sink and leaned against the counter. "I really cannot let Knox's death consume my life again. God, just when I had begun to move forward."

He came to her, put his arm around her shoulder. "What can I do?"

"Let's go get something to eat like regular people, okay?"

"Belle, it's midnight."

"Oh, is it really?" She squinted at him. "Why are you here so late?"

He shrugged. "I couldn't sleep and then I saw the article and I thought you might need a little company. All your lights were on, so I thought you must be up."

"Do you have something to tell me?"

He stared at her for a long moment, then placed his palm on her cheek. "No, I don't have any idea whatsoever who was on that plane, okay?"

"Okay . . ." Annabelle touched his hand on her face, and he quickly removed it. "Doesn't Pizza Plus have twenty-four-hour delivery?"

"I guess it does." Shawn picked up the phone.

Annabelle sat on the bar stool. "Shawn, do you think Knox cheated on me? I mean, really cheated—not just some unfaithful thought or flirting, but a girl on the side he snuck off with, needed and loved, and then returned to his family. Is that even vaguely possible?"

Shawn lifted the Hendricks' bottle. "Annabelle, that is this bottle talking, not you."

"I asked you a question."

Shawn ordered the pizza and then sat down next to her. "No, he couldn't have cheated on you. He wouldn't have been able to tolerate himself, living and loving his family and friends like he did."

"People do it all the time. Have affairs and then go back to living their regular lives, no one the wiser."

Shawn broke eye contact, stared through the back window into the darkness. "Not Knox."

Even in her fog of gin and half-sleep, Annabelle knew Shawn well enough to recognize the gap between his words and his emotions, but she couldn't tell what he was really saying. "Did you ever . . . cheat or . . . ?"

"This isn't about me." He turned back to her. "But, Annabelle, he was never gone, always here."

"No, he went on business trips, hunting trips. And when he was here . . . what if it was because he was supposed to be, not because he really wanted to be?"

"You can't go on believing in your own made-up reasons. You can only trust what he said—then."

"An affair is too terrible a thought to consider," she said, "and yet I am. What is worse than anything is thinking that he might have been with me not because he longed for me, but out of a sense of obligation."

Shawn released a shiver, put his arm around her and pulled her head to his shoulder. She felt something in him tremble. "You okay?" she asked.

"Yes," he said. "Sometimes what is worse is not being able to be with the person you long for."

"Exactly . . ." She lifted her head. "Are we talking about you?"

He shook his head. "No. I have everything I need." He released her.

"So, what if Knox longed for *her*?"

"No, I would have known. I know what that terrible

feeling looks like and acts like, and it didn't look or act like Knox Murphy."

Annabelle nodded as the doorbell rang with their pizza. Shawn answered the door and paid, then handed the box to Annabelle. They each ate a slice in complete silence, comfortable as only old friends can be.

Shawn stood, stretched. "I need to get on home. You get some sleep, okay?"

"Okay," she said, and hugged him. "Thanks for checking on me . . . and feeding me."

He touched her arm, then squeezed her hand. "Good night."

Annabelle locked the door behind him, and climbed the stairs to Keeley's room. She knocked lightly, and when there was no answer, she slipped the door open and saw Keeley's body beneath the yellow quilt. Annabelle walked in, brushed the hair off her daughter's face. Just as Annabelle's life had become uncertain and full of doubt, so had Keeley's. Like the magnolia tree outside, their roots were intertwined. Annabelle sat on the edge of the bed.

"Oh, Keeley," she whispered. Keeley appeared younger with her face scrunched up against the pillow, her features reminiscent of the toddler who'd listened to Dr. Seuss before bedtime.

Annabelle lay down next to Keeley and thought of their life like a lopsided sand fortress built by a pack of children at low tide: a sandcastle built on the belief that Knox had truly loved her and their family, that she knew everything there was to know about him.

Keeley stirred beside her, opened one eye. "Mama, what ya doing?"

"Couldn't sleep."

"Oh," Keeley said, rolled over and returned to her own sleep. "You can lie here."

Whatever Knox had been doing *then*—on that plane with that woman—was affecting them more now than it had at the time he was doing it.

Starting tomorrow, she would face her neighbors' questions and odd looks with smiles of false certainty, with expressions of a faith and bravado she didn't possess. And maybe if she faked the feelings long enough, they would become real.

SIX

ANNABELLE MURPHY

*P*ushing a full grocery cart, Annabelle ticked through a mental checklist of items she needed for the dinner party that night at Cooper and Christine's house. She was in charge of the appetizers. Although only three days had passed since the last dinner party, the group had decided they needed to get together again. Annabelle wasn't a bit fooled by their talk of a free night and "Why not just meet tonight?"—they were worried about her. Keeley was being asked questions at school, and Jake hadn't returned any of her calls in two days, but she would tell her friends she was doing just fine, thank you for asking.

A calm she couldn't explain had come over her, a sense that all would be well. If the ache and longing for Knox were here to stay—so be it. The possibility that she could move on, maybe love again, now seemed foolish. Some people lived their entire lives loving someone they couldn't have. She could, too. The plane's discovery was a simple reminder that for her love was a once-in-a-lifetime event. She needed to get on with the business of living, yet it would forever and only be Knox who dwelled in her soul.

Whoever was on that plane could stay on that plane, not enter her life—past or present.

She dropped a block of St.-André cheese and a package of water crackers in the cart. After this, the dry cleaner, the garden club meeting (they'd forgiven her for forgetting flowers for the retirement home), then preparing for the dinner. In between these chores she needed to finish her advice column.

She felt a tap on her shoulder and turned to face Kristi Miller, the owner of the local art studio. "Hey, Annabelle," she said.

"Hi, Kristi. How are you?"

"I'm good. Just wanted you to know I've been thinking about you."

"Thanks," Annabelle said.

Kristi leaned in. "Did they find out who the woman was?"

Annabelle had thought she'd fortified herself for these questions, had even rehearsed the answer. *Oh, of course I'm fine. I'm so grateful they found his plane.*

It's a relief. Then she'd nod and smile, almost console the person who had asked. But staring at Kristi, she felt the tingle of tears behind her eyes. "No, they don't know yet."

Kristi touched Annabelle's arm. "I don't know how you're doing it, but please know how much we all loved Knox. He was a terrific supporter of the Marsh Cove Art Studio, and we remember him with great fondness."

Annabelle nodded, and walked toward the checkout counter. A treble vibration of something resembling anxiety filled her gut; she attributed it to the mention of his name by yet another well-meaning friend. Yes, Knox had been a grand supporter of the Marsh Cove Art Studio in downtown, had even invested through the years. But he had done this with many new businesses. If he thought they'd benefit the community, add to the town's charm and bring in tourism, he'd invest.

Annabelle glanced at Kristi, who now stood with her back to Annabelle, grabbing orange juice off the shelf. Even in the grocery store, she was reminded of Knox and the good things he had done. See, she told herself, there was nothing about him to doubt.

Annabelle pushed SEND and off went her advice column in response to the woman who had written asking if she should let her eighteen-year-old son's girlfriend spend the night with him in his bedroom. Annabelle had to make up for her last sarcastic column, which had received e-mails and phone calls of complaint. She had promised Mrs. Thurgood a particularly sensitive answer.

It always baffled Annabelle that full-grown women asked questions they already knew the answers to. Mrs. Thurgood often told her they just wanted to hold the column up to their friends or the offending party and say, "See, Southern Belle said I was right."

A sudden, piercing thought made her laugh: she wanted to write in and ask Southern Belle what to do about the woman on Knox's plane.

Annabelle glanced at the clock: six p.m. She had an hour before the dinner party, was already dressed and ready, the appetizer in the warming drawer, Keeley dropped off at her friend's house to do homework. She could be early for the party, or read a book, or take a walk. She and Knox would have sat on the front porch, talked about their day and then strolled the two blocks to Cooper's house.

Annabelle sat back down at the computer, clicked open the untitled novel she'd started the year before Knox's plane went down. As it popped up on the screen, she thought again that writing a book was just a dream for her. She hadn't taken writing courses in college, had no formal knowledge of how to compose a full-length novel. An advice column was about all she could handle. But this story—one about a woman who was a battlefield archaeologist—had seemed like a good idea when she'd started it.

She'd never told Knox about the book—clearly they

hadn't told each other everything. Maybe there were other secrets they had kept from each other—harmless secrets, or not so harmless ones.

She hadn't said anything to Knox about the book because she wanted to wait for the right time, or until she finished, or until she was absolutely sure it was something she wanted to do. Or—and this thought brought a stab of truth—maybe she just wanted something that had nothing to do with family, house and work. Maybe she wanted something that was all hers. Maybe that was all he had wanted, too. . . .

The words on the screen blurred in front of her eyes. What if Knox had just wanted something that was all his—something that didn't fall under the scrutiny of family?

Annabelle rubbed her eyes and read the two paragraphs she'd written all those years ago, poised her finger above the DELETE button, but couldn't push it. Maybe one day she could return to this story.

Instead of deleting, Annabelle typed another paragraph:

Unearthing evidence of past events thrilled her in a way she couldn't explain to other people. Why would she want to dig around in old fields to find out how a battle was fought? So much work for so little information. But others didn't understand that unearthing the truth was akin to creating it: something new and profound appeared where it hadn't been before.

Even as she typed, she felt a shimmer of excitement as she captured a sliver of insight in the words. If writing a single paragraph felt like a miracle, how would it feel to write an entire novel?

The phone rang across the room and Annabelle jumped, hit SAVE and closed the document as though the person on the other end of the line might see her foolish endeavor.

Shawn was calling to ask if she wanted a ride to Cooper's; he was close by and could pick her up. Annabelle waited on the front porch with her appetizers wrapped in tin foil.

He pulled his convertible in front of the house, jumped out and opened the side door. She climbed in. "So," she said, "this early and impromptu dinner party is to soothe me, eh?"

"Oh, you think it's all about you?" he teased.

"Yes, I do." She grinned.

He exhaled. "I guess we all need a little soothing. It's been a tough few days on everyone, and Cooper thought a get-together would do us all good."

"Hmm . . . but I'm really fine, Shawn. A girl is allowed a few days of freaking out, right? Then she's fine."

At a stop sign he gazed into her eyes. "Are you really?"

"I really am." She touched his hand. "Come on, let's go. I hate being late to Christine's. She gets that look on her face."

Shawn pulled the car forward. "What look is that?"

"Can't quite define it, but it has something to do with my personal inadequacies."

Shawn parked in front of Cooper and Christine's cedar shake house and smiled at her. "Do you have any?"

"More than you know."

"I guess we all have our secrets, don't we?" He laughed, got out and opened the door for her.

And although she knew he was joking, she felt his words vibrate below her heart as she entered the lively house.

Christine's table was set with family china that Annabelle had always been afraid to eat off. It was an old Wedgwood design of cobalt blue ships set against a cream background. The chicken and asparagus dinner lay splattered across the porcelain sailboat as though it had drowned in a sea of green. Annabelle pushed the food around her plate, then took another swallow of red wine. After focusing on kids and work, the conversation eventually turned to Knox.

Cooper, at one end of the table, folded his hands. "Belle," he said. Everyone fell silent. "Any new information about Knox's plane since the article came out?"

"No," she said, twirled her fork on her plate, where it made a high screeching sound.

"Nothing?" Mae asked.

"Nothing," Annabelle said, leaned back in her chair. "Unless someone comes forward and tells us they know who she was, we'll be left to make up our own story about her." She smiled to let them know she was okay with this.

Christine stood, grabbed another bottle of wine from the credenza behind her and handed it to Cooper with the wine opener. "Well, someone *has* to know." She glanced around the table, and then as though the glance was contagious, everyone took a quick look at everyone else.

"Listen, Christine." Annabelle lifted her hands. "We've been through so much together—I can't think of much else a group can go through and still remain as we have. If there was something to be told, I hope it would have been told by now."

"Yes, I'm sure it has been." Christine glanced at Shawn.

Frank, who was usually quiet and unobtrusive, stood. "I've thought of a hundred memories of our friend, and I just can't believe this woman was on that plane for a terrible reason. The Knox who could coach his son's baseball team in the middle of working on a high-profile embezzlement case, or the Knox who helped old lady Morgan fight the scam artist who almost took her life savings—that Knox would not be—"

"Cheating," Annabelle said.

"Exactly," Frank said, and then sat down. "He just couldn't. I don't believe he was capable of being two different people."

Christine leaned back in her chair. "I don't think we can ever know what anyone is capable of. . . ."

The energy at the table changed that quickly, and Annabelle stared at the empty plates and half-empty glasses and felt drained of any and all answers. She stood and stared at Christine. "Yes, I'm sure we *all* have our secrets," she said, and then grabbed a few plates, headed for the kitchen, hoping Christine would understand she was talking about the time two years ago when she'd seen Christine behind Bubba's Shrimp Shack crying and holding Mark Rider's hand while she stepped from his shrimp boat. Christine had seen Annabelle, turned away, then later made a curt comment about how sad it was that Mark had lost his shrimp boat to a big commercial concern, and how it had made her cry.

Yeah, sure.

Annabelle leaned against the kitchen counter and took a deep breath. Shawn came in, put his arm around her shoulder. "You okay?"

Annabelle nodded.

The conversation rose in the next room, and Shawn and Annabelle looked at each other. "Listen," she said. "I really don't want to talk about this anymore. Please stop looking at me like a little kid who just lost a parent or something. I don't need pity or reassurance or anything else. We've all lost Knox; I'm not the only one who has been forced to think about him all over again. My kids are missing him. Y'all are wondering about your best friend. . . . I don't need anything."

"We all need something," Shawn said.

Annabelle smiled at him. "I did need something.

And I had it." She touched his arm, knowing that what she would say might hurt him after losing Maria all those years ago. "We all want someone to walk into our life and touch our soul, enter our heart and stay there. I had that. That's all that matters now."

He closed his eyes. "Yes." Then he opened them and stared at her. "And sometimes we get to keep them and sometimes we don't."

"Exactly," she said. "Please tell everyone to stop asking after me, checking on me. Okay?"

"Okay." He stepped back, and together they walked back into the dining room.

The wineglasses were all empty—a sign that someone would eventually say something they regretted. But even if they did, all would be well; this group forgave, moved on and laughed about it at the next party. Like the time Mae told Cooper he really shouldn't have cut his hair because it made his head look like a bowling pin, or when Christine told Mae she was off her rocker to own a horse farm without horses. Well, maybe not everyone forgave her that one, but it hadn't been mentioned since.

Annabelle helped clear the table and dully heard the conversations through a blur of red wine and one martini—straight up—that Shawn had made her before dinner. He did this, she knew, to soften the tumultuous emotions, but actually alcohol only intensified everything she felt, gave it the sharp edges of broken glass. As she watched the married couples lean in for private jokes or the other two women laugh about their husbands, her lonesomeness increased, her sense of isolation keen.

She headed toward the kitchen with a handful of empty plates, heard Cooper's and Shawn's voices in a familiar melody. She stopped before the kitchen door, leaned up against the wall to listen, their hushed words filtering through the doorway.

She heard Cooper say, "It's her, old buddy, isn't it?"

Silence was the answer and Annabelle wished she could poke her head into the kitchen, see the expression on Shawn's face. She should never have alluded to Maria. Now Shawn's past heartaches had come to visit also.

Annabelle clung to the plates for fear she would drop them, shatter Cooper and Christine's family china and give away her presence.

Shawn answered, "It's always been her . . . then and now."

"I'm sorry, buddy."

A long, drawn-out silence followed, and Annabelle stayed frozen behind the swinging door—if she entered, they'd know she'd heard. She tiptoed back to the dining room, set the dirty dishes on the table. Christine, Mae and Frank looked up at her. She walked to her purse and picked it up. "I gotta go, okay? Christine, thanks for having me. It was a great night. I'll get my serving dish tomorrow."

"You're walking home?"

Annabelle nodded at the ever-responsible Frank. "Yes, it's only two blocks. I'll be fine."

Outside, the moist air hit her with an awakening jolt. Just as it would always be Maria for Shawn, it would always be Knox for her. They'd been married for eighteen years, dated for six before that. If she did the math, he'd been gone for less than ten percent of her entire time with him, and she'd never been with anyone else. There was only one time when her and Shawn's friendship had crossed the line into the realm of other possibilities.

She'd had a final exam the next morning, and the house she rented with three other girls was in the full throes of a party. She'd gone to Shawn's house to study—it was the semester Knox was away doing an internship with a state senator.

She and Shawn had driven the hour back to Marsh Cove. His parents had been out of town. They studied in the large library until her eyes started to close; he quizzed her on some remote French treaty in a time and place she didn't much care about. And she'd told him so.

He came to sit with her on the couch, wrapped his arm around her—which wasn't unusual. He continued to study while she dozed on his shoulder, as if his knowledge would filter over to her. She'd awakened to him staring at her, pushing her bangs off her forehead and then holding his hand to her face.

It had seemed the most natural thing to kiss him. Even later, when she wanted to regret that one kiss, she never felt the guilt she supposed she should—after

94

all, Shawn was Knox's best friend too. The remorse never came and another kiss never happened.

But in that brief moment, something blossomed inside her that she hadn't thought possible—an attraction to someone besides Knox Murphy, with his ragged curls, his brown eyes, his deep laughter. This feeling was not something she wanted or needed and so she shoved it away.

They awoke the next morning on the couch, crooked and cramped, drove to school with only seconds to spare before the history final, and both aced the exam to make the dean's list.

Nothing was ever said about the kiss again. Was it just another secret she hadn't realized she'd been keeping?

Once, in a quiet moment long after her and Knox's rushed wedding, she'd caught Shawn's eye and he'd smiled. And in that small space, right below her breastbone, she'd remembered that long-ago kiss. Then she'd reminded herself of the pain and misery she'd felt without Knox, when she'd been unable to find him during Hurricane Hugo.

And for almost two decades, she hadn't thought about that kiss once.

With all the broken pieces of her life scattered or misplaced, she felt incapable of desiring anyone but Knox. The deepening knowledge that she would forever wonder who was with her husband on the night of his death destroyed anything of want or longing inside her.

How, she thought as she climbed the stairs to her front porch, was she to ever love again? Trust again? Believe in herself and what was true in her life?

The weight of her questions collapsed on her as she sat down in the wicker rocking chair, stared at the pewter-colored blending of water and sky: there was no horizon to disappear into tonight—only darkness.

Footsteps echoed on the sidewalk. A figure walked with swinging arms, stopped at her stairs and hesitated to come to the porch: Shawn. He didn't see her in the rocking chair. She watched him under the streetlight and felt like a voyeur, yet couldn't bring herself to call his name.

He stood there for long minutes, turned to leave, then moved back until he finally continued down the street and rounded the corner back to Cooper and Christine's. Relief and loneliness spread through her as she rose and entered her empty house.

She wanted to scream out at Knox, *What were you doing?*

She had to do something, find something. Just walking around vowing to keep it together, faking a smile and feigning bravado were causing her to falter. She entered the kitchen and slammed her palm down on the counter. Helplessness unraveled her heart, and she felt consumed by a need for control. On a piece of white notepaper with the cutesy quote "My heart will always be in a cottage by the sea," written in script on the bottom of the pad, she began to list the facts she knew.

Fact One: Knox flew out on a Tuesday afternoon to go hunting in Colorado at a ranch in Durango where he'd been ten times before (or at least he said he'd been there ten times).

Fact Two: He stopped in Newboro—refueled, filed a flight plan to Durango since he intended to fly by instrument into the evening.

Annabelle's heart paused and the name *Newboro* entered the space before the next beat.

Newboro.

A tingling began at her temples and moved downward to her stomach, then feet. Fragmented ideas fluttered across her mind. Her heart beat as though it couldn't decide whether to stop or quicken, changing its rhythm with each thought.

She ran to her bedroom, pulled the suitcase out from under the bed and began packing, the tingling sensation still running through her body. She would go to Newboro. This was insane, yet her body was acting independent of her thoughts and feelings, as though she were running for an answer she wasn't sure her mind and heart wanted to know, yet she had to go.

SEVEN

SOFIE MILSTEAD

*B*eing separated from Bedford was usually hard for Sofie, but this time she welcomed the reprieve. She'd been in bed sick for two days, heat and ice spreading alternately through her body. Bedford was off in Raleigh for a lecture series that would last only three days. She hadn't told him how she was feeling; she didn't want him to worry. She longed to be alone with this illness, which caused her to dream in multicolored images of dolphins talking, of land and sea melding together.

Sofie pulled her hair behind her head and thought she needed to take a shower, get something to eat. She wasn't sure how she'd gotten sick—either the rainstorm, or the news about the historian, or both had left her vulnerable to a virus. She and Bedford didn't talk much when he wasn't with her in Newboro. She only stayed in his place when he was in town.

She rose from bed and walked to the far corner of her condo. Sofie and her mother had lived here together for more than eight years, and her mother's last canvas lay on an easel in the back of the room, covered with beige muslin. The oil paints in their tubes were dry and cracked.

In an urge she hadn't felt in months, Sophie lifted the muslin off the canvas and stared at the unfinished piece. It had a breathtaking allure. She found herself touching the corners as she exhaled. She sat on the metal stool in front of the easel and picked up a dried brush, attempted to break apart the paint that held the bristles together in a two-year-old memory of when it was last used. Her mother must have taken off in a hurry to leave behind an uncleaned brush.

Her mother's art lessons had infused Sofie with an ability to paint, but not the desire. If, and only if, she added to this painting, picked up a new brush and began to complete the starfish . . . "No," she spoke out loud, put the muslin back over the canvas. If she ruined the art, if she destroyed what her mother had started, she'd never be able to fix it or go back and do it again. You only had one chance to do things right— her mother's advice ingrained in her as permanently as her eye color.

This unfinished painting represented so much that was lost, and deep down Sofie knew that nothing really mattered—people died, they left, they loved and weren't loved back. All of it was spit in the wind, all of it meaningless, and it was ridiculous to try to make sense of senseless chaos. Even her work with the dolphins didn't amount to anything. No matter how she tried to quantify, list, chart, graph or prove her theories, the truth was that none of it meant much in the larger scheme of things. Her life and her work were just specks in a swirling world, and this was just an unfinished painting. Just one.

There was a single cure for her when her thoughts

became trapped in these hopeless thoughts: her dolphins. She grabbed a Windbreaker off the hook by the door.

She headed to the research center, where she always went to calm her inner turmoil. If she stood on the rocky outcropping at the very edge of the harbor, she could see nothing but water, nothing before her to the right or to the left. It was all she could think to do when she reached this hollow, hopeless place.

The water was calm, in harsh contrast to her churning mind. Fever raged in her veins, in her muscles and behind her eyes where a headache throbbed. She sat on the rock, leaned forward and despite her dizziness, she basked in this vista of sea and sky.

She willed the dolphins to appear. Finally, the still water rippled, and they rose above the surface, blew air from their blowholes; two jumped and flipped as though for her enjoyment. The other two swam sideways, glancing at her. It was Delphin's family with his pregnant mate. Sofie smiled and longed to jump in and swim with them.

She shivered inside her Windbreaker, suddenly chilled underneath her pajamas. She leaned farther out, watched them with the acute eye of the researcher. She sensed they knew she was sick—they were sympathetic. She had no way to verify her belief so it would be accepted by the scientific community, but still she felt it to be true. Could love be quantified and put on a chart? Could desire be graphed? Could grief be summarized with bullet points?

She rose and stared down at her dolphins, held her hand over the water to acknowledge their presence. She knew without a doubt that these animals had a name for her.

Sofie's mother had told her many times the story of her real name and why it had had to change. She longed for her mother now to come and tell her the story again. She wanted to curl up on the couch and hear about her mother's love, and how they'd been rescued.

When she returned home, she unplugged the phone and placed the teakettle on the stove. Today, she would remember the story as though she were telling it to herself, as though her mother sat on this couch with the muslin off the canvas, with the sweet smell of paint remover settling in the corners, Bocelli on the stereo, the windows open so she could hear the splash of water against the dock and of boats against the waves: this was how her mother had loved to live.

Sofie clicked PLAY on the CD player, opened a far window and curled beneath her quilt with a cup of hot tea. Her mother was always one to tell stories, use them as another would use salve or medication to heal a sick child. She told fairy tales, myths of gods and goddesses, stories of running and being saved. Sofie couldn't pinpoint the exact moment when she realized that one in particular—about the man who had saved them—was a true story.

Sometime during her childhood, among the telling and retelling, Sofie began to recognize a change in her mother's voice when she told the story of their rescue.

But with her tea in hand, Sofie fell asleep without recalling the entire tale—remembering only the feeling of safety and love.

While she slept, the fever ebbed like an outgoing tide, and Sofie woke to a knock on her front door. Something important had drifted through her in sleep, and yet she couldn't find it when she awoke.

She jumped for the door—maybe Bedford, worried about her, had come home.

But a stranger stood on the threshold dressed in a suit and tie, and holding a briefcase. His eyes squinted at her, giving him an intense and tired appearance, like a weary traveler.

Sofie pulled the blanket tighter around herself, aware now that she was in her pajamas. "May I help you?" she asked, closed the door another inch.

"Yes, I'm looking for a woman named Sofie Milstead."

"I can't help you." Sofie pushed the door.

"Will you let me finish, please? This will only take a minute." The man removed a card from his pocket, handed it to her. "I am Michael Harley. I'm an art historian. I was told that Sofie Milstead lives here and that she's the daughter of the woman who used to own the Newboro Art Studio."

Sofie's fever was gone now, as if her mother had soothed it away with her presence at her side all afternoon. Strength filled her as she told the truth. "I'm Sofie. There is nothing I can tell you about the art studio. It was my mother's and . . . she is gone."

"Please." He put his foot in the doorway. "Can you tell me if you know anything about the artists whose work she bought? Did she keep records or addresses?"

"No, I sold the studio, including the records, to a new owner—Rose Cason. I have nothing to do with any of it."

He took in a long breath. "I already talked to Rose—she gave me your name and address. I don't think you understand how important this is to me. I have been searching for a particular artist for years. I own five of her pieces. Her name is Ariadne. I'm writing an article about her." He spoke so fast he ran out of breath. "All roads have led me to you."

If Sofie let herself, she might feel sorry for this man and his desperate quest, which she was stopping in its tracks.

"Have you seen her art?" he asked.

Sofie stood stock-still, not wanting any movement to suggest a yes or no.

"Have you?" He stepped back now, offering her the opportunity to shut the door, but something in her wanted to hear what he had to say next. "It is sublime. She . . . or he . . . was a master at background." He shook his head. "If you don't know who she is or where she is, I've reached the end of the line."

Sofie could repeat the words her mother had taught her, the words she could recite in perfect order, but so far the false story wasn't needed. She leaned against the doorframe, stared at this anxious man. "I'm sorry," she said, tucked his card into her pocket and shut the door.

When the metal door at the end of the hallway resounded with its familiar slam against the door-frame, Sofie returned to the canvas, removed the cover and stared at the words below the half-formed image. Her mother had painted around the words, which weren't in any order. There were repeated phrases about secrets, longing and loss. Sofie made a list of the words in a sketchbook, put the muslin back over the painting. Her mother had taught her one thing well: the man they ran from must never, ever find them, must never know Sofie existed. Sofie had meant it when she'd told Michael Harley she was sorry that she couldn't help him find Ariadne, but fear was a stronger emotion than sympathy.

Sofie wished the world would slow down so she could take measured and deliberate steps to find her footing once again. She sat back on the coach as the TV droned on, the local news full of tragedies from Charleston to Raleigh and down to Newboro. The local anchorwoman talked about lost dogs, minor arrests and a new condo development on the river being fought by conservation groups.

Knox Murphy.

Her eyes flew open. Was she going crazy or had she just heard his name? She glanced at the TV and saw his face—Knox's beautiful and kind face. She curled her knees up to her chin and leaned forward to listen. A hiking group had found the plane that had crashed two years ago. The bodies of Knox Murphy and an unknown woman had been recovered. The FAA

wanted to know if anyone, anywhere, had any information about the woman on the plane.

"Mother. What am I supposed to do now?" Sofie
cried aloud.

Of course there was no answer.

EIGHT

ANNABELLE MURPHY

*D*arkness, doubt and the dull realization that she was
doing something completely crazy followed
Annabelle on the eight-hour drive to Newboro, North
Carolina. She had called her mother, Grace, who still
lived in the family home that had been rebuilt after
Hurricane Hugo, to come to stay with Keeley. She'd
left a message on Jake's cell phone about where she
was going, and then she'd jumped in the car with two
days' worth of clothes and toiletries.

Who did such a thing, drove through the night to an
unknown destination without anywhere to stay and
not knowing what she would do when she got there?
Her college roommates had raced off to the beach on
a whim, and she had always told them they were out
of their minds. Now look at her, forty years old and
driving to the beach in the middle of the night without
a plan.

Her thoughts became tangled as she steered the car
through the black night. She remembered snippets of
her and Knox's life together in no particular order, as

if she'd cut memories out of a scrapbook, and the pages had been mixed up in the wind of this recent storm blowing through her life.

She recalled Knox taking her to the hospital when she was in labor with Keeley; Knox holding the back of Jake's bike until he couldn't keep up and he let go so Jake could ride on his own; Knox making love to her in their bedroom—silent so as not to wake sleeping children; Keeley running after her daddy's car when he went to work one morning, wanting him to stay home and play Twister with her.

Annabelle examined each memory as if looking for buried evidence, for some hint of Knox's secret life. She took the memories, held them up to the magnifying glass of her mind, to the light of scrutiny, and still found nothing to doubt in their lives, no moment that carried a trace of neglect or betrayal.

She went over the hunting trips he took to Montana and Colorado, how he'd plan them in advance and bring home photos of the mountains, the elk, the riotous rivers where he'd fly-fished. Had he left someone out of the photos?

He'd learned to fly planes when he was in college, taking courses through the local airport until he had his pilot's license for single-engine planes. She'd always begged him not to fly alone. One man, one engine, she'd say—not a good combination. And he'd always told her, with a wink, "I want to live more than you want me to live, believe me."

But when the plane went down it was *not* one man,

one engine. It was one man, one woman, one engine—a vastly different equation.

Maybe she could find the answer if she went all the way back—back to when they were dating, to when he'd proposed. Was there anyone in between the two of them at that time?

In all the years they'd been together, there had only been one gap in time when she hadn't known where he'd been. The weeks before he proposed, she hadn't seen him at all. They'd broken up during a ferocious fight about whether he should take a job out of town or stay in Marsh Cove. Agreeing that they just couldn't see eye to eye on the most fundamental of all choices—where to live—they split up for only the second time in their six years of dating. She was twenty years old, he was twenty-two—she was in her senior year at the College of Charleston; Knox had graduated that past spring, summa cum laude, and was researching law schools.

The breakup had been followed by a period of intense silence. Annabelle didn't hear from or speak to Knox for weeks, as though he'd faded into nothing, as though their years together had never happened. He quit his job at the yacht club, and was traveling to visit law schools and decide his future, which obviously did not include her.

Until his death, she had counted those weeks among the worst of her life. Sitting now in her car, on the way to Newboro, she saw those days clearly and vividly, as though they were a video playing on the windshield.

That September, the start of classes corresponded with a recurring nausea and a dull ache she attributed not only to the loss of their relationship, but to the loss of her dreams for the future.

She carried this grief the way other people bore illness: in her bones, her marrow, her very heartbeats reminding her of a changed life. Not once did she feel the thrill of new possibilities that her friends were telling her about. Belle, they'd say, you can start a whole new life now, dream bigger and newer. You've been dating him since ninth grade, for God's sake. Spread your wings. Meet someone new. Go out. Get drunk, have fun, make new friends.

She couldn't do what her friends suggested. She trudged to classes. Before each day, she threw up in the small bathroom in the house she rented with Mae and two other girls who long since had faded from her memory—girls who partied all night, thought her preoccupation with a high school boyfriend absurd.

The nausea continued, and she visited the college chaplain, believing she needed some type of counseling. The chaplain was kind, bald and looked like Thomas Merton, whom she had studied in her freshman year religion class. He spoke in soft tones, warm words of encouragement about broken hearts and life lessons, about not understanding the meaning of events until one had time to step back from them.

Many words were said, an hour's worth, but all Annabelle took home with her were two sentences: "Just because we don't know why things happen doesn't mean there aren't reasons." This phrase she'd echoed many times in her life to friends and family, so much so that they often repeated it back to her. The second line was "And you need to make sure there's not a medical reason why you're throwing up every morning."

Not once had she considered that possibility—that the nausea was caused by more than heartbreak.

On the way home from the chaplain's office, she stopped by the medical clinic and discovered that her white blood cell count, her red blood cell count and all other counts were normal. They wanted to try a pregnancy test.

She'd laughed. Actually laughed. How could she be pregnant by someone she wasn't with anymore? Until she counted backward and realized she'd missed a cycle.

She knew before they told her, before the nurse came into the examining room with the pinched mouth, the pamphlets on pregnancy options and the lecture on birth control. In a daze Annabelle stuffed the pamphlets into her backpack.

Pregnant.

With child.

Knox's baby.

Each thought shot hope through her—he would return to her now. Then immediately came the dread, the emptiness she'd felt for weeks now. Maybe he wouldn't return; maybe this news wouldn't bring him back.

The thoughts bounced through her as she signed out of the clinic, drove from Charleston to Marsh Cove without stopping by her rental house. During that hour she was lost to her senses and her emotions, which warred inside her mind and soul. This kind of thing only happened to *those* girls—not to her.

So many dreams ruined—so many hopes undone by this simple fact: she was pregnant with her ex-boyfriend's child. A nightmare from which she was not going to wake up, in which all her options were bad ones.

Twenty years old, a senior in college and pregnant.

She rolled down the windows of her beat-up Camaro and let the ocean air wash over her face. It was hurricane season, and rain from a tropical storm was forecast for the next two days.

Annabelle formulated a short-term plan: have her mother call the college and tell them she was deathly sick, tell her parents she'd come home with something akin to the bubonic plague and spend the next days in bed, sleeping and deciding what to do with her life, what to do with her and her baby's life.

The thought made nausea rise as she drove over the river. She watched the water rush toward the sea and she wished, for only the slightest second, that she could follow it far away.

When she pulled into town, she drove past Knox's family's home first, parked and stared at the long, rutted driveway, which led to the farmhouse and then farther back to the barn and stables. Live oaks lined the drive; a wrought-iron fence with a scrolled "M" was shut tight. She got out and walked to the gate, fingered the ironwork. She wanted to push the code to open the gate, run to Mrs. Murphy and tell her everything, beg her to go find her son and bring him back.

The smallest voice inside told her to go home. Whether it was ingrained etiquette, fear of what she'd discover about where Knox was and had been or just complete fatigue, she wasn't sure. She climbed back in her car and drove home through the familiar streets of Marsh Cove.

In college everyone had told her that there was more to life than these streets and lanes, more than these tidal creeks and wide rivers, more than this one small town. Of course she understood that—she just didn't care to go there. She loved learning about other places, reading about them, even visiting them. Her mild obsession with archaeology was an enigma to those who knew she never intended to leave this town, yet she hungered for information about other places and what they revealed beneath their layers of silt and rock.

As she neared Palmetto Street, an extended honk jerked her from her thoughts. She'd driven straight through a stop sign at Route 23 and barely missed being plowed down by a chicken truck. The truck swerved; chicken feathers flew from the caged coops and the driver shot her an obscene gesture, yanked the vehicle to a halt at the side of the road. Trembling, she pulled her car over.

Annabelle grimaced, mouthed, *I'm sorry*. The truck driver shouted expletives and pulled back into traffic. Annabelle sat frozen, afraid to take the steering wheel, to drive. To make a single move right then seemed impossible. The chicken cages jostled back and forth as the truck turned a corner. She felt a pang—as if from seeing a dead deer on the side of the road—and she wasn't sure whom the sorrow was for: the caged chickens or her frightened self.

Her feelings were so misplaced and disquieted she couldn't decide where to let them rest. She drove toward the only solace she could think of: home. Her brother, ten years older than she was, had moved to Texas years ago to run a software company. Her dad would be at work, and Annabelle would have her mother to herself.

She pulled into the driveway, parked her car and came through the back door into the kitchen. Grace Clark sat at the kitchen table, dividing mail into piles. "Oh, Belle, darling, what a nice surprise." She dropped the mail and went to Annabelle's side, hugged her.

"Hi, Mom." Annabelle bit back tears. She wasn't ready to tell her mother her news yet.

"Are you okay? Aren't you supposed to be in class? What's wrong?" She put her hand on Annabelle's forehead.

"I don't feel well at all. I think I'm getting sick." *Really sick.*

"Is it Knox?"

"No," Annabelle said. "I just don't feel well. I went to the nurse. . . ."

"Okay, baby. Go on upstairs. Get in bed. I'll make you some soup while you sleep."

Annabelle dropped her head onto her mother's shoulder. "Oh, Mom."

The fact did not escape her that soon she would be a mom also—that the name she was calling out was the name she herself would soon be called. A single mom. Alone.

Her mother smoothed the hair from her face. "You look terrible. Have you lost weight?"

"A little. I've been sick to my stomach."

"Okay, get to bed. Where are your bags?"

Annabelle shrugged. "I didn't bring any. . . . I came home straight from the medical clinic."

The bed beckoned with sweet denial and Annabelle burrowed under the covers, into the pillow, and found solace in pretending none of this was happening. In this pale purple bedroom with the Eagles and Bon Jovi posters and the cheerleading trophies, with the bulletin board full of old notes, a dried corsage and tiara from homecoming court (she hadn't been the queen, only in the court; Mae had been the queen), she could be fifteen years old and in love, believing in her own Southern belle status, in her own goodness and her love for Knox Murphy.

Some people dreamed of the future and what it held for them, and at one time, she had also. Now she dreamed of the past, of what she could have done *then* to change today.

Sleep finally visited Annabelle, and she drifted off into disjointed dreams of missed classes, car wrecks with trucks and being lost in a maze of familiar marshes and creeks. She awoke to her mother standing over her bed with a tray of soup and toast—a balm for all evils, according to family lore.

Annabelle sat up in bed, rested her back against the headboard. "Thank you." Dreamscapes washed over her, and in the split moment between her mother lifting her hand and reaching to touch Annabelle's cheek, she made a decision to speak.

"I'm pregnant." There were better ways to have said this. She could have prepared a speech, written a letter, asked her brother to tell her parents. She could have said it any other way but this abrupt announce-ment that would surely shatter her mother's heart.

But there they were: the words bold and shimmering in the room, across her mother's stricken face. And just like the night when she'd made love with Knox, she couldn't take it back.

"Did you have a bad dream?" her mother asked, and Annabelle knew her mother fervently wished she'd only imagined her condition.

Annabelle shook her head and waited for the tirade that would surely follow. Maybe it was why she had told her mother in the first place—she needed to be punished.

Her mother hugged her. "Oh, Annabelle."

"I'm sorry, Mother. I am so sorry," Annabelle whispered on choked tears.

"Knox?" her mother asked.

"Of course," Annabelle said, closed her eyes.

Her mother stroked her head. "Have you told him?"

"No, I just found out . . . and came home."

"Try to sleep now. We have a lot to talk about and decide. I'll tell your father when I find the right moment. For now . . . sleep."

For the next two days, her mother offered comfort in measured doses until her father came home early and haggard from a business trip, stating that Hurricane Hugo was headed toward coastal South Carolina and they needed to evacuate immediately.

Evacuate.

Annabelle glanced around her room, at all her belongings, and wondered what to pack. She climbed from bed at her father's prodding, grabbed her suitcase from the back of the closet.

Her room smelled of chicken noodle soup, chamomile tea and lavender—all scents from childhood. In those distressed days of her life, she didn't want to leave her room. Something unalterable was about to occur: she felt it in every part of her body, and wanted to crawl back under the covers. Leaving this room meant a million things, including facing her pregnancy and possible damage to her home, but she felt that her emotions were distilled into one: fear.

Annabelle's hands shook as she lifted the suitcase onto her bed, from the nausea, fear of telling her father the truth about her illness and dread of the incoming hurricane. She'd been through this before: hurricane warnings, evacuation, deciding what was really worth keeping. The last time had been two years before, and all that had come was rain and wind knocking down her childhood tree house.

This time there was more at stake than a tree house full of tea-party paraphernalia. How was she to face possible disaster without Knox? Loneliness spread through her like warm water, left her weak with regret and loss.

"Shit," she said, trying out a word she rarely used. She threw a pair of jeans and a sweatshirt into the suitcase. Then she looked around her room for what she would really miss, what would cause her grief if Mother Nature took it on wind and rain.

She crawled under her bed, grabbed the large box full of Knox's letters, notes and photos. Losing this, above all other losses, would fill her with anguish, and she placed the box into the suitcase along with a few more clothes, her journal and the small oil painting on her dresser, done by Shawn in fifth grade.

Father poked his head in the room. "You ready, pumpkin?"

She nodded.

"Only one suitcase, right?"

"Only one, Dad. See?" She pointed at it. "Do you really think this . . . one will hit?" she asked, already knowing the answer from his pinched mouth and unshaven cheeks.

"Yes, I do. Let's just pray it doesn't hit us too hard. But it's bearing down on South Carolina like a loco-motive gaining speed." He nodded toward the door. "I'm sorry you don't feel well, but we have to go now."

"Where are we gonna stay?" Annabelle slammed her suitcase shut, locked the latch.

"We'll head toward Atlanta and stay with your aunt Barbara."

Annabelle nodded, which made her dizzy and nau-seous. "Can I make one quick phone call before we leave?"

He nodded. "Hurry." He grabbed the suitcase and left the room.

Annabelle dialed Knox's phone number, not knowing what she would say, but needing this one touch point before she could walk from her room and face whatever came next.

Mrs. Murphy, breathless, answered the phone. "Hello."

"Hi, Mrs. Murphy, it's Belle."

"Oh, hello, dear. Please tell me you know where Knox is."

Annabelle's stomach plummeted. "I have no idea. That's why I was calling. I wanted to talk to him before we . . . evacuate today."

"Oh, dear. Oh, dear. That's why we're trying to find him. We're leaving within the hour or we'll be stuck here, and I haven't heard from him in a couple days. He said he was going to stay with Cooper, but Cooper hasn't seen him."

Annabelle dropped to her bed as her knees gave way. "Okay." What else was there to say?

"If you hear from him, will you please tell him we are crazy trying to find him and that we'll be in Columbia staying at his grandfather's house?"

"Yes, and if you find him, please tell him I'm looking for him also. I'll be at my aunt Barbara's in Atlanta."

"Okay . . . okay." Mrs. Murphy hung up without saying goodbye, which she had never done since Annabelle had known her. So much was changing. The world seemed to be turning into a place she didn't recognize.

She stood at her doorway, stared at the bulletin board, the pink bedspread, the pale purple walls—all paraphernalia from her childhood. She swallowed her grief as one does a bitter pill, and she understood, as she had not before, that when she returned to this place neither her soul nor her room would retain anything of their childish airs.

The hurricane hit with an angry force, as though it had a vendetta against the South, against the history and beauty of coastal South Carolina, testing her fortitude and alliances as the Civil War had decades before. And, as always, her people rose to the challenge with determination and courage. It was the Southern way.

Entire houses were washed into the streets of Sullivan's Island, neighborhoods destroyed on Isle of Palms. Charleston was left battered and bruised.

Annabelle watched the devastation from the static-filled TV screen in Aunt Barbara's apartment in midtown Atlanta as the wind and rain whipped through the land she loved. They all sat transfixed as they waited for at least one shot of Marsh Cove, their home or neighborhood. But even the familiar names and streets were unrecognizable in the chaotic aftermath.

They weren't able to go back for at least a week; the authorities prevented everyone from Awendaw to Charleston from returning to their homes. Annabelle felt as though she floated, so dislocated from time and place that she couldn't find her bearings. She'd heard of pilots who spun out of control when they lost all sense of up or down. This was how she pictured herself, spinning, spinning, unable to find the horizon to right herself.

In those gyrating days she almost forgot about the baby, about Knox, her mind never reaching for a solid thought. Until Aunt Barbara took her into the back bedroom.

"Honey, is there something you need to tell me?"

"What do you mean?" Annabelle sat on the edge of the guest bed, fingered the fringe on the quilt.

"You're different, dear. And I know why. I've been there, remember?"

"You mean when Uncle Mark left you?"

"No, when I was pregnant."

Annabelle closed her eyes. There was no way she was showing—no way Aunt Barbara could know unless her mother had told her.

"I hate her," Annabelle mumbled under her breath, and then opened her eyes. "I hate her for telling you."

"No one told me anything." Aunt Barbara took her hand, held it. "There are some things women know. Fortunately your dad wouldn't notice if you came out wearing my old maternity clothes." She smiled, touched Annabelle's cheek.

"For a few minutes, I forgot about it." Annabelle shrugged. "For just a few minutes."

"Tell me everything."

"There's not much to tell. I'm pregnant with Knox's baby, and he hasn't called or talked to me in six weeks. And I can't find him and neither can his parents."

Aunt Barbara pulled Annabelle to her. "He doesn't know?"

"No. Only Mother and the pinched-mouth nurse at the medical clinic. I truly don't know what to do. Mother hasn't mentioned it since I told her, and I figure she's ignoring it or she didn't hear me. All she's done is cook for me and let me sleep."

"Sometimes that's all a mother can do, Belle."

"But so many . . . decisions."

"Well, dear, go ahead and list them."

"The first, above all else, is tell Knox or not tell Knox. Like option A or B in a multiple choice test, and I want to pick C."

Aunt Barbara stroked Annabelle's hair. "I won't ever tell you what to do."

"But I want your opinion."

"Of course you must tell him. You've dated for how long?"

"Six years."

"You find him, and you tell him."

"I can't find him until they let us go home. I have to . . . wait. And what if he's . . ."

"*Shh* . . . don't say that. Sometimes waiting is good."

"And Dad." Annabelle dropped her face into her hands.

"Do you want me to tell him? I am his sister. . . ."

"Not yet." Annabelle's head snapped up. "No one else can know until Knox does. There's something wrong about that."

"Yes, I agree."

Annabelle's mother opened the bedroom door, stared at them. "What are you girls up to?"

"Nothing," Annabelle said, wiped a tear from her face.

"Oh, oh . . ." Her mother entered the room, shut the door. "Please, Barbara, don't tell Garner yet. He has enough on his mind with the hurricane and whether the house has survived. . . ."

Barbara nodded. "Yes, I know."

Mother sat on the bed next to Annabelle. "How are you feeling?"

"Fine, Mother." Annabelle held up her hands. "Just fine."

"Well, they've just announced on TV that our section of Marsh Cove is open to residents. So, Dad is out there packing the car."

"What if we return and the house isn't . . . there or something?" Anxiety clamped Annabelle's lungs down as she took short breaths.

"We'll figure that out when we get there." Her mother hugged her. "Like we always do and always will."

"Okay." Annabelle rose, and fortified by sleep and family, she felt ready to face what waited in Marsh Cove.

NINE

ANNABELLE MURPHY

The roof of Annabelle's childhood home was gone, as though the house was a movie set with only the walls and interior. Hundred-year-old trees lay across the streets like meager broken twigs. Whole landing piers had floated from the river onto land; half of an unmoored dock lay in front of Annabelle's house as though it had been placed there as a walkway.

Her father parked the car in the cracked driveway and examined the front yard. Annabelle's mother climbed out of the car and went to his side; he placed an arm over her shoulders, and together they stood and stared at the battered house. Annabelle stayed in the car gazing in wonder at the changed landscape, then in awe of her parents standing together, steadfast and still.

They turned to her, motioned for her to join them. She went to them. "It's not as bad as some. The Carpenters lost everything," her dad said.

Annabelle ran for the front door; her dad yelled at her to stop. "You don't know if it's safe yet, darling. Let me go in first." He stepped carefully through the front door.

The blazing sun mocked what had come before. How could a place of such balmy, beautiful, cloud-free days have such destruction wrought upon it?

Annabelle pointed to the garage, where a live oak lay on top of it like a Lincoln Log tossed by a child. "Good thing we put my car in the garage, eh?"

"Oh, Belle."

"Mom? Have you heard about anyone else? Is everyone okay?"

"Your father has been keeping in touch with the mayor, Mrs. Barkley refused to evacuate and still hasn't been found. She is presumed—"

"Dead."

"Yes, and the Chandlers lost their home and farm, both. Everyone else has severe damage like us. I'm sure we won't be able to stay here. No one is really able. . . ."

"It looks like a war zone," Annabelle said, stretched her hands across the yard. "I don't see how this will ever be cleaned up, how it will ever be the same."

Her mother pulled her close. "No, it won't be the same. Things never do stay the same, do they? But we can rebuild. The South is good at that, you know."

"I know." Annabelle squeezed her mother's hand. "But am I?"

Her mother spoke to her in a voice that resonated. "Now, listen to me. You *are* strong enough. For whatever storm your life brings, you are strong enough to endure and thrive because you are a Clark, and God has granted you an extraordinary legacy of strength. There are worse things in life than what we are about to endure."

"Thank you," Annabelle said, leaned against her mother's shoulder and marveled at the changes that had come about in the ten short days since she'd gone to the chaplain. Ten days—a lifetime.

Her father came to the door. "Y'all can come in, but be prepared. Not much can be saved."

They entered the foyer, which spoke in whispered tones of a receded flood. A thick line of black mud had climbed five feet up the wall. Mold grew in the heat and humidity below the line. The moist odor of mildew permeated the air in a sickening stench.

"Oh, my Scalamandre wallpaper—they don't make it anymore," her mother said, ran her hands along the stairwell and glanced into the dining room. "Mother's dining room table . . ."

The afternoon went on as her mother recounted all that was gone, calculated in a never-ending equation of loss. Then she gathered them together, and made the three of them drop to their knees and thank God for their safety, for this reminder that material possessions were nothing compared to the losses others might have suffered.

When they rose from their prayer, Annabelle asked for the car keys.

Her dad placed his hands on her shoulders. "You can't drive out there, honey. The roads are still dangerous. Lines are down. Martial law has been imposed in some places."

"Dad, I have to know if Knox and his family are okay."

He nodded. "I'll take you."

They drove their pickup truck with extreme caution through the local streets, and then out to Route 23 toward the farm. With a single-minded capriciousness, the hurricane had left the Murphy farm virtually untouched except for a few downed trees and a crushed chicken coop. Annabelle and her dad sat in the truck, stared at the white clapboard house with its pale blue shutters: a house Annabelle knew as well as her own.

"Looks like all is well here," her dad said.

She nodded. "Do you mind waiting while I see if they're home?"

He shook his head, got out of the truck and leaned against it, lifted his face to the sun. "Take your time. Not like I'm in any rush to get back. Aunt Sissy is picking your mama up right now, taking her to her town home, where we'll meet her."

Annabelle stepped around scattered tree branches to the front door. Her hand shook as she knocked on the door.

Mrs. Murphy immediately opened it, as though she'd been anticipating her visit. "Hi," Annabelle said, lifted her fingers in a half wave. "I'm so glad to see your house is okay. . . . I wanted to check."

Mrs. Murphy placed a hand on Annabelle's arm. "And yours?"

"Mostly gone." And for the first time since they'd driven past the U.S. marshal on the entrance to the county road, tears filled Annabelle's eyes. "Oh, there are some things Dad thinks we can save, but . . ."

"Oh, dear. I am so sorry." She opened the door wide. "Come in, have a cup of sweet tea and . . . you must be exhausted."

Annabelle glanced over her shoulder and saw her dad lying on the hood of the pickup truck, his eyes closed and his body slack. He was obviously asleep.

"Okay . . . ," Annabelle said.

Mrs. Murphy followed her glance. "Should we wake him up and ask him in?"

"I think he's fine." Annabelle took a step into the pine-scented kitchen and asked the only thing she wanted to know. "Is Knox here?"

"No." Mrs. Murphy shook her head. "But I do know he's okay. I was hoping you could tell us where he is. He came home two days ago and ate like he hadn't eaten in days, told us he was fine and had survived the hurricane outside Charleston . . . and then he left again. We haven't seen him since then. I don't know where that boy keeps going, but a mama can't follow a twenty-two-year-old around."

"Oh." Annabelle sat down at the oak table, where she and Knox used to do their homework, eat fried chicken, hold hands while they read.

Mrs. Murphy sat next to her, placed a tall glass of tea on the table. "Dear, I'm sorry I can't help you. I know you miss him, and I know how torn up you must be about this breakup, but sometimes you just have to let things go to see if they return to you."

Dear God, how many times had Annabelle heard that? Let them fly free, and if they're really yours, they'll fly back. She'd even seen a poster with the saying and a flying bird. Maybe that was true about birds, but she didn't see, in any way, how it applied to Knox Murphy.

She took a long swallow of tea and smiled at Mrs. Murphy. If Knox returned in the next few days, she didn't want Mrs. Murphy telling him she had been morose, looking for him. "I'm fine, really. I was just worried about all of you, so was Dad, so we drove out here to make sure you were okay. God knows when the phone lines will be up."

"Where will you stay tonight?"

"I don't know. . . . I guess Aunt Sissy's—that's where Mom is right now."

"Your aunt lives in a one-bedroom town home."

Annabelle shrugged, leaned forward. "There don't appear to be a lot of options left in Marsh Cove. Dad wants to start emptying and cleaning the house as soon we can."

"Your family must stay here. Please. We have four

bedrooms, and we're only using one. Daniel and I were wondering who we could help—and lookee here, the good Lord answered us right away—you and your family came knocking." She grinned as though Gabriel himself had just come down from heaven and told her to take care of the Clark family.

"Oh, no . . . really."

"Oh, yes, and as soon as Daniel is finished helping at the docks, he can help your dad with the house. We have been blessed with such little loss, we can surely help those who have lost so much more."

"I can't . . . I can't stay here if . . ."

Mrs. Murphy touched her face. "Yes, you can. You have been like a daughter to me for the past six years, and now I can help you and your family."

Annabelle nodded, overcome with the thought that she was carrying this woman's grandchild, how Mrs. Murphy would be housing her own flesh and blood without knowing it. She turned from Knox's mother and bit back the tears.

"Please don't cry, Belle—we'll all get to the other side of this. Now go tell your father."

Annabelle finished her tea, wondered if caffeine was okay to drink and rose to tell her dad they could stay here on this huge farm while they rebuilt their house and lives. Her heart lifted, like that bird on the poster, at the thought that eventually Knox would come home and she would be right here. They'd take a long walk to the barn . . . talk, and she'd tell him.

Shortly, soon, he'd know.

Two weeks of naked sun and throbbing heat passed. Long days of manual labor left Mr. Murphy and Annabelle's father so exhausted they fell asleep each night immediately after Mrs. Murphy's home-cooked meals. Annablle hadn't seen Knox's mother so animated in years—she had people to take care of, and by God, she'd do just that.

Mrs. Murphy did their laundry, cooked breakfast, lunch and dinner, put ironed sheets on their beds and fresh towels in their rooms, left cold glasses of water with lemon slices at their bedsides and fussed over Annabelle, her mother and dad.

Each day, Annabelle's blazing hope of seeing Knox dwindled to embers and then soot—she had given up thinking that he would return to his parents' home. She lay in bed each night envisioning where he was, what he might be doing and in what foreign place he could be doing those things without her. She went from hopeful, to sad, to angry and back again, like a clock's hands going around and around.

She imagined Knox came home, saw her parents' car, turned and left again.

At the beginning of the third week, when she knew that sooner rather than later she would have to tell her dad about the baby since her middle was starting to strain against her T-shirts, Knox walked casually through the kitchen doorway, as though he'd been gone for an hour.

Smiling, radiant at the sight of him, Annabelle felt

the immediate joy of his presence like a balm. She jumped up from the kitchen chair, ran to him, knocked over a full bowl of snap peas and threw herself into his arms. For this first time in her life, she didn't care what the others thought of her, or why she went to him with such abandon. She only cared that he was finally there.

It would all be okay now.

She buried her face in his neck, in his chest, and inhaled him, listened to his heartbeat. He held on to her, and the world righted itself until she pulled back from him, saw his face. Confusion crossed his features like a school of menhaden startled in the river—quick, jumping and chaotic.

He stepped back and glanced around the room. "Hey," he said.

Mrs. Murphy jumped up from her chair; Annabelle moved to allow her to hug her son. "Where have you been?" his mother asked.

"I've been helping in Charleston, crashing with friends." He hugged her back, then draped his arm over her left shoulder as he faced the table. "You think it's bad here, you should see Charleston and the islands. Almost complete devastation . . . with mold."

Mrs. Murphy grinned at him. "I figured you were doing something like that."

His father rose, hugged Knox. "Damn glad you're safe, son."

"I'm sorry I haven't been in touch—not much in the way of phones out there, and whenever I finished, all I could do was sleep."

Annabelle took steps backward toward the table.

He glanced at her, then at her parents. "How are y'all? Your house?"

"We and the house have been in better shape." Annabelle's father stood, walked to Knox and shook his hand. "We're glad you're safe. These have been hard days and we were all worried about you."

"I'm sorry to have worried anyone. I told Mama I was all right."

"Yes," she said. "Yes, but it is good to see you. Sit, have some dinner."

Annabelle watched as he walked to the cabinet, noting something different about him when he reached for a plate and then set it on the table. Although it couldn't be true, he seemed to have become taller or wider, as though something of substance had been altered inside him.

He sat at the table, in the chair they'd kept empty for him during the past weeks. The evening spilled shadows into the room, morphed the shapes of the trees, tractor and birdhouse outside. The water pitcher on the table, sliced lemons floating on the surface, shook when Knox sat, the only movement in the room.

He glanced around the table. "What's wrong?"

"I think we're all just glad you're home," his father said and passed the plate of chicken. "Don't know what to say . . . been waiting on you. You know, we could use your help around here, too. The Clarks' house was almost destroyed. After two weeks, all we've managed to do is haul the furniture to the dump, box up the salvageable items."

Knox took a large bite of the fried chicken, closed his eyes. "So good, Mama. So much better than the protein bars and canned soup I've been living on." He looked at Annabelle, finally. "Can the house be saved? Have any contractors been by or seen the damage?"

Annabelle shrugged, still speechless in his presence, the only words she wanted to say to him almost spilling out of their own accord. Her father spoke up. "We finally found a contractor from somewhere up in Asheville who is willing to come down and help us and the Carters. What survived was the most important things. My family." His voice quavered; he looked away toward the wall. "The Carters lost their seventeen-year-old son when his car slipped from the road into the river."

"Buddy Carter is dead?" Knox dropped the chicken onto his plate. "No."

"Yes, I'm afraid so." Mrs. Murphy reached across the table to Knox. "And a few more of your classmates haven't been found yet . . . but they hold out hope that, like you, they are somewhere safe but just can't call or come home yet."

Knox closed his eyes. "I'm sorry about Buddy."

"We all are," Annabelle said, her voice soft and frail.

Knox squinted at her. "Are you okay, Belle?"

She nodded. "It's been a long few weeks, Knox."

"Yes, it has." He picked at his peas with the fork. "It

feels like a year or more. . . . So much has changed, it seems like more time should've gone by."

As Annabelle watched him say this, she knew, absolutely knew, that he was talking about more than the external landscape; he spoke of his internal terrain. Fear wrapped around her, and instinctively she rose from the table and left the house. She couldn't look at this boy she had loved for years, this boy whose baby grew inside her, this boy who suddenly and surely seemed a man sitting across the table talking of change.

She let the screen door bang shut behind her and ran toward the barn at the far end of the property. She couldn't see it, but she knew where it was, where the hayloft provided a respite, a place to be alone. Her mother had found many excuses why Annabelle couldn't work alongside the men in the heat of the day, still not wanting to reveal her daughter's condition to her husband. Why hadn't Annabelle thought of the hayloft before? She could have sat up there, passed the hours in "their" place instead of staring out Mrs. Murphy's kitchen window waiting for Knox's Jeep to come into view, or hiding in the bedroom in the wee hours of the morning, hoping no one but her mother heard her vomit in the cramped farmhouse bathroom.

She ran in bare feet over sharp gravel, across broken glass from a toppled tractor, through mud and around a litter of kittens until she reached the edge of the field where the old barn sat atop a hill. She bent over to take a deep breath; dizziness washed over her. Despite having once been on the track team and jogging miles a day in college, she had not moved much beyond the house and yard in the past several weeks. She attempted to take another stabilizing breath, and fell to the ground in a heap.

She couldn't tell him now. The real Knox was gone, and a new man had appeared, a man she would never tell, a man distant and different, gone into some new internal place where she did not belong.

She added up the days: they hadn't seen each other for seven weeks, longer than anytime she'd ever been apart from him before they met.

The cool grass felt good against her cheek, and she faded into it, let the tears take her longing for Knox Murphy into the earth, away from her. Oh, if only it could work that way, if only she could release this need for him into the dirt, but the ground was still saturated with rainwater and seemed unable to absorb more than it already had.

She rolled over onto her back, spread her arms and legs, felt a dull pain where glass had cut into the arch of her foot. The branches above her were like a net across the sky, also catching whatever she wanted to release and sending it right back down to settle into her soul. The Spanish moss danced in a swaying motion that made her dizzy again. She closed her eyes.

The earth shook with subtle steps, careful steps. She didn't want to see her mother, her father, the Murphys; she didn't want to explain why she'd run away.

But when the footsteps stopped at her side, she knew before she opened her eyes that it was Knox who stood beside her. He knelt down, touched her foot. "You're bleeding, Belle."

She opened her eyes. "I know," she said.

He lay down next to her, took her hand and held it in silence. Long moments passed, the only sounds the wind, whispering moss and, far off, frogs singing to the approaching twilight. Then he spoke into her ear. "I'm sorry."

His sweet voice, his lips against her hair and his hand on hers released the withheld emotions, and she turned toward him. "For what?"

"I know these have been rough weeks for you and your family, and I wasn't here."

"The weeks were rough before the hurricane, Knox." She touched his face, his familiar face.

"I know, Belle. I know. But we agreed, didn't we?"

"Yes, we did."

He ran his hand through her hair, down her spine and then around to her middle. He held his hand to her stomach while they faced each other on the grass.

His eyes asked a question and she answered it for him. "Yes," she said, knowing that someone who had held her for years would notice those weeks of growth on her small frame.

He seemed to hold his breath as he asked quietly, "Yes, what?"

She closed her eyes, not wanting to say the words,

not wanting to make him do or say something he didn't want to do or say.

"Knox?" she asked.

"What?"

"Did you come out here to get back together or just to say goodbye?"

His hand cupped her abdomen, stayed there. "What do you mean?"

"Today, right now, when you came after me, said you're sorry—was that to say goodbye?"

He pulled her to him so she couldn't see his face. "Oh, Annabelle Marie Clark. I've loved you since you were practically a child."

"And now?" she whispered over his shoulder.

"And now . . . you carry my child, don't you?"

She pushed him away. "Knox, you have to answer me. You have to tell me—did you come to say goodbye or to return? Tell me. . . ." Her voice cracked, broke on the last word, into a million pieces.

"I'm here. I'm here."

"I know you're here, but why?"

"This is where I live. This is my family." He pulled her close. "My family."

And she didn't have the will to ask again—to discover if he had truly meant to return to her, or if he had only now decided, with the news she still hadn't spoken out loud. He stood, pulled her to her feet. "I love you, Belle. I always have. I always will. There are a few things I have to do. Trust me."

She nodded. He dropped his forehead to hers, kissed

her, then ran back toward the house. She watched him and marveled how they had just had an entire discussion about their future with so few words. It had always been this way with them—understanding without words, without argument.

But had he come to say goodbye or to return to her? She would never ask again because the answer would never be truer than it would have been before he touched her stomach, before his eyes opened wide with knowledge.

His body disappeared behind the hill, on the other side of the farm, and she walked back toward the Murphy home, repeating his words with each step. "Trust me, trust me, trust me. . . ."

Twenty-four hours—one day that felt like a year, a lifetime. He'd said *Trust me* and disappeared behind a rise in the land and had not yet returned. Annabelle sat on the edge of the bed, bent over her knees, wanting more than anything to be in her own bedroom, getting dressed for a party or date, for church or a luncheon. She wanted to be doing anything other than sitting on the bed waiting for the nausea to subside and wondering once more where Knox had gone.

She stood and went down to the kitchen, where they were calling her name for dinner. No one had asked what happened between her and Knox; no one had pushed the subject or inferred that she had made him leave again. There were other pressing concerns.

Her father pushed open the screen door. He was covered in mud and moss. "Hi, Daddy," she said. "What in the world have you been doing?"

"Just met with the contractor," he said, sat on a wooden chair at the Murphys' kitchen table.

"And?" Annabelle came and sat next to him, took her dad's hand in her own. Her mother sat opposite them.

He looked at both of them, then at Mrs. Murphy. "I cannot thank you enough for your hospitality and the way you've taken care of me and my family. We cannot intrude on you any longer." He turned to his wife and daughter. "We'll have to find somewhere else to live for a while—the house will have to be torn down. The foundation is completely rotten. The contractor said that the house probably wasn't in very good shape to begin with because of its age, and that the water and mold ate through what was once worth saving. Insurance will cover rebuilding, but it will take a long time, at least a year, and we can't stay here that long. It's too much of an imposition." He turned to Mrs. Murphy. "Our son, Charlie, is coming home to help us for a few months. He took a leave of absence from work. . . ."

Mrs. Murphy came to sit at the table then, placed her hand on Grace's. "I know you'll want some privacy, but it has been more than a pleasure having you here. I didn't realize how lonely I'd been until you came."

"Daddy, I'm so sorry about the house. Can we build the exact same one?" Annabelle asked.

"Once the foundation is ruined, you can never build

the exact same one, but we can try and make it look similar. Make it feel the same."

Annabelle's mother lifted her hands. "As long as we're all in it, it is exactly the same. Home is not about the stuff. I might have thought that at one time, but it is never, ever about the stuff. It is about the people."

Mrs. Murphy rose, placed dinner on the table. Annabelle had become accustomed to this routine the way a child becomes dependent on a lullaby and a back rub before sleep: the call to dinner, the sitting down at the handmade pine trestle table with the mismatched ladder-back chairs, the linoleum floor with the single crack below Annabelle's chair, where she ran her toe.

A place was set at the far end for Knox. Annabelle didn't know if this was because his mother knew he was coming, or hoped he would show up.

Trust me.

Mr. and Mrs. Murphy grinned at Annabelle simultaneously. "Is something wrong?" She touched her face, her hair.

"No, dear. Let's eat."

"I love your cooking, Mrs. Murphy, but I'm just not very hungry tonight." Annabelle stood. Her chair scraped across the floor. "I think I'll go lie down."

"Please sit, my dear," Mr. Murphy said.

And because Mr. Murphy had never ordered her to do anything, she sat. "Okay," she said, glanced at her own dad, who shrugged his shoulders.

Mrs. Murphy passed the ham and potatoes, then the green beans and sweet tea. Silence blanketed the table with a humid quilt of unsaid words. Rain began to fall onto the metal roof, pings of intermittent drops that quickly became a full cacophony.

Then the screen door scraped open and Knox walked into the room, grinning and shaking rain off his coat and umbrella. "Hey, sorry I'm a bit late. . . . Weather hit around Awendaw."

All five faces looked up at him in question, but none more than Annabelle's wide eyes.

He walked toward her, then knelt. "Annabelle Marie Clark," he said, "all the loss and death have made me realize that nothing is more important than those we love."

Annabelle stared down at him. "I love you, too. Get up off the floor, silly."

"Because you and the people in this room are more valuable than any I've ever known, I wanted to ask this in front of the entire family. Belle, will you marry me? Be my wife? Stay with me forever and build a life with me?"

All the words she'd ever dreamed of hearing were being said, and the moment didn't seem real. She wanted this proposal to be more authentic, more alive than anything she'd ever experienced, but a surreal feeling came over her.

She dropped to her knees next to him. "Are you sure? Are you really sure? I don't want you to . . ."

He placed his finger over her lips, pulled a diamond

ring from his pocket and offered it to her in an open palm. "Don't say anything except yes." The ring was his grandmother's—he'd been to the safety-deposit box to retrieve it with his parents' permission.

"Yes," she whispered, fell onto his chest.

They married almost immediately beneath the oak tree where he'd found and held her that night he discovered the life growing inside her body. They blamed the hurricane for the rushed wedding, for their sudden desire to live together. There were so many things one could blame on the cursed hurricane.

Annabelle became Knox Murphy's wife and never dwelled on the events that immediately preceded his proposal; she merely relied on the love they held for each other in the years that came before, and all those that followed.

TEN

ANNABELLE MURPHY

*O*n the road to Newboro, Annabelle's anger returned. She thought she had conquered this particular emotion a year ago—rage at Knox for leaving them, for dying while flying a plane she'd begged him not to fly. Now her memory of the weeks when he was lost to her cut through her mind like a jagged knife. Had those days been long enough for him to have an affair, to have fallen in love with someone else?

Annabelle banged the steering wheel, stepped on the

gas until her SUV crept toward ninety miles an hour in the middle of the night somewhere on a bleak road in the Carolinas. Blue lights lit up behind her and her anger spiked. Damn!

She pulled the car over, and a policeman appeared at her window, shining a flashlight into her face. She held up a hand to cover her eyes.

"Driver's license, insurance, registration," he said.

Annabelle rolled down the window, reached for her purse on the passenger seat, yanked the license and insurance card from her wallet, then dug the registration out of the glove compartment. She handed them to the bald man in uniform.

He looked at the documents, then at her. "Do you have any idea how fast you were going?"

She shook her head and felt the sting of tears and fatigue behind her eyes; she hadn't been pulled over in twenty years.

He leaned down to the window. "Ma'am, are you okay?"

She nodded. "Yes, I guess I just . . ."

"You were going eighty-eight miles an hour."

"Oh." Annabelle reached a hand to her mouth. "I've never gone that fast. I'm so sorry."

"Where are you headed in such a hurry?"

"I am trying to get to Newboro, North Carolina." Annabelle stared out into the dark night. Her lips quivered as righteous anger and indignation ran out of her as though she'd opened a drain, leaving her limp, exhausted while this policeman stood at her window and held her papers. She was suddenly unsure if she could drive one more mile. She glanced at the clock: three a.m.

"You still have a few hours to go until you get there, ma'am. You need to slow down before you hurt yourself or someone else."

Annabelle leaned back on the seat. "Do you know where the nearest hotel is?" she asked.

He handed back her documents. "Follow me to the next exit. There's a Hampton Inn."

Annabelle looked at him. "No ticket?"

He laughed. "When was the last time you got a ticket?"

"Probably twenty years ago." She smiled.

"Ah, hell, I don't want to break that kind of record. Follow me." He walked back to his car.

Annabelle pulled the car into the traffic lane, followed the county police car to the next exit, where HAMPTON INN blinked in neon lights beside the highway. When she pulled into a parking space, she wasn't sure she had enough strength to get out of the car, check in at the front desk and then drag her bag to a room. Examining her and Knox's life over the past six hours had been more exhausting than running a marathon.

The police car pulled up next to her as she climbed out. "Be safe, Mrs. Murphy."

"Yes, sir. Thank you."

She had an odd thought as he drove off—what would it feel like to be with a man who didn't know her now and hadn't known her since kindergarten, a man who hadn't heard all about her and her children, and wouldn't look at her with pity because her husband had gone down in a plane, leaving her all alone?

She checked into room 623, crawled into bed fully dressed and fell asleep before one more thought could carry her down the spiral pathway of doubt.

Daylight filtered through the blinds, hit Annabelle's face. Confused, she squinted into the light and lay still, trying to remember where she was and how she'd arrived there: somewhere in North Carolina on the way to Newboro. She rose from the bed, an ache stretching along her back from the drive and the unfamiliar mattress. She walked to the window, threw open the curtains to look at her view of the parking lot.

She picked up the folder on the desk and saw that she was in Holly Ridge, North Carolina. The clock blinked seven a.m.

She drank the instant coffee provided in the room while out loud she talked herself through what she would do next. She'd call Keeley and Jake and soothe their worries about where she was. Then she'd call Shawn. And then what?

She'd decide when she got there.

The bridge to Newboro spanned a river with the deep basin of a marina, the quaint town below. She'd only been here once before—to pick up Jake from sailing camp—and then she'd been in such a rush to get home, she hadn't stopped to appreciate the outrageous beauty of this place and its harbor, homes and boats. Now the possibility that she'd lived her entire life too fast, without noticing important things, filled her with regret.

When she'd spoken to Jake he'd been concerned, but quiet. Keeley hadn't cared about her mother's absence as long as Gamma didn't try to boss her around.

Annabelle turned off the bridge and into a town surrounded by water. Public parking was available along the waterside streets; she pulled into a spot, shoved coins in the meter without any idea what to do next except get out and walk around.

Live oaks lined the roadways through the middle of town, as though the trees had been planted a hundred years ago with just this day in mind. They framed the town square while midday sun filtered through the Spanish moss. Bed-and-breakfasts in hundred-year-old homes were scattered up and down the block. There was an art studio, a bookstore located next to a coffee shop and a corner drugstore that claimed to be the first to sell Pepsi. Annabelle entered the coffee shop and paid for a large black coffee and toasted bagel with cream cheese to go.

She walked out onto the sidewalk, then across the street to where a wrought-iron fence surrounded a massive stone church. She stood eating outside the gate and stared at the stone building. The words on an iron plaque described the history of a town founded before the signing of the Declaration of Independence, proclaiming with pride that this town was older than the country itself.

People were walking into the church, and Annabelle realized it was Sunday. She marveled at all these people believing and having faith when her world was falling away.

A man and woman passed, smiled and nodded at her. Annabelle swallowed the last of her hasty breakfast and followed them into the sanctuary. Maybe her faith would be fortified in this stone structure, in a place older than the country, than her marriage, than her doubts. She went in and sat in the back row, where she could see most of the congregation without being seen herself.

A slight, tall young woman entered the sanctuary. Her presence caused a tingling in Annabelle's neck. She was a fragile blonde with pale skin and a haunted expression. She clung to the arm of a man who looked to be her father; he led her into the far left pew. Annabelle couldn't take her eyes off this woman.

In the way people know someone is staring at them, the woman turned to Annabelle. Their gazes held longer than a stranger's would and a deep chill, not caused by the air-conditioning but originating deeper inside, ran through Annabelle. She had once known this woman. She closed her eyes, mentally scrolled through time until she reached ten years ago. Her eyes flew open—this young woman looked like Liddy Parker, but younger. Liddy Parker had once owned the art studio in Marsh Cove, and then abruptly moved away.

Disorientation overcame Annabelle. Liddy Parker and her daughter, Sofie, had moved here? Had she known that? Had Knox ever mentioned them again? Or was fatigue making her delusional?

Liddy had had a young, beautiful daughter who had been . . . ten when they'd moved. Recognition came in a single knowing: this woman was Sofie Parker all grown-up.

The blonde looked away, as if Annabelle had said her name out loud; then she whispered to the man next to her, rose and walked out a side door. Annabelle scooted from the pew, ran out the front door and around the church to the outdoor courtyard, where she had stood only moments ago.

Frantic, Annabelle glanced around the courtyard, ran to the far side, where a children's playground had been set up next to an ancient graveyard—an anomaly that seemed sacrilegious: a plastic play set alongside the worn stones of the dead founders of the church and town.

The young woman's ponytail fell over the back of the stone bench where she sat facing away from Annabelle. The playground and graveyard were in front of the bench, and Annabelle could not see what the woman was staring at until she got closer, walked around the bench and saw that Sofie was gazing at her hands. Annabelle's feet made a crunching noise in the gravel, and Sofie looked up, offered a single nod.

Annabelle sat on the bench, turned to this familiar stranger. "Are you Sofie Parker? You look so much like—"

"Yes," Sofie said, quiet and trembling in her voice and body. "But it's Sofie Milstead. . . ."

"I thought I recognized you. . . . Do you know who I am?" Annabelle whispered as one would to a child one wished not to scare away.

"Mrs. Murphy," Sofie said.

"This is the oddest coincidence," Annabelle said, rubbed her temples. "How long have you lived here?"

"It's not so much of a coincidence," Sofie said. "Not really."

Annabelle straightened up. "What do you mean?"

Sofie turned now and looked directly at Annabelle. "My mother and I lived here for a long time, and your husband visited frequently, so I figured you'd show up eventually."

"My husband . . ." Annabelle's pulse knocked against her wrists in an erratic beat.

"Mr. Murphy. Knox. He helped a lot of people around here," Sofie said.

Annabelle smiled; she would pretend she knew what Sofie was talking about. Her real world at home in Marsh Cove began to fade into sepia shades as this world in Newboro became too bright, too crisp with the image of Knox living in it.

"So," Annabelle said, "you do know he . . . passed away two years ago."

"The plane crash," Sofie said. "Yes, I do."

"Do you know his plane was recently found and that a woman was traveling with him?"

"Yes, I'm sorry. I saw it on the news." Sofie looked across the playground. "This is my second-favorite place in Newboro. Isn't it beautiful? The old stones that have been here for hundreds of years, the old souls that lie beneath this land, the children—when they're here—defying death with their laughter."

Annabelle took a deep breath. "Is that your father in the church?"

Sofie's gaze flashed back to Annabelle; her mouth attempted to move into a smile. "No, that's my boyfriend."

Annabelle nodded. "Oh, sorry. How is your sweet mom?" But even as she asked the question, something moved toward her from the corner of her eye: a knowing as wispy as smoke.

"She . . . left," Sofie said.

"Oh," Annabelle said. She wanted to chat longer, ask personal questions that would draw information out of this fragile young woman, but the only question she could voice was "So you must know who else was on the plane?"

Sofie nodded. "Yes, he was helping a woman. . . . She was in some kind of trouble, and he was taking her to Colorado."

"What kind of trouble?" Annabelle asked.

Sofie stood now. "I always knew I'd see you again, but I thought . . ."

"What?" Annabelle looked up at Sofie, the sun

backlighting her, blacking out her face and leaving only an impression of a woman, without substance. "There's more, isn't there?" Annabelle whispered.

"There's not more that I can tell you," Sofie said.

"Yes, I'm sure . . . I'm sure there is." Annabelle stood, wanted to grab Sofie, shake the information out of her. "This doesn't make sense." Annabelle brushed the hair out of her eyes, felt her flesh grow hot and then cold as confusion overcame her.

"His flight was a mission trip of sorts," Sofie said. "Mrs. Murphy, I really can't tell you more."

Annabelle's body shook as though it was October and a gale wind blew through the harbor to the courtyard. Sofie glanced around the yard, and then took quick, small steps back to the church. "Sofie . . . please," Annabelle called after her, but Sofie opened the wide wooden doors and disappeared into the sanctuary.

Annabelle sat back down on the bench and felt herself free floating, as though someone had just loosened her tethers to the earth, letting her rise above her body and the stone bench, taking her to an unknown land where her husband flew to Newboro, North Carolina, and picked up a woman for a mission trip of some sort.

The realization that Knox was "doing good" spread relief over her like warm water: her dear husband was helping someone; he died while doing a good deed. Her tight fists unclenched; the muscles around her mouth relaxed, and she was able to take a deeper breath.

She exhaled in a loud huff, dropped her head into her hands. The dread she had voiced to Mrs. Thurgood—*What if nothing I believed about my life was true?*—was now answered. Her beliefs were true. Knox was true. Their marriage was true. Questions remained, prodded at Annabelle's heart, but she rested in one sure thing: Knox had come here to help someone.

The hotel air conditioner coughed and sputtered through its coils cold air that smelled of mildew and salt water. Annabelle sat on the nautical-print bedspread and allowed the chill to cool her off. She called her mother to check on Keeley, but heard only the monotonous recording of her own voice saying to leave a message. Annabelle told her mother and Keeley she loved them and what hotel she had checked into, and then she fell backward onto the bed.

For days, memories of Knox had arrived unbidden and without warning. Annabelle remembered when he'd taken the family to Colorado for spring break to ski the great Aspen Mountains. Jake was almost fourteen and about to enter high school, and Knox wanted a great family trip before their older child began navigating the tumultuous world of adolescence. They'd gone together to the nearest outlet malls and purchased ski apparel for the entire family. In their matching goofy white-and-silver ensembles, they had looked like an ad for one brand of ski wear.

Annabelle closed her eyes and saw the hot tub, the

kids laughing at dinner; Keeley making a new friend from California (which seemed like another planet to her) whom she still kept in touch with; Jake sneaking out one night to meet a girl at the bottom of the slopes. Annabelle and Knox had lain in bed and laughed because Jake thought he was pulling one over on them when they knew exactly what he was doing.

They had made love, talked about how lucky they were to have this family, this life. The next day with patience and good humor Knox had taught her to snowboard. She'd given up and gone back to the lodge to drink peppermint schnapps and wait for her family to join her next to the fire.

No matter what situation Annabelle remembered or where she placed Knox on the time line of their life together, she could not find a single moment to sift doubt into the sieve of her memory. She would find out who this woman was and how Knox had been helping her, but her essential faith in him was restored.

She curled fully dressed beneath the bedcovers. After driving most of the night and then seeing Sofie in some bizarre time-warp experience, she had hit her limit. Sleep came quick and dreamless.

Jake's voice called her over and over. Annabelle opened her eyes, attempted to focus in the evening light of the strange hotel room. She must have dreamed about him, of his needing her. She rolled over, rubbed her face and heard his voice again.

"Mom? Are you in there? Are you okay?"

Her mind took a while to catch up with her body. For a moment she listened to her son call her name and wondered if she was in some alternate world. Then he called again; Annabelle bolted from the bed, ran across the room and opened the door to face Jake. He stood in the green-carpeted hallway with the fluorescent light shining down on his concerned face. He wore a pair of wrinkled khaki shorts and a frayed golf shirt that had once been his father's. Annabelle threw her arms around him. "Why in the world are you here?"

"Mom, are you okay?"

"I'm fine . . . fine." Annabelle stepped aside to let him into the room. "What are you doing here? How did you find me?" A welling up of love flowed through her body at the sight of Jake's face. "Are you all right?"

"I'm fine, Mom. The big question is, are you okay? You pretty much have everyone in a total panic. You ran off in the middle of the freaking night. Who does that?"

"Not me, usually." She smiled at him. "I called everyone, got Gamma to come for Keeley. No one should be worried. I'm fine." She glanced around the room. "How did you know my room number?"

Jake shrugged. "I told the cute girl at the front desk that I was your son—I did show ID. She told me your room number—but I didn't have enough charm to get a key out of her. Shawn . . . Mr. Lewis wanted to drive up here, but I told him I could take care of my own mother. Luckily you told Gamma what hotel you'd be in or I'd be wandering the streets."

"Oh, Jake, I don't need to be taken care of." Annabelle stretched. "But I am so glad to see your face. What time is it anyway?"

"Six o'clock."

She ran her hands through her hair. "I'm starving. Give me a second to freshen up, and we'll go grab something to eat."

Jake sat in the sole chair in the room, dropped his arms over the sides of the starfish-design upholstery. "Mom, what are you doing here?"

"Jake, I need some food in my stomach before I try to answer that. Okay?"

"Does it have anything to do with Dad?"

"Yes, but I'm not sure how yet." Annabelle walked toward her son, who was now taller than Knox had been. His dark curls fell below his ears, and dark stubble covered his chin. The remnants of adolescent acne were long gone.

She was selfish for believing that this dilemma was affecting only her, not everyone else in the family. She walked into the bathroom, hoping to wash the fatigue and stress off her face. When that was unsuccessful, she dabbed on some blush and lipstick, ran a brush through her hair, then leaned close to the mirror. "That's as good as it's gonna get tonight."

In the past two years she'd often found herself wondering if Knox could see her, could watch the family from heaven. At times she'd wished this were true, but right now she hoped it wasn't. The last thing she wanted him to see was her, bedraggled, panicked, running around like an insane woman trying to find out about "the woman." She looked up at the water-stained ceiling. "Oh, Knox, I do love you, but what were you doing here?"

She came out of the bathroom. "Let's go. I'm starving," she said to Jake.

He followed her outside without a word. Communication between her and Jake was often like this. Annabelle understood he was angry, yet trying to control it enough to discover what this trip had to do with him, with his dad.

She led him down a side street to a restaurant she'd noticed after leaving the church. She wound her arm through his as they entered a packed room that smelled of fried food and warm salt air. They were told there would be at least a half-hour wait. Annabelle leaned against the wall and let out a long breath.

Jake pulled on her arm. "Come on, Mom. I'll buy you a drink."

She lifted her eyebrows at him. "You aren't legal to buy me a drink." She poked at his side.

"Two more months and I will be."

"How did that happen?" Annabelle spread her hands apart. "How did I come to have an almost-twenty-one-year-old son?"

He shrugged, blushed, then walked toward the bar. Annabelle listened to him order her a Chardonnay and a Coke for himself, his gestures and tone of voice so like his father's. Her heart hurt as though it were breaking all over again as she watched him take money from his wallet, smile at the waitress.

She accepted the glass of wine he handed her, took a long swallow and then sat on a bar stool. "Thanks, Jake."

"No problem. Tell me what is going on. Please."

Annabelle leaned her elbow on the counter, pushed a stray hair off her son's forehead. "I remembered that your dad stopped to refuel here. I thought I'd come and ask some questions. But it didn't take very long. . . . You're not going to believe who I saw in the first couple hours I was here."

Jake shrugged.

"Sofie Parker. Remember her?"

He stared off at the wall, paused and smiled, turned back to her. "The little girl who used to live above the art gallery with her mother. The lady whose painting is in our foyer . . . right?"

Annabelle took a sharp breath—the painting in the foyer. She had forgotten Liddy Parker had painted it. Annabelle felt her eyes squint, her brow furrow.

"Did I say something wrong?"

She shook her head. "No, I just haven't eaten."

Jake rose and walked toward the maître d', then returned. "Come on. We have a table now."

Annabelle laughed. "What'd you do, bribe him?"

Once they sat down, the room around them faded like the blurry background in an old photo. Annabelle spoke in quiet tones. "Anyway, she knew your dad's plane was found—she heard it on the news—but when I asked if she knew who was on the plane with him, she was very skittish, scared almost. She told me your dad was helping some woman—a mission trip. She wouldn't tell me the woman's name, but in a small town like this, that shouldn't be hard to find out . . . I guess." Annabelle leaned back in her chair and marveled how some sleep and reassurring news could completely change her outlook on life.

"I remember Sofie from elementary school, and her cool mom who ran the art studio. Sometimes when Dad picked me up from school, we'd drop Sofie off there, and Dad would look at the art, talk to her mom about it."

"Well, that little girl must be twenty now. You two were the same age."

"I still don't get it."

"Neither do I, but it must've had something to do with his pro bono work."

"Yeah . . . I guess." Jake leaned back in the chair. A waiter came and took their order, placed a basket of hush puppies on the table. Annabelle ate two. "These are wonderful." She pushed the basket toward Jake.

He popped a hush puppy into his mouth, chewed while he stared at the restaurant crowd. "Weird."

"Yes."

"Well, maybe I can talk to Sofie, find out something more."

"You can try—she wouldn't tell me anything else. I

have no idea where she lives or works or anything."

Jake scooted back to allow the waiter to place water glasses on the table. "What else did she say?"

"Listen, Jake, I don't have anything else to tell you. That's all I know right now. Let's talk about you. How is school going?"

"I dropped out of the semester."

Annabelle's drink slipped in her hand; Jake grabbed it before the wine spilled.

"Sorry, Mom. That's why I've been avoiding your phone calls. It's why I bought you that drink." He smiled at her and made a face. "Don't lose your cool, okay?"

Oh, God, how she wanted Knox here. She wanted to look to him for the proper words to say, for how to respond to her precious son in a way that wouldn't ruin this fragile moment.

"Jake, why?"

"Mom, I didn't like the prelaw classes at all. I think I want to teach. Or write. History probably. I'm not really sure. But I know I don't want to be a lawyer."

It was as if the news about the woman in the plane had upset a precarious equilibrium, tipping out a mess of confused goals, beliefs and misunderstood motivations.

"Honey, you've wanted—"

"I know. But I don't now."

"Okay, then let's talk about what you do want."

"That's the biggest problem. I'm not sure. I just know what I *don't* want. I know this is crazy for you to

158

hear, Mom. I know this isn't the way your brain works. And I've practiced this speech five hundred times, but it still isn't coming out right. I know you can't support me while I figure it out, so I promise I'll get a job. If we're supposed to do something with our lives that inspires us and others, then I want to teach history." He held up his hand. "I know that doesn't make much money. But I love it. I love everything about it."

Annabelle looked across the table at her son in this strange town, in this foreign land where she had come to find out what her husband had been doing right before he died. "Jake, if you love history, then teach it, write about it. You do not need to choose a career to satisfy me or your father."

She spoke about Knox in the present tense, as if he were still there looking over them, judging Jake's decisions. A new freedom came over her, freedom mixed with a sense of betrayal; she didn't need to think about what Knox would say or how he'd react—he wasn't there. "Jake, you've loved history since you could read. While everyone else was reading the Hardy Boys, you read about the Crusades. While others did their school projects on the popular sports figures, you did yours on some Roman battle I don't even remember. While others dressed up at Halloween as John Elway, you dressed up as a gladiator. Don't try and please *me* with your choice of career or school." She grinned at him. "I never want you to blame me for whatever misery you bring on yourself. You already have enough to blame me for."

Jake looked toward the other side of the restaurant, but a mother knew the look on her son's face when he was fighting back tears. She couldn't tell what they were for—her mention of Knox or her release of his life—but she reached across the table and laid her hand on his forearm. "Hey, you okay?"

He looked back at her. "Mom, I have never blamed you for anything. Ever."

She smiled. "That was meant to be a joke, but you know what? Keeley does blame me. She hates me now. Do all sixteen-year-olds hate their mothers?"

Jake nodded. "That's what I've heard. Mom, I just think she is still really, really mad at Dad for leaving us."

Annabelle sat back in her seat. "I guess I've seen it, but ignored it, hoping it would pass."

The waiter returned, placed their plates on the table. Jake took a bite of the pecan-encrusted grouper he'd ordered, chewed and spoke simultaneously. "Mom, are you sure you don't know where Sofie lives now?"

Annabelle shook her head, laughed. "Don't talk with your mouth full." Then she looked away from him. "No, I don't know where she lives. I drove most of the night to get here, and then found her by accident at the church. Guess I'll have to do some sleuthing."

Jake stood abruptly and went to the bar, came back with a phone book. Annabelle laughed. "I would've thought of that . . . eventually."

Jake leafed through the pages until he came to the Ps

for Parker. He looked up. "Nothing here with the names Liddy or Sofie, or even the initials."

"She said her name is Milford or Milstead now, something like that."

"Did she marry?" Jake sifted through the pages.

"I doubt it. In the church she was with an older man she called her boyfriend. She's awfully young to marry."

"Hmmm . . . don't I know someone who married the love of her life when she was twenty?"

"That was different," Annabelle said. "Very different."

"I'm sure it was." Jake laughed. He flipped through more pages. "Here's an L. Milstead with an address and a phone number."

"Liddy."

"You have a pen?"

Annabelle pulled a black Sharpie from her purse. "Here," she said.

Jake scribbled the name, address and phone number on a napkin. "She must still live with her mother."

"She told me her mother left. That's all she said about her."

"Mom, this is all way weird."

Annabelle took a sip of wine, attempted to ignore her son's comment as she looked out the porthole window to Bay Street. Sofie Milstead knew more than she had told, and the information was like a stranger Annabelle was unsure she wanted to meet.

ELEVEN

SOFIE MILSTEAD

*B*edford stroked Sofie's back, muttered the words she loved to hear. She never understood all that he said, yet she got the meaning—she was loved and adored. And above all else—she was safe.

He told her of her beauty and how her life had been made for his. If she examined this idea, if she probed for reciprocal feelings within herself, she couldn't find them. There was not a space inside her that Bedford filled—only the dolphins did that for her. She understood there was something wrong with her, this failure to return his deeper love, but she basked in his adoration and assumed that eventually her immaturity would diminish and she would be able to truthfully love him back, tell him that he completed her.

Bedford dozed off with his hand flat on her stomach, and Sofie thought how the hours that had passed that Sunday somehow added up to more than one day.

The humidity outside had settled inside her veins, her very blood bringing on a languor. When they'd set off for church that morning, she'd felt slightly guilty for not having told Bedford that Michael Harley, the art historian, had come calling. Bedford had looked down at her and kissed her on the forehead.

They had walked into the church as they had every Sunday since the first time she met him. He was a man of habit and of conscience, and these two qualities conspired to make him a churchgoer, if not a man of faith. This had baffled her at first—how could this man demand such strict church attendance when he found it hard to believe anything that couldn't be empirically proven? Then she realized that the familiar liturgy, the same words repeated in the same order week after week, appealed to his need for order even as they called to her heart.

They had walked toward their seats, the air dusty and stifling. Sofie had leaned against Bedford's shoulder and allowed the calm of this place to comfort her. People had filed into the church, sat in their regular seats and nodded hello to Sofie and Bedford, whispered, "Humid out there, eh?" as if no one else knew. Sofie had stared at the doorway, where the refracted light fell in a single path along the blue carpet; she thought how it looked like the path a dolphin might make in the water. A sadness rose in her, in a lump below her throat. She had started to look away, but a woman who walked into the shaft of light had caused Sofie to stop and stare.

She had dusty blond curls that fell wind whipped to her shoulders, and the awed, disoriented look of someone who had never entered this church before. She'd rubbed her hands together, then looked left and right and sat in the back pew to one side, her legs poised as if she might run at any minute.

Then the woman looked straight at Sofie, stared at her, through her. Electricity ran through Sofie and caused her body to quiver beneath Bedford's hand on her knee as she recognized Annabelle Murphy—Knox's wife.

Bedford patted her leg. "Are you okay?"

"Yes," Sofie whispered. "I'll be right back. I have to go to the ladies' room." She stood and walked down the aisle, avoided this woman's stare and entered the courtyard through a side door. This was it—this was when the consequences of her lies and secrets caught up with her.

The bench at the end of the church courtyard faced a playground surrounded by gravestones. Sofie sat and stared at the date on one of the stones: 1875. She counted inside her head: how long would it take Annabelle Murphy to come outside, find her?

She made it to fifty when Annabelle sat next to her, said her name as though they were intimate friends.

Sofie stared at Annabelle Murphy in wonder and dull amusement. This woman had always seemed little more to her than a name—more a concept or picture than a person. Knox Murphy's wife. The woman who had kept Knox from her mother and from her, a woman who only allowed Knox into their lives in small doses, none of them big enough.

The few words said between her and Annabelle replayed in Sofie's mind as she lay in her own bed next to Bedford and thought of all the events that had occurred that day. Chaotic feelings swirled while sleep eluded her. She rolled over and stared at Bedford's face as though he had brought all this upon her;

then she rose, wrapped her robe around her middle and walked to the window. Moonlight spilled over the sidewalks and bushes in the front yard. He rarely slept at her condominium, and his presence there now filled the space to overflowing.

Sleep would not visit. She took her car keys off the dresser, tiptoed around the condo. Confusion and chaos always drove her to the water, to the research center. In less than ten minutes, she pulled into the empty parking lot. In the absence of streetlights, the stars shone as though the heavens had turned up their brightness.

She walked to the seawall. Although she couldn't see them, she felt the presence of dolphins below her. She lay down along the length of the wall and listened for their cries and calls. "Hello," she said in a whisper. The thought occurred to her that maybe they didn't want their names to be known—that they didn't want the human world to know they had individual souls. Hadn't Sofie's mother hidden her and Sofie's real names for a reason? Why wouldn't these brilliant animals do the same?

Sofie sat up, swung her legs over the wall and stared into the vast darkness. The crunch of gravel and the squeal of brakes caused her to turn around, stare over her shoulder. A squat dark car pulled into the lot and parked. A tall man unfolded himself from the front seat, looked around and then walked toward the research building.

Sofie sat on the edge of the seawall and watched the

man place his hands on either side of his face and peer into the windows. She held her breath until he went to the south side, out of sight. She stood, walked to her car, sidestepping stones so as not to cause noise in this quiet, starlit night. Whoever he was, she didn't know this man or his purpose for being at the research center in the middle of the night.

The car door squeaked as she opened it; she stood frozen, afraid he would come around the corner. She wanted to leave, call the police. She had never felt afraid here before, and she was unsure how to react now. The man didn't return as she climbed behind the wheel, thinking she was a fool for not bringing her cell phone.

She released a long breath, started the engine. A knock on her window startled her so that she jammed the car into drive instead of reverse and rolled into the yellow concrete barrier in front of the tires. The man jumped back, laughed. Sofie stared at him through the driver's-side window, tilted her head in confusion. She *did* know this man, and something in his face caused all fear to empty out of her in a rush.

He smiled at her and leaned down to the window. His face was full of a warm smile, stubble on his chin, tousled brown hair moving in the breeze. There was something safe and calm about him. She opened her door and stepped out, but didn't say a word, just stared at him.

"Are you okay?" he asked in a voice she didn't remember, but found familiar nonetheless.

"I think so," she said, walked to the front of the car, looked at the bumper. "Just a scratch." She turned back to him. "Do I know you?"

"Yep, you stole my crayons in first grade and blamed it on Chandler Hoover."

Sofie's mind reeled backward. "I didn't . . . live here in first grade."

"No, you lived in Marsh Cove."

Memories came to her in random order, half-remembered like the words that were painted under layers of paint on her mother's canvases: phrases and pictures that were covered up and masked.

The man tapped his chest. "I'm Jake . . . Jake Murphy."

Her hands flew to her face, her mind registering that a single news story was causing an ever-widening ripple of events over which she no longer had any control. Her initial reaction was wrong—totally wrong. Jake Murphy meant danger, not peace. She backed away from him.

"Don't you remember me?" He held his arms apart.

"Of course I remember you," she said, glanced around the parking lot as though expecting to find someone there to help her.

"Don't be afraid of me. I shouldn't have followed you—don't freak out. I went to your condo, then saw you leave. . . ."

Sofie nodded, trapped now with the keys still in her car.

He rubbed his forehead. "Wow. You know, you look

the same as I remember you. I mean taller, of course, and all that, but same cute face."

She felt herself blush and hoped the meager starlight was not enough to let him see. "I have to go . . . please." She stepped toward her car.

"Please, just wait." He moved away from her even as he said this, as though he were trying to prove he wasn't a threat.

"I can't," Sofie said.

"Okay," Jake said, and strode off toward the water. Sofie meant to climb in the car, shove it in reverse and leave, but without thinking she followed him.

They reached the seawall and stood next to each other without speaking. Then Sofie turned to him. "You look just like your dad."

"That's what they say." Jake ran a hand down his face. "We really weren't much alike, though."

"In what way?"

"Oh, in the things we liked and didn't like. But we got along great." He turned to Sofie. "I mean, we used to get along great."

"I'm sorry about your dad. I really am. I loved him, too, you know." Her words came as a surprise to her. She held up her hands. "Not like . . . that."

"Did you know him . . . here?"

"Yes, he did some legal work for the underprivileged, helped . . . people."

"Why here?"

Sofie battled within herself whether to tell him the entire truth, but the ingrained need for secrecy and safety held her tongue as surely as it ever had—as though her mother had locked the truth shut and taken the key with her. "I don't know," she lied.

Jake sat on the seawall, and then as Sofie had done only moments ago, he lay down along its length and stared into the southern sky. "Triangulum," he said, traced his finger along the stars, and then lowered his hand to the right. "Pegasus." Then to the right again. "Delphinus."

Sofie sat down next to him. "How do you know the constellations?"

He craned his neck to stare up at her. "Oh, I don't know all of them—just the Greek gods. I haven't seen stars this bright since I went skiing in Utah last year. Are they always like this here?"

"Not always, but yes, we can see them better out here where there aren't any city lights." Sofie traced her finger along the same figure in the sky that he had. "Delphinus," she said. "That's the only one I know besides the Big Dipper."

He took her finger and traced it along a path. "That's Pegasus. He is a complicated constellation and sits right next to Delphinus. One story says he is the son of Poseidon."

"God of the sea," Sofie whispered, dreamlike, untethered from the logic of night and day.

"Yep, and Delphinus is the constellation Poseidon put in the sky to honor the dolphin that brought him his wife, Amphitrite," Jake said.

Sofie picked up the story of redemption and love

that she knew so well. "Amphitrite was hiding in a cave and wanted nothing to do with Poseidon when the dolphin Delphinus came and found her beyond the Pillars of Hercules, in the depths of the sea. Delphinus convinced her that Poseidon was the brightest of all gods and that she could be Queen of the Sea."

Jake sat up. "And then Delphinus performed the marriage ceremony."

Sofie traced the constellation again with her finger. "And Poseidon placed a constellation in the sky to honor the dolphin."

Jake smiled at her. "There are nine stars just like there are nine muses."

"Now that," Sofie said, "I did not know."

"Glad I could broaden your horizons," Jake said.

Sofie released a long breath. "Some versions even say that dolphins were once men. . . ."

"We have all these myths about the dolphins. Do you think they have myths about us?" Jake asked with a laugh.

A sudden feeling of lightness came over Sofie; she could not remember the last time she'd laughed. Jake knew about her love of dolphins without her having to speak of it. What alternate world was this?

Jake pointed upward. "So, you're into Greek mythology?"

"Nope," she said. "Not at all. Just dolphins."

Jake waved toward the building. "Thus the research center."

She nodded, although she wasn't sure he could see

her. "Yes, I work here—for school. I go to UNC, but here at their satellite school. My major is marine conservation technology."

"All about dolphins?"

"No, my studies cover all marine animals. . . . Dolphins are my side work. So . . . where do you go to school?"

"University of North Carolina," he said. "Funny, huh? I went to the main campus in Chapel Hill—but I just dropped out for this semester."

"Dropped out? Why?"

"I was in prelaw and hated it. History was my minor, my side work. But maybe I'll make my side work my main work."

She stood now with the sudden awareness that Bedford was probably awake, looking for her. Guilt filled the back of her throat with a metallic taste. "I have to go. . . ." What was she doing talking to this man?

"Sofie, will you please tell me why my dad would come here—if you know?" Jake stood with her.

She stared at him, wanting to do two things she didn't understand: touch his face and tell him the entire story of his father. But she didn't do either; she said goodbye and then took slow, deliberate steps to her car and drove from the parking lot with shaking hands and liquid legs.

When she looked in her rearview mirror, she saw that he was still standing where she'd left him, staring up at the night sky.

The lights were on in the windows of her condo.

Sofie looked at the digital clock in her car: twelve thirty. She parked and ran back into the building, took the stairs two at time. When she entered the bedroom, Bedford sat on the edge of the mattress punching buttons on her cell phone.

She stopped short, stared at him. "What are you doing?"

He started, looked up at her. "Trying to figure out where the hell you could've gone in the middle of the night without your purse." He pointed to the dresser, where her purse lay open. "Or your cell phone."

"I couldn't sleep and didn't want to wake you. I went to the center, sat on the seawall. You know how I do that . . . nothing else."

He placed her cell phone on the bedside table. "You scared me." He patted the bed for her to come sit next to him. "You're upset about something."

"No, just work." She sat and laid her head on his shoulder. What was she thinking, talking to Knox Murphy's son about dolphins, myths and school? It was as if their encounter only moments ago had been a dream from another life.

"Let's just go to sleep," she said. "I'm tired now."

Bedford laid her down and held her. Sofie rolled over and allowed sleep to come.

In her dream the dolphins were calling her name in their language, and Jake Murphy dove into the water with her to hear them. She jolted from her light sleep and stared across the room to her open purse and the shadows of gnarled branches from the live oak falling onto the dresser, floor and bed. She rose and waited for morning as she stared out the window to the east.

Bedford awoke at first light to find Sofie standing in the kitchen with a cup of tea. He rose and absently kissed her on the cheek, not caring that he'd missed her lips, then rushed off to his own home to get ready for his day.

Sofie stared at her condo as though last night's conversation with Jake might have changed something, but everything was the same: the covered canvas; paintbrushes sticking out of a jar: the mussed-bed proof of her restless sleep beside Bedford. Her closet door was open, and Sofie stood in front of it, clothes hanging haphazardly. She slipped on a pair of jeans, a green tank top and a long silver chain necklace with a single peridot.

She grabbed her purse and headed out the door with the hope that routine behavior would return normalcy to her day, but she had the lingering feeing that her contact with Annabelle and Jake Murphy was already altering her life in imperceptible ways.

TWELVE

ANNABELLE MURPHY

Morning sunlight replaced the shadows of the previous night; the town emerged as a new place washed clean. Annabelle walked along the sidewalk checking addresses, looking down at her torn paper, then back up again to the numbers on the buildings. Jake hadn't risen this morning no matter how hard she pounded on his door, so she had ventured out to find Liddy Parker's address on her own. She needed to ask Sofie a few more questions—she didn't want to scare the girl, just find out who was on the plane.

Annabelle stopped in front of a brick condominium building with a metal plaque stating that the structure dated from 1773. A flash of something Knox once said came to her. They'd been in Paris on vacation, just the two of them, drinking too much red wine, going to art museums and historic places, eating food they couldn't pronounce and making love to the sound of Parisians on the street below.

Later, she and Knox had stood in front of a building with a plaque on it. He'd shaken his head, touched the date. "Eight hundred years old. And we think we have old buildings in South Carolina," he said, kissed her on the lips and then they'd entered the café.

Now Annabelle ran her hand along the plaque on a North Carolina building, shook off the feeling that her Knox could have had another life in this building, another life in which she didn't know where he went or why.

She stepped into a narrow hallway and glanced at the list of names and numbers for each condo. The Milstead sign was exactly the same as the others, but with the number 7 stamped in black. Annabelle glanced up and down the hall. She touched a brick, ran her fingers along the grout, wondering if these walls had seen her husband come and go. Her purse slipped from her fingers, the metal chain clanging on the tile floor.

A woman poked her head out of a door, blue curlers sticking from various angles under a hair net. She pulled her bathrobe tight around her chest, squinted at Annabelle. "May I help you?"

Annabelle stood straight. "Yes, I'm looking for Sofie Milstead."

"She lives upstairs. I am about sick of sending people up to her condo. So irresponsible the young are these days—don't you think?" The woman picked something out of her teeth with her pinky nail, then looked back at Annabelle. "Now why would you be looking for Sofie? You into the art, too?"

"No, I'm an old friend from where she used to live."

"Colorado? You don't look like someone from Colorado. Not that I'd know what someone from Colorado looks like."

Annabelle stepped back; her stomach plummeted as a strange knowing took shape in the corner of her mind. "No, from South Carolina."

"Oh, then you must have the wrong girl. Her and her poor dead mama were from Colorado."

"Dead?" Annabelle said, although she didn't hear the word come from her lips.

"Her mama died in a car wreck out there in Colorado, and she left poor Sofie all alone here in Newboro. Guess I can't blame her for being a little spacey sometimes. Guess I would be, too, if my mama left me all alone in the world."

Annabelle put her hand on the woman's door, afraid she would shut it. "She died in a car wreck?"

"Yeah, guess she went to visit her own mama, who was dying." The woman shook her head. "Just terrible."

Annabelle closed her eyes, fought backward in time to a conversation she'd had with Liddy years ago about how she'd lost both her parents in a train crash in some state north of the Mason-Dixon line. Annabelle opened her eyes, stared at the woman. "Are you sure?"

"Oh, yes. Very. We had a memorial service for her right there on the harbor. She was buried with her own mama in Colorado, but I'm shootin' sure about the memorial service. I was there."

Annabelle believed in the woman's certainty, which only meant that what she thought she knew about Sofie and Liddy was wrong. "Where is Sofie's condo?"

"Number seven, upstairs—has the best view in the building. Stairs are there on the left. I keep on telling Sofie that if she's going to spend the night out at her boyfriend's so often, I'd like to buy her condo, but she refuses. I heard the two of them making quite a racket leaving early this morning."

Annabelle nodded at the woman, took the stairs up, hoping her knees would hold as they shook beneath her. At the top of the staircase, she shoved open a metal door and went halfway down the hall before she stood in front of number seven—a door painted bright blue. Annabelle took a deep breath and knocked. She waited at thirty-second intervals and continued to knock, although she knew it was a futile effort.

What next? She had banged on the door once more when Jake appeared at the top of the stairs. "Mom?"

Annabelle startled, stepped back. "Guess great minds think alike," she said, went to her son and hugged him, let her head rest on his broad shoulder. Then she leaned back. "She's not here. Her neighbor told me she thought she heard her leave pretty early this morning with her boyfriend."

"Oh."

"I tried to wake you earlier."

"I was out late."

"Doing what? We got home at ten p.m. Where could you have possibly gone?"

A hinge creaked, and Annabelle and Jake turned to see a young woman standing in the doorway of the next condo. "You two planning on talking and banging around for a long while now? Or are you about done?"

Annabelle placed a hand over her mouth. "Oh, I'm sorry. Were we disturbing you?"

"If you don't count the incessant banging on the door, no."

Jake held up his hand. "I'm sorry. We're leaving."

Annabelle took a step forward. "Do you know Liddy and Sofie?"

The woman moved into the hall, held the door open with her foot. She was a beautiful young woman with long, dark curls, round violet eyes and full lips that needed no makeup. She pulled her hair back from her face, then wound her arms around her small waist so that it appeared as though she were hugging herself or had a stomachache. "Of course I know them—I live next door. Well, I *knew* Liddy. You know she died."

"Can I ask you a question?" Annabelle spoke in a soft voice.

"Seems like people been asking a lot of questions about them lately. Listen, Sofie still lives here—if you want to know something, you should ask her."

"I'm trying," Annabelle said, stepped forward, distracted by her need for more information. "Do you know if there was a man who came here frequently? A man named Knox?"

The woman smiled. "How would I know? Listen, Liddy Milstead had men. If I started naming names, now wouldn't I be able to send some people reeling?" She looked at Jake and smiled.

He smiled back, and Annabelle saw him turn on the light inside him that made things happen, that charmed all those around him. Knox had also had that light, one that could be turned up or down at will, but never off. "Listen, we're just looking for information about a man named Knox and wondered if he'd been here," Jake said.

The woman shrugged. "I really don't know." Jake kept his eyes on hers until she added, "But I can tell you the name of Sofie's boyfriend, Bedford Whitmore. He's a professor, lives about a block over on

Floyd Street. And beides the men who came and went, Liddy's best friend was Jo-Beth, who owns the knitting store called Charmed Knits."

"Thanks," Jake said. He walked toward Sofie's door, shoved a small piece of torn paper under the door; then he took Annabelle's arm. "Let's go, Mom."

They reached the sidewalk, and Annabelle was filled with love for this man who was her son. When she looked at him, she saw all the ages he ever was—not just the man he was at that moment. This was what people without children didn't understand; you were never just looking at or talking to the ten-year-old, or the fifteen-year-old, or the full-grown man. You were also seeing the infant, the toddler, the child you loved from the moment you had known he grew inside you, part of you but separate.

Annabelle spoke first. "What did you put under her door?"

"A note," he said. "I'm going to go look for Sofie; why don't you see if you can find the best friend?"

"You think you'll do better with Sofie? Do you even remember her?"

"I know where she works, Mom. I found out last night. . . ." He looked away, as though he had something else to say, then turned back to her with that light in his eyes. "Let me do this—you already spoke to her once."

"Well, the woman we just talked to confirmed what a woman downstairs told me," she said.

"What?"

"Liddy is dead. But the woman downstairs told me she died in a car crash in Colorado . . . and that she was from Colorado. . . . I don't get it."

"Mom, don't go jumping to conclusions. I'll find Sofie. . . ."

After they hugged goodbye, Annabelle yanked her cell phone from her purse, called information and asked for Charmed Knits. The operator searched for the address while Annabelle felt as though the unknown past was now rushing forward in time, moving toward her with a runaway power she couldn't stop.

THIRTEEN

SOFIE MILSTEAD

*P*risms of light flickered across the water and reflected off the land. Sofie stopped her car at the harbor and stared out to where the sun hung naked and low in the morning sky. She parked her car, and then stood on the seawall, used the sight of water to calm her mind, her spirit before taking a mile-long walk around the harbor park. She didn't have to be at the center for another couple hours, but she thought she'd sneak in some of her private work in the quiet office.

After her walk, she was inside the center, the iron door slamming behind her, before she realized she'd left her logbook at home. "Damn," she said to the empty corridor as she turned around and ran back to her car. She drove the few blocks back to her condo, blaming her forgetfulness and preoccupation on the disruptive presence of Jake Murphy.

A car pulled out of a parallel parking spot in front of her condo building, and Sofie drove in right behind it, slammed the gearshift into park and jumped out the driver's side. She ran into the hallway. Her pounding feet brought Ms. Fitz to her door. It was the last thing Sofie needed this morning. In Sofie's humble opinion, Ms. Fitz needed to get a hobby that did not involve knowing the ins and outs of Sofie's life. Sofie turned and smiled at her. "Good morning, Ms. Fitz."

"My, my, you've been a busy girl. You've had non-stop visitors." Ms. Fitz smiled. "I'm glad to see you're getting a social life."

Sofie bit the inside of her cheek. "Thank you." She turned and moved toward the stairwell.

"Don't you want to know who's been calling on you?"

"No." Sofie opened the stairwell door.

"Hmmph."

Sofie thought this must be Ms. Fitz's favorite response because she used it on every possible occasion. She opened the door, turned to nod at Ms. Fitz. "Have a good day."

"Well, you had an art historian named Michael, a woman named Anna or something like that and a young man named Jake. They all seemed quite interested in seeing you and asked after your dead mom."

Sofie felt the slap of the word "dead" like cold water

thrown over her body. She shivered, turned away from Ms. Fitz and slammed the door, although she knew she'd pay for it when Ms. Fitz called the owner of the building and complained about Sofie's visitors and loud living.

A sheet of white paper lay on the pine floor just inside Sofie's front door; she picked it up and read:

Please meet me for coffee—I'll be waiting at the Full Cup. Jake.

Sofie stared at the paper as though it were an ancient document intended for someone else.

"I can't," she said out loud as if Jake could hear her. "I have to get to the marine center. I really do." She looked up and caught her reflection in the far mirror: her pale face, her hair pulled back into a ponytail. She released her hair, shook it out to let it fall over her shoulders, dabbed clear gloss on her lips. She spoke out loud: "I can't meet you for coffee. I must get to work."

The canvas behind her blinked in the mirror, and she turned around, took small steps toward the painting and ran her finger along the edge. This was a unique piece; she had seen it in the way her mother bent over the canvas, her eyes often filled with tears, her bottom lip bitten in concentration.

Her mother had used tiny brushes on this piece, painting words that Sofie could barely read through the large, translucent starfish imposed over the letters.

182

Sofie knew what the words were about, but she couldn't form sentences from them. She compared it to the dolphin's language—knowing the essential message, but not the exact words.

This canvas was the most beautiful piece her mother had ever done, and yet she had never finished it. Sofie had had a million heartbreaking realizations about her mother's death, but the biggest one was that her mother had been unable to finish her favorite project; she'd left her work in a corner of a room, waiting for her return.

When her mother had been working on this painting, Sofie had had a deep conviction that this canvas would break her mother free of her sadness, free of yearning for the man she couldn't have. It would allow her to love again.

In the end, her mother did break free—but not through her art.

A tube of pale blue paint lay on the easel—just as her mother had left it two years ago. Sofie reached out, touched it, then picked it up while her heart pounded against her chest. She rolled the tube between her palms, then placed it back on the easel.

Sofie turned away from the canvas, grabbed her purse and drove directly to the Full Cup. Her hands shook as she sat in her parked car. This was outrageously foolish—meeting the son of the woman who wanted to know the whole story. The son of Knox Murphy.

Anger at having to keep her secrets, at having to lie

again, overcame Sofie. The therapist Bedford had made her see for a while should have told her that sorrow and fear resembled each other so closely that you could barely tell one from the other. But she also knew anger, and she welcomed it.

She was angry at Bedford for being so clinical, angry at Ms. Fitz for being so nosy, angry at her mother for leaving her, angry at Annabelle Murphy for showing up in Newboro. The cure, oddly, seemed to be to meet Jake Murphy for coffee.

Most of the tables were empty, although there was a long line of customers getting their coffee to go. Sofie saw Jake at a corner table and tilted her head to observe him. He was reading the newspaper and hadn't looked up yet. A thin sliver of memory returned to her.

She and Jake had both missed the bus while they were playing capture the flag in the school playground. The day was unusually cold, and she'd pulled her hood around her face, tied the strings so tightly that only her eyes and nose showed. Jake had run up and pinched her nose. "You look like one of my sister's dolls all wrapped up like that. A little tiny china doll."

She had felt a strange thrill, as though he had just told her she was the most beautiful ten-year-old on earth. He'd run off, and then they both realized they'd missed the bus. After they'd gathered their books, they'd walked to her mother's art studio, only two blocks away, to call Jake's mom to come get him.

They'd sat on two stools and sipped hot chocolate from cracked mugs, rejects from the potter who sold his wares at the studio.

Sofie looked at Jake. "Are china dolls pretty?" she wanted to know, needed to know.

Jake laughed, then squinted at her. "Of course they are." Then he'd jumped off the stool to run to his mother coming through the front door.

That same boy, now a man, looked up from the newspaper he was reading, stared directly at Sofie. He smiled, placed the paper down on the table. A chill ran through her: this man had the potential to make her tell secrets she hadn't told Bedford, secrets her mother had so insisted she keep that they had become part of her family's DNA. She walked toward Jake, sat down and nodded, not trusting her voice to say anything that made any sense.

"Hi, Sofie."

"Hello." She waved toward the coffee bar. "Do you want something?"

He laughed and the sound was deeper than she expected, as though he had more substance than it first seemed. "I've already had my share of caffeine while waiting for you. Would *you* like something?"

"I think I would," she said, glanced up at the board.

"Let's wait until the line goes down a bit."

She laughed. "Yeah, when you're the only coffee shop in town, it gets a little packed before work."

"Only one?"

She shrugged. "There's pretty much only one of

everything here. One bookstore. One coffee shop. One pharmacy. One—"

"Art studio," he finished for her, leaned his elbows on the table.

She needed a change of subject, and as she often did when she was nervous, she began to speak too fast. "Well, there are four restaurants, and two gift shops . . . so there's more than one of some things."

He nodded. "I stopped by the art studio, but it was closed."

"Yeah, Rose took it over a couple years ago and she sort of sets her own hours. No one is sure exactly what they are, but . . ."

"I remember you and your mom at the studio in Marsh Cove."

Sofie's stomach fluttered. She stood. "Listen, I didn't want you waiting all day for me. I didn't want you to waste your time, but I have to go to work now. Okay?"

Jake patted the table. "I'm sorry. I shouldn't have brought your mom up like that. I should know better—I hate when people do that about my dad. It's like they want to tell me they care about and think about my dad, but all they're really doing is reminding me of everything I've lost. I'm sorry."

"You know I lost my mom?"

"Yeah, in a car wreck?"

Sofie felt the speech on her tongue—the one she'd repeated so many times that the story was more real than reality itself. She felt the robotic quality to her words, but they must be said in their precise order, or something bad would happen. Simple, but absolute truth.

"Yes, when we moved here from Colorado, we left my sweet grandma there. Then my mother opened the Newboro Art Studio, but she often went back to visit her mother. They were in a car wreck and died together. I decided to stay here since my life is bound to the water."

Jake squinted. "Sofie, you lived in Marsh Cove, not Colorado."

She blinked. Of course Jake knew that . . . of course. How could she alter the story? Her heart pounded; her head ached; her hands clenched into fists under the table. "Yes, before Colorado."

"Oh," he said. "And your mom painted here, too?"

"My mother didn't paint. She only owned the art studio."

"We have a painting of hers. . . ." Jake leaned back in his chair, twisted his mug in circles on the table. "I'm confused."

"I don't want to talk about my mom—it's too hard," she said. "Can we change the subject?" She'd said this line so frequently that she was able to say it now with a sad smile on her face.

"Okay," he said, paused. "Then tell me about your work at the research center."

Panic ebbed like a receding tide. She had said the correct words in the correct order—she was out of danger now. "What do you want to know?"

"More about your research with the dolphins. I think it's fascinating."

"Well, I gather data to help determine when, how and why the dolphins get captured in commercial fishing nets so we can find ways to make sure they don't. Did you know about three hundred thousand dolphins die that way every year? Not everyone knows that."

"No, that's a new one for me," he said. "A sad fact."

"But privately, on my own, I am studying their . . . language."

"You mean, how they talk to each other?"

She nodded. "Some experts say that their language conveys more emotion than information. Others say that dolphins can communicate very precisely. Some say they know how to use syntax, and others that we can understand the evolution of our own use of language by better understanding theirs. . . ." She took a sustaining breath and sat back in the chair, as if she'd just run a race at full sprint.

"So," he said, and laid his palms flat on the table, "do they talk to each other?"

"Oh, yes. They use certain clicks and squeals to identify each other—names if you will. Or at least I think so. And they can send warnings and tell each other where food is." She leaned across the table and added in a whisper, "I think they have names for us, too." Words were coming out of her mouth so fast she couldn't stop them. What was she doing?

"Well, I guess that makes sense. If they call each other, wouldn't they want to call to us, too?"

She straightened in her seat. "Exactly. Exactly." She glanced around the shop, realized she was speaking loudly. "Want to meet some of them?" She had no idea why she was doing this—stepping freely and willingly into a danger zone.

"I'd love it. Am I allowed in the research center?"

"With me you are. Come on."

Jake stood, and Sofie glanced out the window at the people passing by, at the customers in line. Marty Thompson waved at her. She waved back. What was she thinking? By noon, Bedford would call wanting to know who she had been talking to at the Full Cup when she was supposed to be at work.

Jake followed her in his car, and in five minutes they pulled into the parking lot of the Marine Research Center. She felt about this glass-and-metal structure the same way others felt about their cedar shake homes or their cottages on the dunes. Her condominium was only a place to sleep, a reminder of her mother's absence. Bedford's place wasn't hers either, and she was still a visitor there, despite the years they'd been together. She'd been working or volunteering in this building since she had been fifteen years old; it was home.

Jake stood beside her as she swiped her card and the door buzzed. She walked with him down the brightly lit hall and tried to see the place through his eyes. Posters of dolphins and sea turtles lined the concrete-block walls until they came to the stairs. "The offices are upstairs. Down here are the research center and injured-animal tanks. There are dolphins, turtles, other sick marine animals."

She opened a large door and Jake followed her down metal stairs, their feet clanging. When they reached the bottom floor, a diffuse light wavered across the tanks. It was quiet this morning; feeding time was over and the staff would be upstairs now. One veterinary assistant—Marshall—sat on a stool at the far end of the room.

"Hey, Marshall," Sofie called out. "Just showing someone around."

Sofie gave Jake the tour, explaining the kinds of sickness and injury a turtle or dolphin was apt to sustain, how research could be done on them before they were released.

Jake leaned against a water tank, crossed one leg over the other and stared at her. "Do you do all your research in here? Because if I were a dolphin, the only thing I'd be saying is, 'Get me out, get me out, get me out.'"

"Maybe that *is* what they're saying." She tapped the tank. "But these dolphins need a bit more care until they can go. I do most of my research out on the water from boats, or while diving."

"How do you hear them?" Jake said.

"Recording devices . . . and dolphins come up for air, you know. They cry out and call when they're above water, too."

Jake took a step toward her, and instinctively she backed up. "What do they call you?"

"What?" She lifted her hand to her face, where she felt a flush rise.

"The dolphins. What is their name for you?"

She shivered. How many times had she asked herself this same question? She wanted to know her name: her real name and what they called her when she arrived on the seawall, when she dove into the cold water and reached her hand across their bellies. She wanted to know what they called after her when she left them.

She turned away from Jake, because this was the one question she wanted to answer and couldn't.

He came up beside her. "Guess that's hard to figure out?"

She noticed his eye color for the first time. Someone once told her that you never really knew someone, or could claim to have truly listened to them, unless you could tell what color their eyes were. Now she knew this wasn't true, because she'd been listening to him all along and yet just now dared to stare into his eyes: hazel with brown flecks that seemed to delve far below the surface until the flecks not so much disappeared as became something she couldn't see.

"It's very hard to prove." She shrugged. "Maybe impossible."

He tapped on the tank. "It looks like they're always smiling."

"Everyone assumes that dolphins are always happy—but they only look like that because they don't have cheeks."

He laughed. "Guess we have to be careful what we think we know because of a big old smile." He gave an over-exaggerated grin, showing all his teeth.

She laughed. "I wouldn't exactly call that a smile— and I'm not sure what anyone would assume about you if they saw you like that."

Jake looked back at the tank. "Well, they do look happy . . . and also as if they really want to tell us something—like they're about to speak."

"I know . . . ," she said, walked away from him and out the back door to the parking lot.

He followed her to the seawall, jumped up next to her. She pointed toward a pod of dolphins coming toward them. "That is the Alpha pod," she said.

"I bet they don't know the names you have for them, just like we don't know the names they have for us," he said.

A quiver trembled below her breastbone, as if someone had shaken only that very particular part of her body. "What?"

"They don't know what we call them, so I guess it's only fair that we don't know what they call us." He made some loud clicking noises that sounded nothing like a dolphin.

She held in her laugh with a hand over her mouth. "They're probably calling you Dumb Human about now."

"That or maybe Big Stud."

She sat, swung her legs over the water. "Yeah, prove it."

He positioned himself next to her. "Some of the best things in life are impossible to prove."

She turned to him, her laughter gone. "Name one."

"The existence of God. Real love." He clapped his hands together. "There's two right there."

She ran her finger along the stone wall. "Well, whether dolphins talk to each other or not ought to be something we can prove empirically."

He shrugged. "Maybe." Just when she thought the danger had passed, his next words sent a shock wave through her body. "Can you tell me who was on the plane?"

She stood. "I can't. . . ." She wrapped her arms around her middle, hugged her body. "I have got to get to work." Yet when she looked at his face, she wanted to relieve some of his pain. Her hands fluttered in front of her, as if she meant to take his hand or touch him, and then she dropped them to her side.

He nodded. "Of course." He held his hand out for her. "Please stay another minute."

"Jake, I have to go to work."

"Do you remember the day you found out your mom had died in a car crash?"

She closed her eyes. "Of course."

"Well, it's like that for us all over again. Just when we thought maybe, just maybe, there was life beyond the void of his death, the emptiness returned. It's like he died yesterday or an hour ago all over again. All the questions. Don't you remember how desperately you wanted to know the answer to all the questions?"

His face was contorted in a sad, beautiful way as he continued. "Don't you? Why did they crash? What happened? Was it the engine? Was it the weather? All those questions that will never be answered. Now, here my family is with new questions. Who was on the plane and why? And it seems you're the only one with the answers."

Sofie shut her eyes against the growing sadness. "It doesn't matter."

"Yes, it does." His voice was deeper, and she opened her eyes to look at him.

Her heart ached for Jake, like a bruise under her ribs. A crack opened inside her, where she kept all her secrets, and she said the words before she understood their implication. "It was my mother. My mother was on the plane." She covered her mouth with her hand to stop the words already released.

Jake stumbled backward. "I think I already knew this."

"They weren't running off together or anything like that. He was taking my mom to visit her mom—my grandma, who was sick." Sofie's words came rushed, tumbling over one another in her need to explain. "I'm sorry. Please . . . you can't tell anyone else."

"Why? My mother has to know. The FAA will find out. . . . The truth will come out anyway. What are you hiding?"

"I'm not hiding . . ." Panic faded and flowed in her chest, the word "truth" sounding like a foreign language.

"You don't think you can trust me."

"It's much more complicated than that, Jake."

"We both lost a parent that day," he said, moved toward her.

"Listen, Jake, I don't want you to think . . . that he was my father or anything weird like that. He wasn't. I wished he were sometimes, but no, he wasn't."

Jake looked away. "I don't think I thought that . . . or maybe I did. I don't know. I can't even absorb all this yet. . . ." He faced her and then did something she was completely unprepared for, yet somehow hoping for. He drew her into his arms, held her against his chest. For a brief moment, until a car screeched to a stop in front of the seawall, they were one, fused in grief. Why else would she have told him this secret but for this brief moment of respite?

"What in the living hell is this?" Bedford's voice echoed across the parking lot. Sofie broke away from Jake so abruptly that he almost fell.

Bedford stalked toward them; Sofie had never seen him so angry and she stepped in front of Jake. "Stop," she said in a voice she hadn't used with Bedford before.

"What?" He lifted his hands, took another step forward. "Did he hurt you?"

"No," Sofie said. "He's an old friend from where I used to live."

"Colorado?" Bedford stepped around Sofie and glared at Jake. "You're from Colorado?"

Jake moved to stand directly in front of Bedford.

"Maybe." He turned to stare at Sofie, and she closed her eyes as if to beg him to answer in the affirmative.

Bedford hollered, "What kind of smart-ass answer is that? You stay away from her—you understand me?"

"Not sure I do," Jake said. "You her father?"

Sofie spoke between them. "Stop it now, both of you."

They both turned toward her. Bedford spoke first. "Tell me what's going on here."

"I ran into an old friend—from sixth grade—at the Full Cup. We got to talking, and he wanted to see where I worked, see the dolphins. He's majoring in Greek mythology and is interested in dolphin history—so I brought him here. He was hugging me goodbye." Sofie glanced at Jake. She had just given him an excuse for being there, but also revealed how easy it was for her to lie, to make up a story full of half-truths, on the spot.

She felt dirty, almost obscene, as though she'd betrayed him. She looked away from his pained face and stepped toward Bedford, touched his arm. "He was just going," she said.

Jake walked away from both of them, leaving Sofie with a desperate loneliness.

When Jake's car pulled from the parking lot, Bedford took Sofie in his arms and became once again the man she knew: soft, caring. "Darling, what was that all about?"

"I just told you."

"You recognized a boy from sixth grade?"

196

"No, he recognized me—said he'd heard we lived here from a friend of Grandma's and had thought my mother still owned the art studio."

"And then you decided to show him the research center?"

"He asked," she said, feeling as though each half-truth she told destroyed a piece of her soul. But she saw no other way. Her mother had taught her well. Very well.

"My sweet girl," he said, stroked her hair.

"Why are you here?" Sofie took one step away from him. "I thought you were writing today."

He stuffed his hand into his pocket and pulled out something blue. "You left your computer's memory stick at my house the other night. I keep meaning to give it to you."

She stared at it in slight wonder. How could she have possibly left her precious work unattended? Hadn't she put it in her purse? She took it from Bedford, clasped it in her hand, held it tight. She must never let her mind become so preoccupied that she forgot something this important.

"Sofie," he said, "I looked at the work on it. You're writing a book about how dolphins can talk."

"Oh," she said, blood flowing from her face to her toes in a rapid rush.

"Please tell me you aren't going to try and publish something about speaking dolphins."

"It's a children's chapter book," she said. "And I didn't want to tell you about it until I had finished it."

She looked sideways at him. "Your opinion means so much to me, and I didn't want you to see it until I had polished it all up."

"A children's novel?"

"Just a fantasy story about dolphins. Nothing important."

Bedford leaned down and looked into her face. "You believe that dolphins give humans names. We have been through this a hundred times. You cannot prove the unprovable. You just can't. There is no empirical evidence to support your theory, and jumping off boats and recording sounds is not going to change that, Sofie."

The truth of his words blended with her hopelessness, and she turned away from him. He was all she had left in this meager life she lived. His love. His protection. His adoration. And she was about to lose it all.

"You're blowing things out of proportion, Bedford. Really you are." She kissed him. "Come on. I've got to get to work. We'll talk at dinner, okay?"

"I just wanted to let you know your work was safe." He walked to his car, got in and slammed the door with more force than was necessary.

Sofie stayed on the seawall after he was gone, stared out at the water and thought of her mother's painting, of the words below the pale, translucent starfish. One word came clearly to her: "Loss," written in small, slanted letters beneath the starfish's middle right arm. She clenched her teeth to keep the tears from rising.

She was a fool for allowing herself to reveal so much to Jake Murphy. Something had happened between the myth of the dolphin and the reality of her research, and her heart had split wide enough to allow Jake Murphy to enter her world. She would not let it happen again.

Control was her goal now—force Michael Harley to leave town; hide her research from Bedford; make Jake go away; remove the disapproval from Bedford's face. If she focused, she could do it all.

FOURTEEN

ANNABELLE MURPHY

*T*he Charmed Knits shop was located on a corner lot directly across from the church where Annabelle had run into Sofie just yesterday. Or was that a lifetime ago? A life in which she doled out advice in a newspaper as if she were the queen of knowing, as if she knew exactly what to do in every situation, as if her life were in perfect order.

Behind a plate-glass window, sweaters, booties and scarves hung from flowered mannequins. Rolls of yarn in candy colors were arranged on a large antique chest, tempting Annabelle, who had no interest in knitting, into thinking she, too, could walk into this store and make a sweater worthy of being worn when the next cold front went through.

Annabelle pushed open the door; a bell tinkled a

hollow sound and an overactive air conditioner blew cold air in her face. She rubbed her hands up and down her arms and then walked to the back of the store, where a group of six women sat in a circle talking in another language—knitting language. Annabelle had no idea what a stockinette or garter stitch was, so she cleared her throat.

An older woman with a knot of white hair on top of her head, and a wide smile, which made her look younger than the color of her hair suggested, glanced up. "May I help you?"

"Yes," Annabelle said, nervous as the other women stared at her. "I'm looking for Jo-Beth."

"Guilty," the woman said, and stood.

"May I talk to you in private for a moment?"

"Sure thing." Jo-Beth walked toward Annabelle, her long peasant skirt swishing, her hand-knitted shawl flowing behind her as Annabelle imagined her hair would if it were released from the knot.

She followed the other woman to the other side of the store. "I'm so sorry to bother you while you're teaching . . . but I want to ask about an old friend."

"You want to ask about Liddy," Jo-Beth said.

"How'd you know?"

Jo-Beth shrugged. "A good-looking fellow came in here asking about her earlier today, and I figured this was just a follow-up." Jo-Beth leaned against the counter, picked up a pair of knitting needles looped with brilliant red yarn. Jo-Beth's hands worked even as she looked directly at Annabelle; the needles seemed to be an extension of her hands. "So shoot. Whatcha need?"

"A man was looking for her?"

Jo-Beth picked up her glasses, which were hanging off a beaded chain on her neck, put them on. "You're not with him?"

"Not unless he was a very young man—twenty or so."

"No, this was an older man looking after Liddy because he thinks she knew something about some famous artist named Ariadne or something like that. I told him the same thing I'll tell you. Liddy owned the Newboro Art Studio, but she never, ever told me who Ariadne was. She herself didn't even paint."

Annabelle shook her head. "Yes, Liddy did paint."

Jo-Beth set her knitting down on the counter. "No, really, she didn't. She took photographs, did some knitting and even wrote poetry, but she didn't paint."

"I'm telling you I knew her when she lived in Marsh Cove, and she painted. Beautifully, actually."

"We must not be talking about the same woman. Liddy was from Colorado and didn't paint."

Annabelle reached behind her for a chair, but met empty air. Jo-Beth leaned forward, touched Annabelle's elbow. "Are you okay?"

"This Liddy you knew—did she have a boyfriend? A husband?"

"Oh, Liddy always had a man." Jo-Beth pulled two stools from behind the counter. "Here, you look like you need to sit a spell."

Annabelle sat and leaned over, her elbows on her knees. "Did she ever tell you the names of her . . . men?"

"Well, I knew the ones here, but I don't think I could tell you any more than that."

Annabelle's lip quivered, and she tried to cover it up by lifting a hand to her mouth. "I really am sorry to bother you. It seems as though you have been pestered enough, but I'm not sure how to tell you how important this information is to me, to my family. It is more important than you can imagine." Annabelle took in a deep breath. "Did she ever marry?"

"No. Liddy was not one to talk about her past. The only thing she told me was that they were from Colorado and that Sofie's father was dead. That's it. I don't know how much help I can be. As I told the other gentleman, we all loved Liddy, but she was very private. She showed up ten years ago with her daughter, opened a much-needed art studio in town and became one of us until we lost her two years ago. Even if I could tell you more, I wouldn't. I don't know you and we all loved her and I want to honor her desire for privacy. She was . . . beautiful in her own eccentric and heartbreaking way."

"What do you mean by that?"

Jo-Beth looked up at the ceiling, then over her glasses into Annabelle's eyes. "I can tell that you're desperate for something I can't give you. Liddy lived in some combination of real and imagined romance, constantly searching for a peace within herself that she never found. She loved deeply and impulsively, from one moment to the next, from one person to the next. Sofie is the one who can give you names if you need them. Liddy never once mentioned any names from her past. I respected her and never probed, although our friendship was deep and lasting. I'm sorry I can't help you any more than that."

Annabelle touched the woman's knee, as if this might release more information. "I know I sound desperate—I am. Did she have someone, a man, who came to see her from her old hometown?"

"The only thing she ever told me about her past and old town was that she had one true love and one sad affair—neither of which worked out."

Annabelle gathered a deeper strength to ask, "Do you know if the man she deeply loved and the man she had the affair with were the same person?"

Jo-Beth smiled. "No. I asked her—once—and she stared off toward the water for so long, silent tears pouring, that I thought I had broken something in her that could never be fixed. She didn't answer and I never asked again. You have to understand that even though she is gone, her memory is very dear to me and I have no wish to betray her. I don't know what your family situation is, or why you need the information, but please respect that I have told you all I can."

"Yes, thank you." Annabelle stood, and walked to the front of the store. Hushed voices from the women in the knitting group followed her, and she longed to join them, to sit down, pick up a ball of clean white yarn and make something with these women whom she didn't know: to fashion something soft and new with her hands.

She pushed the door open and gulped fresh air.

One true love.

One sad affair.

Annabelle said these words out loud, yet found them empty of meaning. She leaned against a brick wall and attempted to right this world, which spun out of her control.

Annabelle didn't eat for the rest of the day as the sun moved high and brutal in the sky. A quick, warm wind came without warning around corners, off the harbor and into her face. She walked out onto a pier that extended far over the water and counted the moored sailboats she passed—twenty-seven.

When Jake called on her cell phone, she knew it was not good news. After her son quietly told her that Liddy Parker was the woman on the plane, that Knox was taking Liddy to see her own mother, Annabelle sat at the end of the dock and attempted to stay her weeping. The love of her life, her husband, Knox Murphy, had flown to this town to be with Liddy Parker, and then he'd died with her. What Sofie had described as a mission of mercy no longer seemed so simple, or so innocent.

How was she to absorb this truth? She wanted to run back to the stone church where she'd first seen Sofie, burst inside and beg the preacher to give her back her faith in her life, in her husband, in her marriage.

Such faith was now wavering. She rode on a rapid river, toward another shore of doubt and grief. Her past beliefs could no longer anchor her amidst this tumult.

The day seeped away as Annabelle wandered the streets of Newboro and tried to find a trace of her husband, wondering if he could have been here or there with Liddy Parker. She even stopped by the art studio, but it was closed.

For the second time in her life, Annabelle didn't have a way of navigating the waters of her life. It was as if the world she knew had been swept away. Questions that had never before come to mind now wandered through it freely and openly, as if they'd always been there and she had just not acknowledged them.

The sun sank on the far side of the harbor, casting shadows across the water, over the sailboats. How had an entire day gone by while she merely *thought*? She'd remembered days and years she'd spent with Knox, things he'd said, motions he'd made, places he'd gone. She just wanted to find one moment, one single moment when she could say, "Aha, that is when he was with her. That's it, right there."

Had she edited her memories like some people edited their family history for their Christmas letter? Let me tell you about all the wonderful things our family did—I'll leave out how Johnny was suspended and Janie came home with a police escort. Had she done the same thing? Once, she'd actually written an advice column on this subject. She'd told her readers that they didn't need to brag in their Christmas letters. No one liked to hear how perfect your family was when their own family was fighting over something as silly as which brother-in-law would cut the Christmas turkey.

Through the years, had she done the "Christmas Letter" to her life memories with Knox, leaving out the spaces in which he could have loved another woman? If finding his plane two years after his death with another woman inside was possible, then anything was possible.

She hadn't even kissed anyone else but Knox—except that one brief and impulsive kiss with Shawn. Oh, and in fourth grade, Mitchell Lawson had caught her behind the long slide, pinned her against the metal bar and smashed his mouth against hers. She'd had a big crush on him, and the other boys had dared him. She didn't have a crush on him after that—he'd tasted like ravioli from the lunchroom, and the kiss had made her nauseous. So much for experience. She'd started dating Knox at fourteen, and that was that. No more ravioli kisses for her.

In all the years that she'd been faithful, had Knox been kissing someone else? Had he done more?

She stopped; her mind was going in random and lopsided circles. She lifted her cell phone to call Jake. She needed food and wanted to eat it with him—a touchstone of family. He answered on the second ring. "Hey, Mom."

"Where are you?"

"Back at the hotel."

"Want to meet for dinner?"

"Sure, but . . ." His voice trailed off and Annabelle slumped forward. Of course he didn't want to meet his mother for dinner.

"Forget it," she said.

"Mom, I'd love to, but I really think Sofie trusts me, and I want to talk to her some more."

"Jake, if you can't meet me for dinner, I need you to tell me what else she said." Annabelle shivered in the warm air.

"Not much, really. We talked about her work, and, Mom . . . this is really hard to say, because it is such a terrible thought, but she did tell me that Dad is not her dad—you know what I mean?"

"God, Jake, I hadn't even gone there."

"I know, I don't think I had either, but she told me anyway. There are things, something she's not telling me . . . and I think she will."

"Maybe," Annabelle said, "it's best if we don't know. Maybe we should let this go. I need to get home to Keeley . . . and . . ."

"Mom, maybe you *should* go home. I can stay here and try to get some more information out of her."

"No, Jake, this situation is bizarre and ridiculous. Let's just go home and get on with our lives. We're never going to prove anything."

"Everyone wants proof, don't they?"

"What does that mean?"

"Nothing," he said. "I'll call you later, okay?"

"Okay." Annabelle hung up. She stood, walked down the dock and counted all twenty-seven sailboats again. Some things were provable, countable, stable and sure. She once thought their lives were, too.

FIFTEEN

ANNABELLE MURPHY

*A*nnabelle huddled in the far corner of the restaurant bar and sipped a cup of hot tea. Everything in her hurt: her heart, her bones, her head. She stood to get a table when a conversation with the bartender caught her ear.

A man who stood four stools over, leaning across the sleek bar, had uttered "Liddy." Annabelle inched closer, tried to look away as she eavesdropped. He was asking about Liddy Parker, if she had painted or just owned the Newboro Art Studio. Annabelle stared at him, weighed her choices. This had to be the art historian who was looking for Liddy, the one Jo-Beth and the woman at Sofie's building had mentioned.

He looked about Annabelle's age, or slightly older, with dark, wavy hair that fell just past his ears and a goatee of dark hair mixed with gray. To Annabelle he looked more like he should be in a band playing guitar than doing research as an historian. He turned from the bartender and caught Annabelle staring at him. He wore glasses with round silver wire frames. The overhead lights lit the outside of his glasses, and she couldn't see his eyes.

She tilted her face away. She'd wanted to hear what he was saying, but not get caught. She felt a movement, and pulled her purse closer to her body. "Excuse me," a deep voice said.

Annabelle met his gaze. "Yes."

"Do you live here?"

"No," she said, shook her head, and then stood to walk away. When she reached the end of the bar, she stopped. What if this man knew more about Liddy Parker than she did? What if he could tell her something, anything? The need, the clawing and consuming need to know the answers to her questions, overcame her. She turned back and saw that he had moved to the other side of the bar to talk to another patron. Someone with that much tenacity could most definitely help her find out what the hell Liddy Parker was doing in a plane with her husband.

The dim lighting and weary sense of unknowable secrets weighed upon Annabelle as she approached the man. "Excuse me, but I couldn't help overhearing that you're looking for Liddy Milstead, and I thought maybe . . . well, maybe we could help each other." Annabelle felt as though her moving lips did not match the words she said; she felt disoriented, disconnected from reality.

He smiled. "Did you know her?"

"Yes. Though not well." Annabelle sat on a bar stool and gazed at the bottles of gin, vodka and whiskey reflecting the bar lights. She wanted to be rational, to speak with care yet all she felt was a reckless need to know mixed with righteous anger. She dug her nails into her palms in an attempt to fight the madness welling up inside her like a living thing.

"She was with my husband on a private plane. They were supposed to be headed for Durango, but the plane crashed and she died with him. That was two years ago in a remote region of Colorado where rescue helicopters couldn't find them."

"Oh." He sat on the bar stool next to her and pushed his glasses up on his nose. "I'm sorry . . . for your loss. I was told she died in a car wreck visiting her mother. Were you close to her?"

Annabelle felt the mad laughter rise, then catch in the base of her throat. "Close? No. I hadn't seen her in ten years. Now, my husband? I guess he was close with her. Everyone here thinks she died in a car wreck—but her daughter, Sofie, said that her mother was the woman in my husband's plane." Annabelle leaned forward. "And Liddy Milstead was not from Colorado, as everyone around here seems to think. She was from Marsh Cove, South Carolina, where I live."

He squinted and Annabelle saw now that his eyes were gray with an underlying blue, like the water in Marsh Cove Bay on an overcast day. As she averted her gaze, he touched her shoulder. "Where she used to live . . . in Marsh Cove, do you know an artist named Ariadne, or did Liddy? I promise I don't mean to pry into your personal lives; I just want to finish my research article, find more of this particular artist's paintings and move on. I won't interfere. . . ."

"Interfere?" Annabelle asked. "Interfere?" Her voice rose. He leaned back, glanced around the bar. Annabelle took a breath and smiled at him. "Listen, you're not interfering. You want information about Liddy, and I want to know why she was on that plane with my husband. That's all. I thought you might know more about her than I do."

He stared at her while Annabelle thought about all the things she truly wanted to know: who Liddy really had been, why she had changed her name when she moved to Newboro and then lied about where she came from, why Liddy had been with Knox, why she had left a daughter alone in this world . . . why the hell Liddy had lived in Marsh Cove and then left.

The man tapped on the bar. "I don't know much more about Liddy than you do."

Annabelle realized she hadn't even told him her name. She held out her hand. "By the way, I'm Annabelle Murphy."

"Michael Harley. Nice to meet you." He shook her hand, held it a moment longer than necessary. "Here's what I do know. I am writing about an artist named Ariadne, and I came to Newboro because her paintings once hung in the local gallery. When I got here everyone told me the former owner, Liddy Milstead, died in a car wreck in Colorado. The new owner knows nothing about who Ariadne was . . . or is. She said that she hasn't received a new painting from her in over two years, and that Liddy Milstead was the only woman who knew who she was."

"Did you ask her daughter, Sofie?"

"She slammed the door in my face."

Annabelle nodded. "Did you go to her place or her boyfriend's?"

"She has a boyfriend?"

"Yeah, a professor named Bedford Whitmore—or at least that's what her neighbor told me."

Michael ran his finger along the edge of the bar, and Annabelle saw the paint under his fingernails.

"Do you paint?" she asked, touched his hand before she gave any thought to her action.

He held out his palm, and her finger fell into his open hand when she had only meant to touch the edge of his thumb. Flesh on flesh. She hadn't felt the potential and imminent need for touch in a long time. She allowed her finger to stay there a moment before she withdrew her hand.

"Yes, I paint. Not as much as I'd like, but I worked today. The landscape here is breathtaking and a challenge to capture because it changes with every breath. It might be the most fluid environment I've ever tried to paint. Quick movements of cloud or wind, a shift in tide, and the entire picture alters."

Annabelle laughed. "Where are you from?"

"Philadelphia. I'm a teacher at the art school there."

"Well, that explains it. . . ."

"Explains what?"

"Your accent."

"I'm not the one with the accent—you are." He grinned.

Annabelle gestured with her hand. "I think if you ask every single person in the bar, they'll tell you that you're the one with the accent."

He laughed loudly and several people turned and stared at them, yet he didn't seem to notice. "Just because a bunch of people say it's true doesn't make it true. You can't take a vote on everything, you know."

She wondered if he was talking about more than her accent.

Without removing his hand from her arm, he leaned closer. "Everyone here says Liddy Milstead knew the artist Ariadne. I think Liddy Milstead *was* the artist. What do you think?"

Annabelle shivered, shrugged. "I don't know anything except that when I knew her, she was Liddy Parker. She lived in Marsh Cove for about ten years with her daughter, Sofie, and she painted and had an art gallery. She signed her own name to her paintings. I have one at my house in Marsh Cove. The woman I spoke to here said Liddy didn't even paint, that she came from Colorado. It's like we're talking about two different people."

"What were her paintings of?"

Annabelle visualized the Liddy Parker painting hanging in their foyer. Dizziness overwhelmed her. Her head dropped into her hands; her tangled hair fell over her hands and onto the sticky bar. Michael lifted her hair, whispered, "Let's get out of here."

Annabelle followed him out of the restaurant. When

they stepped into the clear night, she moved away from his guiding hand.

"Are you okay?" he asked.

She turned her back to him. "I don't even know you; I should never have told you all those things." She faced him. "Listen, I don't know any more than you do. I was hoping you could tell me something."

"Let's see. . . . What can I tell you? I'm a teacher at the Philadelphia School of Art working on an article for publication. I'm single. No kids. I grew up in Philadelphia, and this is the first time I've been to this area of the country, which, by the way, I have fallen madly in love with." He laughed. "So there you go— you know who I am."

Annabelle looked at him in the light of the gas lamp and thought she just might know more about him than she ever had about Liddy Parker. "Oh," she said. "I'm sure there's lots more to you."

"Yes, but that's the fun part—getting to know some-body's story."

"I don't have a story, or if I do—right now, it's a tragedy."

"I doubt that. You are too . . . exquisite to be part of a tragedy."

His kind words, the way he said them and then moved closer to her, made her breath catch on that lump in her throat that had been there since the day the sheriff arrived to tell her they'd found the plane. She took in a long breath of fresh sea-scented air and admired the way her lungs expanded, filled the dreaded tight spaces that had occupied the middle of her chest. She wanted to give a witty answer to his words, but nothing came to mind.

He motioned toward the bay. "Let's walk, okay?"

She nodded.

They strolled in silence under the gas lamps, over the cobblestone pathway toward the water. The quiet felt like a warm soothing blanket, peaceful, seductive, and Annabelle hoped she wouldn't have to speak again for a long time.

Michael placed his hand on the small of her back and led her down a side alley that ended at the water's edge. They stood watching the tide move in, the sailboats rising with the floating docks, the stars growing brighter as their eyes became accustomed to the darkness. The horizon blurred, became indistinguishable. Annabelle stared until she could just make out the line separating sea and sky.

"I always imagined I would disappear into that line—that thin line right there." She pointed across the bay.

"The horizon?" he asked.

"Yes, the horizon. Isn't it an appealing thought—to just disappear into that line?"

"Seductive, yes. Now, why would you want to disappear?"

"My husband died."

"Yes, you told me that."

"Seemed like a good solution at the time." She laughed at her own absurd words.

"And now?"

She shrugged. "Not sure."

He stayed quiet for long moments, then said, "Tell me about the painting you own."

She answered in a whisper. "It's beautiful. It's been hanging in my foyer for twenty years now. I'd forgotten who painted it." She closed her eyes, floated into her house with its broad-planked hardwood floors, lovingly cared for by her and well worn by children racing in and out, adults crowding together for parties. On the right side of the hallway stood a hunting table, where mail was dropped. In a tiny pottery dish that Keeley had made in fourth grade, keys had accumulated over the years—Annabelle didn't know which locks some of them fit into. A large photography book of the antebellum homes in Marsh Cove took up the right corner underneath a milk glass lamp, once her grandmother's. Hanging on the wall above these family items was the framed painting.

Maybe all along its presence had been a hint—family mementos in the entranceway of her home eclipsed by Liddy Parker's painting. Nausea shimmied and danced along Annabelle's gut, and she pulled away from Michael, looked at him. "Listen, I'm not sure what you're really after here, but the painting is just like a bunch of others in coastal homes. It's a beach scene with sand dunes and sea oats, a pathway leading to the beach. Nothing spectacular. Really."

"Are there people in the painting?"

"No."

"There never are."

"What do you mean?"

"She never puts people in her paintings. Animals, sea life, inanimate objects, never humans. For the last five or six years, her art has included words below the translucent paint—suggesting she was trying to say something, but wasn't sure she really wanted anyone to know it."

Annabelle shrugged. "Maybe she didn't know how to say it."

"No, I think she didn't like people all that much."

"Oh, you think you know this artist even though you never met her. You have her completely figured out through her paintings? Some mysterious woman who needs you to save her or—"

"Sometimes we know strangers better through their art than we know the people we live with. Art is often an expression of an interior life, a subconscious life."

"Is that your premise for your article?"

"No, just an observation. We can drop the subject."

"Can you tell me what you know about her?" A wind rose inside Annabelle that she felt would carry her away if she didn't hear something, anything to secure her to the ground, to reality.

Michael faced her. "I first found her art in a fellow faculty member's house ten years ago. He had bought the painting in a studio in Charleston. It was an image of sand dollars on the beach, large and blurry with masterful brushstrokes. It was signed with the name

Ariadne. I called the Charleston studio and asked if they had any more of her work. They told me that her paintings came in at odd moments through a patron— a man who wouldn't tell them her real name. He took care of the money, deliveries and communication. They didn't know his name or how to get in touch with him. He stopped by about once a year to pick up payment, if something had sold, and drop off anything new if he had it."

Annabelle shivered with a sudden and outrageous conviction: Knox. She didn't speak his name out loud, as it might shatter the universe, splinter her very world to know or speak his name in association with something so secretive.

Michael leaned against a light post, crossed one leg over the other in a relaxed pose. "So . . . several years later, this studio called me and asked if I was still interested in an Ariadne piece as two of them had just come in."

"When was this?" Annabelle asked.

"Seven years ago or so . . ."

"And?"

"I had them fax me a color copy of the paintings and bought both on the spot. I couldn't afford them, and it was crazy that I bought them without touching or seeing them, but there was something about the art that made me have to have it. I was intrigued by not only the art, but also the fact that the artist had this much talent and yet wanted to remain anonymous."

"Oh." Annabelle shifted her weight on her feet.

"Ariadne is the name of a Greek goddess."

"Goddess of what?"

"She's called the goddess of the labyrinth. Do you know the story?"

Annabelle shook her head.

"Ariadne lived in a castle with her father in Crete. He had a labyrinth with the Minotaur, who was fed seven young men and seven young women every nine years. But Ariadne fell in love with a man who was to be eaten that year—Theseus. She helped Theseus escape the Minotaur by offering him a red thread that he would carry into the labyrinth, then use to find his way out. There are many versions of this myth, but after Theseus survived the Minotaur, he took Ariadne with him, as he'd promised, but then left her on a deserted island. There she met and fell in love with a god, Dionysus, who saved her. After learning she had named herself after this goddess, I decided I would do my article on artists who hide their real identities. And I came looking for her because I figure she is the only one who can tell me why she hid her name."

"Well, Liddy can't tell you any more. She's dead," Annabelle said. The words tasted bitter, harsh, and yet it was satisfying to spit them out.

Her mind filled with the crazy thought: if Knox had had an affair with Liddy all these years, there was nothing wrong with her kissing a complete stranger; if Knox had cheated on her, she would prove she was still desirable, she was still a woman other men might want and need. But her heart wouldn't allow her to act out of spite.

She drew back. "I must go now. Thanks for the conversation and . . ."

"Please don't go," he said.

"I must." She forced her mind to focus. It was Monday night—she'd been in Newboro since early Sunday morning. She'd left Keeley with her mom. Jake was somewhere in this same town trying to get information from Sofie. Knox was dead. She was talking to a complete stranger, who was looking for a woman who had possibly been her husband's lover. "I've absolutely got to go," she said.

Annabelle shoved past him, and moved toward the street without saying goodbye. When she reached the stoplight, she looked left and right, then felt the vibration of her cell phone in her purse. She grabbed it out of her handbag, and looked at the number: home.

She stood still and stared at the phone until a honk made her jump, move to the sidewalk again. "Keeley?" Annabelle said into the phone.

"No, dear. It's Mom."

"Hi, Mom. How are you? Is Keeley okay?"

"We're all fine. I just thought I'd check in on you."

"I'll come home first thing in the morning." Annabelle was sure of her plans now. She needed to get home, get out of this alternate universe that had gone on before her and would go on after her: this world of art and strange men, of secrets.

"Oh, okay."

Annabelle knew her mom's voice well enough to hear the hesitation. "What is it?"

"Well, I did get a call from school today. I let Keeley drive to school, but they say she never showed up. And when she got home this afternoon, she wouldn't tell me where she went. And I just hate to bother you with this, Belle, but should I let her drive to school tomorrow?"

"Mom, you tell her I said you have to drive her and walk her to her homeroom. She'll yell, scream and probably throw a tantrum, but there is no other option. I'll be home by dinner. Okay?"

"Did you . . . ?"

"Find out anything?"

"Yes . . . did you find out anything?"

Annabelle walked carefully on the sidewalk—avoided the cracks. "I've found out a little, but nothing real clear. If anything, I have even more questions now. We'll talk when I get home, okay? I've got to check on Jake and get some sleep."

"Jake?"

"He's here, too. He was worried about me and arrived yesterday. I told him he didn't need to do that . . . but now I'm so glad he's here."

"Oh, darling, I feel better that he's there with you, too."

"I'll call you in the morning."

"Annabelle, I love you."

"I love you, too, Mom." Annabelle had reached her motel by the time she'd hung up. The night wrapped around her, soothed the rougher edges of her thoughts. She would not, in any way, allow this situation to hurt her family. Knox Murphy would never have cheated on her. It wasn't possible in this world or any other. He wouldn't and couldn't live a double life with another woman. She would have felt the disturbance in the earth, the turbulence in the air. Just like the waves that slapped against the dock when a boat ignored the no-wake signs, his actions would have reached her long before now.

This was what she intended to believe.

SIXTEEN

SOFIE MILSTEAD

*G*olden morning light spilled onto Bedford's hardwood floors. Sofie lay on the soft mattress, curled into a ball, and pretended she was still asleep so she could enjoy the warmth when it moved across the room and crawled up onto the comforter.

Bedford shook her shoulder with a light hand. "Baby, it's time to get up."

Sofie looked over at him. "Not for me. I don't have to be in until noon today because of the board meeting."

"Well, let's not waste the day." He rose from the bed and stretched, kissed the top of her head. "Rise and shine."

"No," she said, burrowed deeper into the covers. This was her favorite hour of the morning—but then she remembered what she'd said to Jake Murphy, the secrets she'd revealed that might unravel her entire life.

"Lazy girl," Bedford said, then laughed as he moved toward the bathroom. Sofie listened to the shower turn on, the pipes sing. Her eyes closed and she waited for the sunlight to move over her body as she knew it would in a few minutes. A sound that didn't belong to her routine morning came into the room: knocking.

She kept her eyes closed and wondered what it could be: construction across the street, Bedford not able to get the shampoo out of the bottle? Then it came again—an insistent knock on the front door.

Sofie groaned, rolled from the bed and slipped her feet into Bedford's house shoes. "Bedford," she called out, but he didn't answer, and she knew he couldn't hear her.

His robe was huge on her, but she pulled it around her and held it with her right hand as she made her way down the stairs to the front door. She'd have to remember to bring her own robe next time.

She stood on her toes and looked through the peephole: the damn art historian Michael Harley. She turned away from the door, rubbed her eyes. She had to get rid of him before Bedford came out of the shower, before he stepped downstairs in his khakis and button-down shirt, looking competent and sure of himself.

"Hello?" a voice called from the other side of the door.

Sofie opened the door a crack, looked out. "There is nothing I can tell you. Please go away and leave me alone."

"Please just give me two minutes—that's all I ask. Then I promise I'll go."

Sofie stared at this man with his round glasses and dark hair, his hands behind his back and his eager face pushed forward. "Okay," she said. "You have less than two minutes. We're down to one minute fifty seconds." Her voice was not her own; she didn't talk this way, but panic changed every word.

"Then I'll get right to the point. I came to you originally because I knew your mother owned the art studio, and I thought you could tell me how to find an artist whose work she sold there. I have come across some new information that leads me to believe that your mother not only knew who the artist Ariadne was, but that she *was* the artist."

An earthquake of exposed secrets split the world into two parts: safe life and dangerous life. Sofie felt herself falling, falling into the space between truth and lies where it was dark, cold. She closed her eyes—yes, it would be better to go to this place than where she stood now. She leaned against the wall to fight the dizziness.

She focused until she understood his words. "Are you okay? Should I call someone? Are you okay?"

It took her a moment to find stability. She poked his shoulder with her finger. "Leave now. Hurry." The sound of Bedford's footsteps upstairs told her he would soon appear at the top of the stairwell.

Michael looked up the stairs, then at her. "Was your mother Ariadne?"

"No." Sofie spoke harshly and in a whisper. "Her name was Liddy Milstead and she ran the Newboro Art Studio. She did not paint. We are from Colorado. We moved here ten years ago to open a studio. Now leave. Leave." Her mind spun—had she said the words in the right order? Had she told the correct story?

He planted his feet wide apart and rubbed his chin. "I thought it was Liddy Parker and she was from Marsh Cove, South Carolina. I was told she died in a plane crash with the lawyer Knox Murphy."

"Who told you that?" Sofie grabbed his shirtsleeve in some desperate attempt to keep from falling. Had Jake told him? Had Jake betrayed her already? Life swelled with imminent danger.

"Listen, you don't seem well, and I don't mean to scare you. I'm just looking for Ariadne. I don't want to freak you out. . . ."

Maybe if she repeated the words one more time, the speech would become truth. She tried again. "My mother was from Colorado, her name was Liddy Milstead and she owned the Newboro Art Studio here because she loved art and the coast. The end. You might want some great story for your article or your weird obsession, or whatever is driving you. But that is all I can tell you. I don't know who is telling you all these lies."

The man backed away. Relief flooded Sofie—he would leave before Bedford came down the stairs for his two scrambled egg whites with whole-wheat toast and coffee.

"Who is telling lies?" Bedford's voice filled the room as efficiently as if someone had pumped the house full of freezing air.

Sofie spun around. "I have no idea, but this man is leaving."

Bedford walked toward Michael Harley; Sofie's thoughts gyrated around one word: *Leave.*

Michael spoke to Bedford. "I am so sorry to bother you. I'm looking for some information about Liddy Milstead, and I was told her daughter stays here. My name is Michael Harley, and I'm a professor at the Philadelphia School of Art."

Sofie understood that like animals in the wild who recognize their own species, Bedford would talk to this professor in his matching clothes and wire-rim glasses.

"Hello." Bedford held out his hand, shook the other man's hand. "What do you teach?"

Their voices blended in Sofie's head until she couldn't separate the words one from the other. They talked about curriculum and whom they might know in each other's universities.

Sofie stared at them: all her stories would soon be futile, insignificant. Her heartbeat was erratic and words she'd stored in an airtight place in her soul now scattered through her mind in random order: *hurri-*

cane; Ariadne; beating; father; Knox; never tell; Parker; shattered bones.

What had she unleashed when she'd told Jake about her mother? Her hands flew to cover her face and she whispered behind her palms, "Mother": a single plea in a desperate moment.

Telling even one person could have made her vulnerable to being found. She'd made the worst mistake of her life.

She ran upstairs, changed into jeans, yanked a T-shirt over her head and grabbed car keys off the dresser. She ran down the back stairs and was in her car before she registered the words Bedford hollered after her. "Stop, stop now, Sofie." She had reached the harbor before the words had meaning and before her body had any inclination to do as he said.

The parking lot of the research center was empty except for the few cars of the board members who were there for the meeting. She glanced around for John's pickup truck. Yes.

She parked the car, ran to the docks and hit the splintered wood before she realized that she wasn't wearing shoes. Her bare feet pounded against the planks as she ran to the end of the dock, jumped onto John's boat. "John," she hollered.

His face rose from belowdecks. "Well, top of the morning to you, Sofie Milstead."

"Hi." She smiled at him, crouched down. "I was hoping I could talk you into taking me out this morning. I just discovered I have a few free hours, and it is so beautiful. I'd love to take a quick dive."

He tilted his head. "When was the last time you dove?"

"Four days ago."

He wiped his hand on a greasy cloth and climbed on top with her. "You don't look like you're ready to go diving."

"I can be in less than five minutes. Please."

"You know they"—he motioned toward the research center—"like you to book the dive so they know who is out when."

"Yeah, but I don't want to interrupt their board meeting, do you?"

He scowled at her. "Yeah, like I want to head into that room."

"Okay." She jumped up from her crouched position. "I'll be back in five. . . ." As she ran toward the research center, she calculated that it would take Bedford five minutes to react to her rapid departure, five to get Michael Harley out of the house and ten to drive to the research center, where he would assume she'd gone. She had less than ten minutes left.

The self-closing door swung back on its hinges as Sofie ran down the hall to the locker room, where she kept her bathing suit and diving gear. She unzipped her pants as she ran, entered the locker room while she yanked her shirt over her head. In a conscious attempt at sanity, she emptied her mind of all thoughts except one: *Hurry*.

In moments, she jumped onto the deck of the boat.

John stared at her with a furrowed brow. "You sure you got everything? Seems like that was mighty quick. You couldn't have checked your equipment that fast. . . ."

"John," she spoke in a slow whisper, "please go. I promise I won't dive until I check the equipment. Just get us out on the water, and I'll do everything I'm supposed to do."

He nodded, moved toward the controls. Sofie held her breath until she felt dizzy; then she gulped in fresh sea air as the engine sputtered to life. "Grab the ropes, please," John called.

"Sure thing." Sofie unwrapped the back nylon ties from the cleats as John did the front ones. Then he pushed the throttle forward, and the boat moved across the water into the harbor.

Sofie sat down and dropped her head into her hands. Although she tried to stem the sudden flow of tears, she couldn't. Subdued sobs rose with a will and force of their own.

A hand came to rest on her shoulder; she looked up at John. "I'm fine. I promise. Just give me one minute."

"Did he hit you?"

"What?" Sofie took a deep breath, then glanced at the shoreline, where John motioned with his hand. Bedford stood on the seawall; he waved in frantic motions and his mouth formed a mute round "O."

"Oh, no. No," she said, wiped at her cheeks. "Nothing like that."

John stared down at her, his brown eyes concerned. "Okay."

Sofie faced away from Bedford so she wouldn't be tempted to go back, to make him calm down until his face became warm with love and approval.

"Do I need to turn the boat around?" John asked, moved toward the steering wheel.

"No, whatever he needs can wait until I've done my dive."

"Are you sure you're feeling okay?"

"I don't think a few tears make a dive impossible." Sofie attempted to force lightness into her voice.

She checked the oxygen level, the tank and the regulator. She called out each checkpoint to reassure John that she was in control and thinking clearly. This was what she needed right now: to delve beneath the surface and listen to the song of the dolphins. She needed this more than she needed air, water, love, food, even Bedford: her consuming urgency grew.

The flippers snapped onto her feet; she fit the mask to her face and took a couple of breaths from the regulator. She gave a thumbs-up to John and bent over the bow.

"How much farther do you want to go?" he asked.

She wanted to tell him miles and a millennium away from here, but she looked over her shoulder and said calmly, "Let's just go about a half mile into the sound. Then I'll begin to look for the dolphins."

"They'll find you. They always do. It's weird, if you ask me." He revved the engine.

Waves splashed against the bow in a rhythmic dance. Entranced, Sofie leaned over, then banged on the side of the boat to attract any dolphins that might be nearby.

John pulled the boat into a tidal creek that Sofie knew cut through to the sea, not the way he usually went. She glanced up at him. "Where're you going?"

"When I was fishing here yesterday, there was a pod running up on the bank, almost beaching themselves, eating fish like they were never gonna get enough. Frantic almost. I've seen that twice before. It's beautiful. Thought they might still be back here for you. . . ."

Sofie nodded. "Strand feeding," she said. "They chase the fish onto the banks, where they can catch them easier. Lazy bums." She laughed. "You know, the only place they've ever been seen doing that is here and around Hilton Head. And only at low tide."

Slowly, surely, Sofie's panic lightened, the memory of the morning's events fading like day into twilight.

The boat purred as John navigated the tidal river. Sun teased along the marsh edges in a silver-flash amusement of light and green growth. Tiny fish jumped near the spartina, causing pockmarks on the water, as if rain were falling from a clear sky. Warmth traveled up Sofie's spine, along the back of her head, where the strap of the mask gripped her scalp.

Droplets of water hit her face, and an alligator raised its knobby head and stared at her. She shivered at the sight of his cold eyes and stealthlike movements. Once, she'd been in a boat with her mother—the small

Boston Whaler they kept on the far shore—when a pair of alligators swam past them toward the marsh. They'd stopped and blinked their bright eyes at Sofie and Liddy. The large one, lumpy and green, its tail slithering like a snake through the water, stared at them as it opened its mouth, moved forward in a movement so quick that the deed was over before Sofie understood that the alligator had just eaten a turtle sunning itself on the mud.

When the mouth snapped shut, when the teeth came down and the crunching sound echoed across the water, Liddy grabbed Sofie's hand and squeezed it so tight that Sofie felt her finger bones rub against one another. When Sofie had pulled her hand away, telling her mother she was hurting her, Liddy had begun to cry silent tears of apology.

Sofie had asked why the alligators scared her mother so badly when they couldn't get in the boat. Liddy answered, "The one in the front—the bigger one—looks just like a bad man before he strikes. The alligators and that man usually attack at night, but you have to be careful all the time, be ever vigilant."

Sofie had whispered the only question that mattered to her. "Mother, does the alligator ever attack and eat the dolphins?"

Her mother had wrapped her arms around Sofie. "Of course they don't eat dolphins," Liddy said. But for the first time in her life, Sofie had not believed her mother. Terror had crawled into Sofie's soul at that moment and had lived there ever since.

Until that day on the water with her mother, it had seemed that her mother's stories were make-believe, equivalent to the boogeyman under the bed. But the alligators made the danger authentic and palpable. Sofie never forgot.

Now the alligator disappeared below the surface and slithered into the marsh grass. Sofie shivered, motioned for John to take the boat out to open water at the mouth of the river. He gunned forward, and they rode the tide out toward the sea.

John stopped the boat, came to the bow, where Sofie stared into the gray-blue depths, picked a barnacle off the side of a buoy.

"Ready? I'll anchor here," he said.

"Okay." She stood, took in enough of the sea's vista to wash the image of the alligators from her mind. "Let's just float for a bit until we see a pod. Don't anchor yet, okay?"

"Okay." He took a step back, and then laughed.

"What?" Sofie screwed up her face, yanked at her mask strap.

John pointed to the water; Sofie looked over her shoulder. The gray-silver burnished back of a dolphin rose from the surface. Joy billowed upward in Sofie's chest. She swung her legs around, gave John a thumbs-up and fell backward into the water.

The sea surrounded her, took her in as she knew it would. She sank with each breath until she swam evenly and without effort just ten feet below the waves, where she heard the dolphins the best. She didn't recognize this pod—but it didn't matter since she didn't have her recording equipment with her.

Some pods never left the rivers, yet this one headed toward open water as she followed it. She felt a kinship with the pods that stayed inside the winding rivers and tidal creeks of the marsh and barrier islands, where everything one needed was within the safety and comfort of the known world; danger lay out in the mysterious, unfamiliar expanse of the ocean.

The mammals called to one another in high-pitched squeals; Sofie craved to know what they were saying. Were they talking to her? This need to understand them was a constant ache that moved through her body like the flu. She followed them to deeper water, listening, touching, diving below and above them, lost in their sounds and silken bodies.

An adolescent dolphin poked at Sofie's side with its blunt nose as if it needed or wanted something. Sofie touched its face, ran her hand down its side until she came to the fluke and flattened her palm against its flesh.

She knew she was crying by the way her mask fogged, by the sounds of her breath in the regulator as the pod pushed forward and she followed. A boat revved in the distance, the engine muffled. A chorus of clicks and whistles filled the air, and the pod dove straight down. Sofie smiled beneath her mask, the rubber digging into her cheeks.

She had no proof, but somehow she knew they had all warned one another of the danger posed by the boat ahead, by the nets that would be trailing it. Still far enough away to be safe, she took long breaths of oxygen, lunged deeper with them.

From where she swam, the crests and dips of the seafloor looked like the mountains of Colorado from the sky. This was what people on land never understood—they thought of the aquatic world as something separate from themselves, apart from the dry, oxygen-laden surface, but the land swept the oceanic floor just as the crests and valleys of dry earth.

She'd first seen the earth from the sky when Knox Murphy had taken her and her mother to Colorado on his private plane. She couldn't have been more than twelve years old, it had been twilight and she remembered staring out at the glorious mountains below her. The image had embedded itself deeply in her mind so that she could still picture it.

The single-engine Cessna hummed, and in that moment Sofie had experienced a peace that she rarely found any other time in her young life. Knox Murphy sat in front of Sofie with his earphones on, his hands twisting instruments. Her mother, seated next to Knox, had leaned her head back on the seat and stared out the window with a calm smile, then patted his leg and mouthed, *Thank you.*

Sofie, caught up in the moment, had never wanted it to end. The mountains below them, the sky above them, all in a quiet place where no one could find them, ask them questions. Knox wouldn't have to leave. Her mother wouldn't be silent for days or even weeks afterward, painting as though she were mad, half crazed with the need to capture a shell or sea oat in perfect detail.

Maybe in the beginning of her dive training, the recollection of how she felt that day in the plane had drawn her to the below-water life: it was the same world that she saw below the gilt-edged clouds. The familiarity and peace she found were only part of why she belonged below the water more than above it—the dolphins were the other part.

Sofie and the dolphins were deeper now. The water teemed with tiny fish, shrimp going out with the tide. Sofie followed the pod as it began to feed on a school of menhaden. She looked down at her depth watch, and calculated how long she'd been there. A monstrous realization struck her: she'd made a cardinal mistake—she'd lost track of time.

Somehow in her sorrow, fear and remembering, she'd forgotten to watch the clock and oxygen level. She glanced at the floating gauge and saw the needle almost buried on the large red *E*. She'd once had a dream like this, awakened herself as she grappled with the quilt, clawed at her empty bed.

This was not a dream. How had she gotten in this situation when she knew better? When it had never happened before? At some point she'd been crying, gulping air in bigger and deeper breaths than usual. The adult male dolphin swam back toward her, nudged her bottom with his nose. *I know. I'm going.*

Sofie kicked upward, too fast, she knew. She

attempted to take slow, even breaths to save the oxygen she had left. Even if she ran out, she could make it to the top while holding her breath, she told herself as she rose. She mustn't go up too fast or she'd get the bends. She'd moved too far away from her own boat, from John, who was probably frantic by now at her failure to return.

The surface came into view, shimmering and light-filled. She took another slow breath, filled her entire body as if with helium, full and expansive. A peculiar calm overtook her mind and body; a tranquillity that told her nothing really mattered. She slowed her kicks and floated; she'd rise eventually.

Images moved through her mind. She saw her mother smiling, Knox Murphy standing at their front door holding a box of her favorite crab cakes, the three of them together on the beach at twilight while Sofie collected shells in a tin bucket. Sofie smiled at these beautiful images and wanted to stay with them, find more of them. There was a storehouse of fluorescent memories in her mind, and she wanted to access every single one of them more than she wanted to rise to that surface. Her regulator must be wrong—there was no way she could be out of compressed air so quickly.

She looked up toward the surface and thought it curious that the bottom of a boat dented the smooth top of her world. Breath released into the regulator, and she heard the hissing of empty sound just as she remembered another moment. She'd been about nine years old, and they'd still lived in Marsh Cove; she was in the back of the art studio making a sketch of a house. Her mother was in the front of the store talking to a customer, laughing and explaining the technique of another artist whose work was displayed in the window. Sofie shifted her gaze from her drawing. She'd just made a perfect front door and wanted to show her mother.

Sofie had run out into the main room and hollered for her mother, the paper held in her hand like a flag. Liddy turned around and her face looked like a stranger's. Instinctively, Sofie dropped the paper and ran to her mother, crying out to know what was wrong.

Her mother had put her hand on top of Sofie's head, leaned down and whispered to return to the back room and do her homework. Everything was just fine out here. But it wasn't fine; the man who stood at the front desk was asking too many questions.

The sea's surface was too far away.

Knox couldn't stay with them.

Her head hurt and the hissing sound grew louder.

A small boy came into the studio with Knox—Jake—and they hid together in the back room while their parents whispered and Sofie heard her mother cry.

The dolphins poked at her with force now—nudging her more than she wanted. Sofie reached down and touched the top of one dolphin's head, ran her hand along the silken flesh, or she thought she did, but she couldn't move her hand; her body wouldn't obey her.

She tilted her head at the animal—it was Delphin; he'd come.

She closed her eyes because she had to, because her body forced them shut. Then she heard it—the soft double click followed by a squeal that she had come to know as Delphin's greeting.

Double click. Squeal.

Double click. Squeal.

Her mother stood in the front of the studio. Twilight surrounded her as she faced the easel, her face smiling, a paintbrush in her hand.

Sunlight fell through the water in thin strips.

Double click. Squeal.

My name, Sofie thought, *a double click and a squeal.* She sank into this knowledge: they did know her. Wasn't that all that mattered?

Yes, her mother had told her that Knox knew them. He knew their real name. Everything else was not nearly as important as the fact that he knew them.

Then, like the news of the plane crash, and the realization that her mother was on that plane, pain shot through Sofie's head, then her body. She released a long breath. In the darkness, she heard one last sound: Delphin calling her name.

Seventeen

Annabelle Murphy

$\mathcal{T}$he road from Newboro to Marsh Cove unwound before Annabelle's windshield. She continued to recall moments with Knox—who he was to her and their family: things he did, words he said. This was her conclusion: she *chose* to believe in Knox Murphy. No matter what the circumstances or scattered facts suggested, she intended to believe in him.

The eight-hour drive went by in a blur of blacktop, boiled-peanut stands, shrimp shacks and her favorite—a barbecue place called the Butt Hutt. Her driveway appeared as though it were a mirage, shimmering and distant, as she drove down the street to her home.

She parked and released a long breath. She was climbing up the porch steps when the front door opened, and Keeley came out with her hands on her hips. Annabelle went to her daughter and reached to hug her, but was greeted with angry resistance.

"Did you tell Gamma I couldn't use the car, that I had to stay in the house until you got home?"

"Well, hello, Keeley. Good to see you. I missed you, too." Annabelle smiled, hoped to defuse the anger rolling across the porch like incoming fog.

"I'm serious, Mom. Did Gamma make that up or did you tell her that?"

"Keeley, you skipped school. You lose car privileges and social privileges when you skip school." Exhaustion crept up on Annabelle, and she wished she could tell Keeley to do whatever she wanted—go take the car, forget school, just don't look at her with such hate; she couldn't take it anymore.

Keeley slumped into a chair on the porch. "I didn't skip. I left school for one period. One. Then I didn't go the day you left because . . . well, just because."

"That's skipping, technically." Annabelle sat down next to her daughter. "What is going on with you?"

Keeley stared at her mother with hard eyes, and Annabelle mourned the lost child with the sweet smile and soft cheeks. "Nothing is going on with me," Keeley said with a closed mouth.

"You hate everything and everyone." Annabelle rubbed her stinging eyes.

"No, I don't hate everyone." Keeley stood, stared down at her mother. "Just you and Dad."

The sentence carried more weight and import than four words strung together should. Annabelle's shoulders sagged, her heart split, and Keeley slammed the front door as she went back into the house.

Annabelle stared across the street toward the bay and thought maybe, just maybe she should have stayed in Newboro. "Oh, Knox," she whispered, "what do I do now?"

Running to Newboro hadn't solved anything. While she'd told herself she was tracking down "the truth," she'd merely been remembering the past. She had recounted and recalled and reconstructed a time that was forever lost to their family.

But she wanted Keeley to remember the truth: who Knox was, how he loved, what his heart was made of. If Annabelle couldn't trust what she'd learned in New-boro, at least she could trust her memories.

Wind trembled through the magnolia tree; leaves plunged to the ground in a twirling ballet. Annabelle stepped off the porch toward the tree. She remembered what the expert had told her—that this tree would not stand for long, that the extra weight and pull of the new offshoots would weaken the main trunk. She hadn't wanted to believe him because to her this tree represented her family. They didn't pull one another down, but held one another up through buffeting winds and storms.

Now it seemed important that she be right about this, that the tree still stood strong and sure, that the leaves and branches were healthy and thriving, that the root system went deep. Annabelle knelt at the tree's base and ran her hand along the knobby ground, up the trunk and through the lower branches, where her children once hid when it was time for chores or homework.

The branches remained firm, the leaves waxy, green. Her relief was so great, she finally allowed the sobs to come—the weeping she had withheld all during the eight-hour drive from the place where Liddy Parker had lived with her daughter, Sofie, the last piece of earth her husband had touched. The ground below the magnolia absorbed her tears of sorrow and confusion, the root system nourished by her own loss and uncertainty.

She leaned against the trunk, allowed it to hold her up as exhaustion followed and her eyes closed. She stretched out on the ground and laid her head on a thick protruding root. Her eyes stung, her head ached as she whispered, "I'm home."

A peace that only comes with letting go washed over her. Trust was moving and breathing again inside her, turning to faith in Knox even though she didn't understand his actions.

Keeley's voice screeched across the yard, shattering the quiet. It took Annabelle a moment to realize what she was saying. "What is wrong with you? Are you crazy? Have you lost your mind?"

Keeley stood with her hands flailing, staring at Annabelle as though she were indeed insane. Annabelle sat up, wiped her face where she felt the grit of dirt and moss on her cheek. "I'm fine, Keeley. You can stop screaming at me."

Keeley turned away from her as though she were ashamed to look at her, to see her dirty face and clothes. Annabelle stood and touched her daughter's shoulder.

Keeley spun around again, her expression contorted with emotion. "What are you doing? Why are you lying in the dirt?"

Annabelle read the trepidation under Keeley's anger. She had lost her father and didn't understand why. And now it appeared that her mother had completely lost her mind. All this time, Annabelle had thought the glittering anger emanating from Keeley stemmed from hate, but the emotion moving, living and breathing in Keeley was fear.

New relief filled Annabelle. She could not cleanse her daughter of anger or hate, but she could assuage Keeley's terror. She touched her daughter's arm. "I'm fine. We're all fine. I was out here rejoicing in the strength of our family, in the strong roots we have. We're okay."

Keeley wiped at her face, as if this could remove the emotions shifting across her features. "What about . . . Dad? He's not okay, and he's not who we thought. What if . . . what if he really was leaving us?"

Annabelle held both Keeley's shoulders in her hands, held her fast so Keeley had to look into Annabelle's eyes. "I know this feeling, Keeley. I've been there. I know what you're thinking."

Keeley shoved Annabelle's hands off her shoulders. "There is no way you know what I'm thinking. You can't read my mind."

"You're thinking this: you're scared to death that everything you've believed about your father is an illusion. That everything that has guided your life, the very foundation of your life, is false, a lie. It's a terrible place to be, a terrible place to live. It's dark and scary and twirling with ugly thoughts, and all of a sudden nothing seems to matter anymore—not school, not friends, not family. Nothing really matters because what you believed isn't true. That's why I ran off to North Carolina." Annabelle stopped and took a deep breath, realized the words had come too fast, too bluntly.

Keeley bent over, placed her hands on her knees. "Stop, Mom. Please shut up."

Annabelle placed her hand on top of Keeley's chestnut curls and remembered holding this child against her breast, shushing her to sleep, patting her back until her breathing smoothed out and she could place her in the crib next to her night-night doggie stuffed animal and let her sleep in peace. Oh, to do that now, Annabelle thought, to place her hand on Keeley's head until sleep and peace came that easily.

"Oh, Keeley. Just remember. Just remember one thing about your father, and you'll know. Think."

Keeley straightened and her hard, wet eyes and clenched, trembling jaw were a portrait of confused emotions. She set her feet in motion and ran barefoot across the lawn toward the road, toward the park and bay. Her frayed jeans, her untucked tank top were too loose on her small frame.

Annabelle watched until Keeley reached the edge of the bay and stopped at the dock. Then Annabelle went after her. When she arrived at Keeley's side, Keeley twirled around. "Leave me alone. I mean it. Leave. Me. Alone."

"No," Annabelle said.

"Why? Why can't you just go away?"

"Because I love you too much, and I can't have you thinking wrongly. You are part of me, Keeley. You cannot, ever, make me stop loving you—no matter what you say or how you act."

"You say that now. But look at Dad—he obviously stopped loving us. And you know it."

"I don't know any such thing."

"Give me a freaking break, Mother. He ran off with some woman. If you call that loving us, you're delusional."

"It was Liddy Parker. She was the woman who once owned the art studio here."

Keeley went still, stared out over the water. "I don't remember her, but I've heard people talk about how she started the art studio. Don't we have one of her paintings?"

"Yes, the one in the foyer," Annabelle said, realizing she still had not stepped into her house and looked at the painting with fresh eyes.

"That's sick. We have Dad's mistress' painting in our house? I think I'm going to throw up."

"I don't think she was his mistress, Keeley. I did think that, but I don't believe it now."

"Then why the hell was she in that plane?"

Annabelle touched her daughter's face and considered reprimanding her for the curse word, but changed her mind. "Your dad was taking her to see her sick mother in Colorado. That is all I know."

"How can you be so sure he wasn't . . . with her?

There isn't any other explanation. Unless you're not telling me something . . ."

"No, there seems to be a lot of mystery around this woman. I went to Newboro because that's where she lived with her little girl, Sofie. And everyone there believes she is someone else entirely."

"Either way, Dad lied to us."

"Or didn't tell us the entire story."

"Same thing." Keeley kicked at the ground. "He said he was going hunting alone in Colorado, not flying with some woman from Newboro."

Annabelle nodded.

"Don't have an answer for that one, do you, Mother?"

"No, I don't. You're right about this, Keeley, I don't have the answer to everything. I can only tell you what I believe."

Keeley took four steps away before she turned around and headed down the bay toward the beach. Annabelle fell into step beside her. They walked in silence until they reached the end of the bay. Together they cut across the wooden boardwalk that was built so no one would walk on the sand dunes and hurt the roots of the sea oats. When they reached the sand, Keeley bent over, rolled her jeans up to her knees. Annabelle pulled off her shoes, placed them side by side on the beach.

They stood, mother and daughter, in silence until Annabelle whispered, "Remember when your dad brought us out here for the lunar eclipse?" She reached down, picked up a smooth shell, bleached white and pure, rolled her thumb into the concave portion, and handed it to Keeley. "Remember?"

Keeley took the shell, held it in her open palm, and then closed her hand around it. "Yes, I remember. He woke me and Jake up in the middle of the night, wrapped us in blankets. Jake walked, dragging his blanket in the sand, and Dad carried me. We lay on the blankets, stared up at the sky, and he told us that story about the god racing across the sky in a chariot."

Annabelle laughed. "That's probably why Jake is so into Greek and Roman mythology. It's all Dad's fault."

Keeley's eyes opened wide. "You know about that?"

"You mean that your brother dropped out this semester because he wants to change majors?"

"Oh, I thought he didn't tell you."

"He told me in Newboro."

"He was there, too?"

"Yes, he was worried about me, which he shouldn't have been—but I was glad for his company. He's still there. He wanted to stay another day or so."

"This is crazy." Keeley bent down, picked up another shell. "Remember when Dad came to career day dressed like a fireman because he thought his real job was too boring for me, and he wanted to make the class laugh?"

Annabelle felt a giggle rise in her belly, and as if it were a loved one returned, she welcomed the feeling. "Yes, I remember."

"It might have been funny in second grade, but this was eighth grade. I wanted to crawl under my desk."

Annabelle reached down and picked up another shell, cream-colored and cracked, held it up to the sun. "Remember when Jake brought home that girlfriend none of us liked?"

"The one with the tongue ring?'

"No, not her. I liked her. The one with the makeup so thick she looked like a mannequin."

Keeley laughed and Annabelle wanted to take that sound, wrap her arms around it and carry it in her heart like a gift. "Oh, Mom, Lilly-Rose was her name. And Dad asked her why her mother named her after two flowers instead of just one, and she told Dad it was because she was double sweet and Dad said, 'Yeah, I smelled that when you walked in the door.'"

Keeley took the third shell from her mother's hand, held them all together and rolled them between her palms until they sounded like wind chimes. "This is how, huh?"

"How what?" Annabelle asked.

"This is how you believe. You just add them all together. All the remembers—you add them together and you believe."

"Yes," Annabelle said; her voice cracked. "We don't know all the reasons yet, but we do know certain things."

Without answering, Keeley began to walk farther down the beach. Annabelle didn't follow—this time it was right for Keeley to walk alone. Annabelle watched her for a few moments as Keeley bent over, picked up a shell, ran her fingers over it. Annabelle turned toward home.

Grace Clark stood in the kitchen emptying the dishwasher; Annabelle came up behind her mother and hugged her around the middle. Grace turned and smiled at her. "Tough trip?"

"Yes," Annabelle said, took two glasses from the dishwasher and placed them in the cupboard. "Take a break, Mom. Sit down."

Together they sat at the counter. Grace held out her hand for Annabelle, who squeezed it. "Thanks for helping me, Mom. I would never have asked if I didn't really need it."

"You know how much I love Keeley. It was no problem at all. You feel like talking about what happened while you were gone?"

Annabelle rubbed her eyes. "Mom, did you ever think Dad was lying . . . or keeping something from you? I know it's a strange question, but do you think we can know everything there is to know about the person we love?"

"No, we can't. We all keep secrets, Belle. Sometimes we won't admit it even to ourselves, but there are spaces in our hearts where we hide things from ourselves and others. Do I think your dad lived a life of integrity and honor? Yes. Do I think he might have kept some things from me? Of course."

"Do you think he ever had an affair?"

"No, I don't think so. But how can we ever really know?"

Annabelle sighed. "That's what I'm trying to figure out."

Grace squeezed Annabelle's hand. "Darling, you don't have to figure everything out. Life is confusing and messy and doesn't always make sense. Remember the hurricane?"

"Mom, how could I not?"

"It was the worst time of my life. I was so worried about you and the pregnancy. Worried about the house. Sick about my family's heirlooms. But do you see how far we've come since then? Who we are?"

"What do you mean?"

"Out of that brokenness, out of that tragedy, came a new and stronger house, a marriage between you and Knox that gave me my grandbabies, a sense of community that had never existed in Marsh Cove. . . . You don't have to figure this all out. You only have to know what you know."

Annabelle stared off toward the hallway, felt the crunch of sand between her toes. She pulled a shell from her jacket, laid it on the kitchen counter.

Grace stood. "I have to get to my garden club meetin'. Call me if you need me." She kissed Annabelle on the cheek and held her in a hug a fraction longer than usual.

When her mother had left, Annabelle took a glass jar from the kitchen cupboard, placed it on the front hall table and dropped her shell into it. She would collect the shells she found. She would gather memories and keep them in a place of honor in her home and in her heart.

EIGHTEEN

SOFIE MILSTEAD

*E*very breath brought sharp pain into Sofie's chest, and when she willed herself not to take another, somehow air was forced into her lungs. She contracted her abdomen, tried to release a cry, but her speech was stopped.

She pried her eyes open and saw the lights—too bright. Her hand weighed too much, and when she tried to lift it to shield her eyes, it wouldn't move. One by one the sensations of her body came to her: needle in the right hand, plastic in her nose, restraints on her wrists. She glanced frantically around the room: taupe drapes closed over what she assumed were windows, a white curtain between her and the next bed. After the freedom she'd found deep underwater, she was now trapped in its opposite: her personal hell, penance for all her lies and deceit.

Monitors beeped next to her ear, but she couldn't turn her head to see what they measured. The most significant pain came from her chest, where each breath burned.

She attempted to piece together the events that had

brought her here. Nothing came to mind except a slight remembrance of waking, of Bedford in the shower, then static-filled noise and no memory.

An empty metal chair faced her bed as if someone had just vacated it. An upholstered chair was shoved in the far-left corner against the drapes. Oh, how she wanted to cry out, to call for someone.

She closed her eyes and told herself to remain calm; she was in a hospital and someone would check on her soon. Then loud voices filled the room—words overlapping so that, like her mother's paintings, she could understand only the general meaning, not the specifics.

The voices belonged to Bedford and Jake. They were arguing about her safety, Bedford saying Jake was not allowed to enter the room. Bedford thought Jake had hurt her, had brought her to this state. Had he?

Confusion spread down her arms and legs in a tingling sensation. She was diving. Yes, she'd been diving and something had happened.

She opened her eyes, tried to sit up, call out to Jake that he was allowed to come in. The door swished open on air hinges, and both men entered the room. Bedford's hand was on Jake's upper arm, attempting to pull him out again. They both stopped in midstep when they saw her staring at them.

Bedford released Jake, came to her bedside. "Oh, baby, you're awake. You're okay."

She attempted to shake her head that she was not

okay, that she needed to pull the tubes out of her nose and arm, but she couldn't move.

"Don't try to talk. You're restrained. I'll get the doctor. . . . Wait, wait. I'll get the doctor." Before Bedford ran from the room, he pushed Jake up against the wall. "Don't talk to her, don't touch her."

As soon as the door swished shut behind Bedford, Jake took tentative steps toward her bedside. "Oh, Sofie, I'm so sorry about this. Thank God you're awake. You have friends out there in the waiting room who are on their knees with worry." He sat in the chair next to her, and she wondered if he was the one who had left it there in the first place.

He wound his fingers through hers, around the restraints. "You're probably wondering what happened, right?"

She attempted to nod, but could make only a slight movement.

"Yes?" he said.

She squeezed his fingers.

"You were diving. You stayed down too long and came up too fast. The doctors say it was a combination of low oxygen and the bends. Then you came up and hit your head on the bottom of a shrimp boat."

Sofie closed her eyes and tried to remember, but found a blank white space, as if her mind had been wiped clean of that day.

"The dolphins . . . they saved you," he whispered close to her ear.

The door swished open again, and a woman in a

white lab coat and stethoscope came into the room followed by Bedford. She reached Sofie's side. "Hello, Sofie. Glad you could join us." She lifted her stethoscope and placed it in her ears as she scanned the monitors.

Bedford grabbed Jake's arm, pulled him to his feet. "I told you not to touch her. Get out."

The woman—Dr. Burke, the name tag said—turned to Bedford as she placed the stethoscope on Sofie's chest. "Not here. If you two have a problem, take it outside. Now."

"I don't have a problem," Jake said, "except that I'm worried about Sofie."

Bedford squared off in front of him. "You don't even know her. Don't say her name. Get out."

"I've known her since she was a child. . . ." Jake touched Sofie's forehead. "I'll be waiting outside."

Sofie's eyes shifted from the doctor to Jake, then back to Bedford and to the doctor again. How awful it was not to be able to say what filled her mind. She wondered if this was how the dolphins felt with her—trying to talk to her but not knowing her language. If only she could tell them all exactly what she wanted to say: *Let Jake stay; tell me what the dolphins did for me; give me a drink of water; my head hurts; am I okay? Is John mad at me?*

Dr. Burke smiled at her. Her gray-and-black hair was pulled back in a tight ponytail. Her eyes crinkled with her smile, and her forehead was etched with deep furrows, probably from looking at patients just the way she was looking at Sofie. "You gave us quite a scare. Your boat captain probably saved your life by calling the coast guard, which was right there when a crewman on the shrimp boat pulled you out of the water."

I thought the dolphins saved me. Jake said it was the dolphins . . . Her mind screamed unspoken words.

The doctor patted her arm. "I know you must have a lot of questions. We'll get you off the oxygen, and then we'll catch you up on everything. Meanwhile, try and rest quietly while I get respiratory in here, okay?"

Sofie blinked as her only response. Bedford sat down in the metal chair, grabbed her hand. Tears filled his eyes. "You scared me."

He loves me. He really loves me.

"I knew something bad was going to happen. Something bad always happens when we lie to each other. I couldn't live without you, Sofie. Please tell me you didn't try and kill yourself."

Kill herself? Had she run from the house to kill herself, and her mind had gone blank at the horrible thought?

She gave a hoarse answer that tasted like fire. "No."

"*Shhh . . . shh . . .* I didn't mean to upset you. I'd just never seen you do anything like that."

What did I do?

He laid his head next to her on the pillow, stroked her hair. "My sweet girl."

Then weariness such as she'd never known overtook her like a wave; she closed her eyes and fell into a sleep where there was water and peace. Sunlight warmed her; dolphins soothed her with clicks, whistles and squeals. Bedford's voice faded into a muffled murmur. Jake took his place, and although she didn't understand what he said, his words were comforting and familiar.

Hours later, she woke. The respiratory therapist was there to explain how they had removed the oxygen tube from her nose, how she'd been in a decompression chamber and they needed to check her blood oxygen levels. They drew blood, listened to her lungs.

Finally she spoke. "Where's Jake?"

Bedford slammed his fist down on the bedside table. "Those are your first words after a near-death experience? 'Where's Jake?'" Anger filled the room like a noxious gas. The doctor and therapist backed away from the bed.

She wanted to explain that the only reason she wanted to see Jake was to hear him explain about the dolphins. . . . What had he meant about the dolphins?

Sofie reached her hand out to Bedford, but he didn't take it. "I just want to ask him about the dolphins." Her voice was raspy, rough—not hers at all, yet coming from her mouth.

"I can tell you anything you need to know . . . so can John. He was there." Bedford took her hand, squeezed it. "Do you remember anything?"

Sofie scooted up in the bed now, for the first time aware of how she must look after being fished from the sea. She ran the hand without the IV through her hair; it caught in the tangles. "I don't . . . remember," she whispered.

The doctor stepped forward. "Before she starts talking, I need to check her vital signs. If you will wait in the hallway, I'll call you in a few minutes, and you can have about twenty minutes with her. But she's had a tough time—she'll need to rest."

"Okay," Bedford said. "I'll go tell everyone how well you're doing. A lot of people are worried about you . . . sitting vigil in the waiting room."

"Who?" Sofie whispered.

"John, who is scared to death. Our preacher, Fred. Your mom's friend Jo-Beth . . ." Bedford walked toward the door. "And that annoying friend of yours from Colorado—Jake."

Sofie closed her eyes as the doctors listened, poked, prodded and asked her questions. When they were done, Bedford returned to the room alone.

When he sat in the chair, she looked him in the eye. "Please tell me everything."

He told her how she'd run from the house, how she'd gone out on the boat with John. When she hadn't returned in the proper amount of time, John called the coast guard. They put out an alert for a diver in the vicinity, and that was what saved her life. The shrimp boat saw her floating and notified the coast guard, which by then was only five minutes away. They brought her in, sent her to the decompression chamber, from there to the hospital room. It had been a full day since she'd been rescued.

"A full day?"

"Yes. I spent the night in this chair." Bedford smiled. "I've slept in better places, trust me. They kept you sedated for a while so you could get proper oxygenation. They said you probably wouldn't remember much, but it seems you went down too quick, ran out of oxygen and came up too fast."

"I wouldn't have gone down too fast. I know better." Every word hurt like a needle.

"You were in quite a state. John didn't realize you were so upset, or he wouldn't have let you go down."

"Upset." This wasn't a question—she knew she'd been upset; even the blank sheet of memory allowed this one emotion to slip past.

"It seems you weren't making your usual good decisions. I tried to stop you, but by the time the research center had radioed John not to let you dive, you'd already gone."

"Upset about what?" She attempted to conserve her words.

"Not now, Sofie. We don't have to talk about it now."

She needed to talk about whatever had made her troubled enough to disregard her own life deep in the water. But weariness spread through her again, and sleep came with Bedford's hand on her forehead.

NINETEEN

ANNABELLE MURPHY

A full day after her return, Annabelle's suitcase still spilled its contents across her bedroom in a mess of mismatched and wrinkled clothes. She threw all of them into the laundry basket. She dumped her makeup case on the bedside table, then sat on the edge of the bed and took inventory of her room. Nothing had been moved since Knox had died: the wedding photograph propped on his bedside table; the Christmas photo of Jake and Keeley next to it; his alarm clock, which hadn't been set in two years. The day after his death, the alarm had sounded at six a.m., and Annabelle had moved her foot over to nudge him, tell him to turn it off.

Annabelle ran her finger along his pile of books, his phone, then picked up the receiver and dialed the cell number on Sheriff Gunther's card. He answered. Annabelle sat on Knox's side of the bed and spoke in a bold voice. "Hi, Sheriff. This is Annabelle Murphy, and I have the name of the woman who was on the plane with my husband."

Silence came through the line, and for a moment Annabelle thought he'd hung up. Then his voice reverberated strong and sure. "Thank you for calling, Annabelle."

"Her name was Liddy Parker. Or at least it was when she lived here. Remember she owned the art studio? She changed her name to Liddy Milstead when she moved to Newboro, North Carolina."

"Married name?"

"I don't think so," Annabelle said. "I think she just changed her name. She owned the Newboro Art Studio there and has a daughter named Sofie, who is twenty now and still lives there. Remember they lived here for about ten years?"

"Were you in contact with her through these years, Belle?"

"No," Annabelle said, took a breath. "But I guess my husband was."

"Do you know anyone else in town who was in touch with her?"

"No."

Wade's breathing was audible in the silence until he spoke. "Well, thank you for your help. I'm going to need her daughter's contact information."

"No problem," Annabelle said. "I have it."

"Can I ask you one more question?"

"Sure." Annabelle picked up the framed photo of Jake and Keeley.

"How did you find her?"

"I went to Newboro because it was listed in Knox's flight plan, and I asked around. . . . It's a small town."

"Thanks. I'll call you if I have any more questions."

Annabelle hung up, then lay back on her husband's side of the bed. She'd kissed Keeley good night and allowed her silent nod to pass without comment. Now she waited for the peace of sleep to arrive. As she drifted off, Knox came to her and held her hand and smiled at her. He was alive and beautiful, confirming his love for her and their life together—not with words, but with a simple touch. When she woke, her heart was both broken and healed in the only way something could be both at once: in love.

The ringing phone woke her early the next morning. She would have liked to hold on to the peace of her newfound belief in Knox, the soft moment when he came to her in a dream, but Jake's voice on the other end of the line began another day.

"Hey, Mom," Jake said, "did I wake you?"

"That's okay. You on your way home or are you still in Newboro?" Annabelle sat, swung her legs over the side of the bed.

"Sofie had a diving accident. She's still in the hospital, but I think she'll go home tomorrow. I feel like . . . well, like I need to stay."

"Oh, Jake, that's terrible. But she has a boyfriend; you don't need to stay."

"Okay, then I don't have to. I want to."

Annabelle was completely alert now, wistful dreams gone like they had never happened. "Oh, Jake, you're always wanting to take care of everyone and everything. She's not a lost puppy. . . ."

"Mom, she almost died. She ran out of oxygen, hit her head. It was bad."

"I'm sorry. Poor Sofie."

"I just wanted to let you know where I am. I'll call, okay?"

"Jake, I love you."

"Love you, too, Mom."

Annabelle had told Shawn that she would meet him for a few moments at the café on the same block as the *Marsh Cove Gazette* offices after she got Keeley off to school. She wanted to talk to Mrs. Thurgood. She wanted to immerse herself in writing her column, get back the busyness and normalcy of her life.

Shawn sat at a back table, rolling his coffee mug between his palms. Annabelle understood he was anxious to hear what she'd learned in Newboro, and she swallowed her irritation at having to talk about it this morning when she wanted to float in her memory of Knox's hand on hers, to stay safe in her firm belief in him. But Shawn was their dear friend.

She took a seat next to him, and had to touch his arm before he noticed she was there. "You're off somewhere, Shawn."

He smiled at her, kissed her cheek. "Sorry. I didn't hear you. How's it going?"

"Good." She leaned back in her chair, grinned at Izzy, the waitress behind the counter, and motioned that she wanted a cup of coffee by pointing at Shawn's mug.

"You look great," he said. "Really, you do."

"I finally got some decent sleep." She brushed her hair back from her face.

"Then it must have been a good trip."

She shrugged. "I don't know, Shawn. It was bizarre. I still don't know how to process all of it. But now it's up to the FAA. I just want to get on with my life. You know?"

"What did you find out?" He leaned forward.

Annabelle gave Shawn the facts of her trip like bullet points in a presentation.

"So," he said, paused to take a long swallow of coffee, "all you know is that he was flying Liddy Parker to see her dying mother. That's it? And you're happy with that explanation."

"Listen, Shawn, I don't know what I'm happy with. If you're asking if he was *with* her, I don't think so. I really don't. Her best friend did say she had an affair when she lived here in Marsh Cove, but I don't think it was with Knox." Even as Annabelle spoke the words, doubt crept like termites into solid wood, slowly eating away her belief. She closed her eyes. "That sounds like denial, doesn't it?"

Shawn shook his head. "No, it sounds like faith."

"Maybe I'm being a fool. Maybe Knox was her lover, and that's why she left. But . . . she's dead, Shawn. And so is he."

"What about her daughter?"

"You want to ask her daughter if her mother had an affair with a married man?"

"No," Shawn said, "I don't." He dropped his chin, and Annabelle reached over, touched his fingers.

"Are you okay?"

"Listen, Annabelle, I need to tell you something. I never wanted you to know this, but I can't have you believing something else."

The café walls moved in a wave; Annabelle's lungs clamped down and she saw a simple V in the road of her life, and she didn't want to take either fork. She could travel to the right—the way of ignorance—and not know what Shawn was about to tell her. Or she could take a left—the way of the truth—and struggle to integrate it into the beliefs she had come to embrace.

She stood, looked down at him. "No," she said. "Don't say it." She held her hand up to stay his words. Maybe, just maybe, like the shells in her jar at home, her memories of Knox were broken, only fragments of the real thing, a contrived attempt to fulfill her own wishes.

Shawn stood. "Let's walk, okay?"

As if in slow motion, Annabelle followed Shawn outside. Her well-laid plans for the day—organizing her house and catching up on her advice column—were all forgotten. She didn't care to hear what Shawn wanted to say; she needed to believe for one more day before her world changed again.

They walked a few blocks in silence before he sat down on a concrete bench facing the bay. She settled next to him; he took her hand.

"I don't want you torturing yourself for no reason. There are things you need to know."

She searched his eyes to see if she could discern the words without him having to say them. "Shawn, here is what I know—that Knox loved me; he loved our kids; he remained faithful to our life. That is what I believe. If what you have to tell me is any different, I'll listen, but I'll still believe that his heart was with us."

Shawn closed his eyes. "We all keep secrets, Belle."

Shame poked out its ugly head as Annabelle thought how she had kept secret from Shawn that she was pregnant when she and Knox got married. "You're right."

He released her hand. "I'm the man Liddy had an affair with."

The air wavered before Annabelle. "Huh?" Her reply came mumbled and soft.

"When I was married to Maria, I had an affair with Liddy Parker. No one ever knew except Maria. No one. Not even Knox. Maria wanted to leave me anyway, so she allowed me to keep secret the catalyst for our breakup."

Annabelle needed to see if this was real, if the man she'd known her whole life could have done this and she hadn't known. She touched his leg, then his arm to see if he was solid and not a vaporous ghost of secrets revealed. "You cheated on Maria." It was not a question. "All these years I thought she abandoned you—I hated her for it. She was a friend; I loved her. I'd known her since third grade, and I thought she was . . . the one who . . . but you cheated on her."

"Yes." His tone was flat. "I'm only telling you so that you won't think Knox had the affair with Liddy. That's all."

Annabelle felt such an odd mix of emotions she

couldn't sort them out. That her best friend had kept this secret from her all these years fractured her belief in their simple and honest relationship. Not knowing how to react, she just stared at him.

"Don't look at me like that, Belle. Please. I can take a lot of things, but not your disapproval. You have no idea what it was like then. It was years and years ago. Maria and I had nothing together—we should never have married. Liddy was a beautiful, magical artist who came to me, and I thought she could fill that empty place inside me. Of course she couldn't and didn't, and then she left. I hadn't thought about her in years."

"What empty place would that be, Shawn? The one where you have a great life, a fulfilling job, wonderful friends and family? That hole?"

"No. The space that can only be filled when the one you love loves you back. When you can't make someone love you. That empty place."

She knew what he meant because she felt it, too: the despair that threatened to overtake her if she thought for more than two minutes that Knox had not loved her as she had loved him, the emptiness that loomed when she thought again, *What if none of what I believed is true?*

She took Shawn's hand, understanding the dark place. "I'm sorry, Shawn. I didn't mean to say it so cruelly. Did you love Liddy?"

"No. I thought I did for a little while, but she was only an escape. I am ashamed to say I was glad when she moved. When I realized that I had used her to leave a bad relationship, I felt terrible."

"And you never told Knox?"

He shook his head. "Never. I didn't tell anyone. Until now."

"Oh, God, how many more secrets are there?" Annabelle dropped her head into her hands. "If you . . . if you did this thing and kept it from me all these years, why couldn't Knox have done the same? If she had that kind of power . . ." All Annabelle's beliefs, which she'd been gathering all day, crumbled. She could talk and talk, and remember and remember, and gather more shells, but what was the truth?

He spoke in a whisper. "That is the only reason I told you. You think I wanted you to know about this? Never. But I could not have you think it was Knox who had the affair. . . . He wouldn't. He didn't."

Annabelle looked up now. "If you could, he could."

Shawn looked away, and she knew it was because her words were true and he had no answer for them.

"Why else," she said, "would he have been with her?"

"I came to relieve your fear, not add to it. That woman told you Liddy had one affair in Marsh Cove; you're looking at him."

Then a possibility crossed her mind like an arrow of such piercing pain that she doubled over. "Shawn, are you making this up to force me to believe Knox was not that man?"

He stood, touched the top of her head. "God, no. I wouldn't do that."

She looked up at him. "I thought you wouldn't cheat on Maria either, that she left you because she was selfish and cruel. Here's the thing, Shawn: we know part of the story, only part of it, and we form our belief around that part. Now you're telling me another piece of the story, and it challenges everything, doesn't it?"

"No, it doesn't challenge everything."

She rose next to him, looked toward the horizon. "It breaks life into pieces I can't put back together, not in a way that makes any sense to me."

"You don't think I'm trying to piece this all together, too? You aren't the only one who feels hurt and betrayed by Knox."

She looked away from the water and sky, refocused on Shawn. For the first time, she saw anger flare in him, where only grief and sympathy had been before. "What do you mean by that?"

"Knox didn't tell me about Liddy, either. He didn't say a word to me about taking her somewhere on a plane. Hell, I didn't even know he had kept in touch with her. You aren't alone in this."

"I wonder if he knew he'd hurt everyone—you, me, our friends."

"I don't think he would ever intentionally hurt us, or anyone for that matter. Listen, what I had with Liddy for that brief time was wrong. It didn't seem that way then, but we both admitted that we had tried to find something in each other that we couldn't get from the one person we truly loved. We even tried to make that okay. Isn't that the worst part? We tried to make it okay that we tried to take our love for other people and give it to each other."

Annabelle stepped closer to Shawn to ask, "Who did she love?"

"She never told me."

"But Maria loved you, didn't she? She was my friend . . . a good friend, and I turned my back on her because I thought—"

"It wasn't Maria that couldn't love me back."

They faced each other, and Annabelle felt a shifting beneath her feet, a crack opening that might expose another secret she wasn't sure she could bear. She asked anyway. "Who did you love like that, Shawn? Who did you love so desperately that you tried to fill the loss with an affair?"

"You."

"Shawn . . ." His name escaped her mouth in a whisper.

He took a step backward. "I am going to walk away now, because I cannot stand to see your eyes."

He turned to leave. She wanted to find words to soothe him, make him come back, but instead she sank back onto the bench. Had she always known this? *Another secret.*

She returned to her car, allowing the obligatory chores of the day to drive her forward without thought. When Shawn's face or words entered her head, she forced herself to think of Keeley and Jake, of her newspaper column, her grocery list . . . anything but his confession.

When she drove back to pick up Keeley from school, she thought how children did this for parents—made them move, forced them to get up and go when they felt incapable of doing one more thing. *This is what love does.*

Keeley crawled into the passenger side of the car. "This is so embarrassing—getting picked up by my mother."

Annabelle nodded at her. "You can start taking the car next week if I don't get one more call from the school."

"No more calls." Keeley leaned against the car door, stared at her. "What did you do all day?"

"Not much."

"I doubt it. You're always going a hundred miles an hour."

Annabelle stopped at a red light and looked at Keeley, and her heart filled all the way to the edges with love. "Well, maybe you just don't know me as well as you think you do."

"Yeah, right," Keeley said.

Silence filled the car and Keeley reached over, turned on the radio, and Annabelle tolerated the music of Ludacris until they pulled into the driveway. "You have a lot of homework?"

"Yeah," Keeley said. "I'll be in my room."

Annabelle nodded.

"Mom?" Keeley opened the car door, put only one foot on the ground.

"Yeah?"

"You okay?"

"Yes," Annabelle said, ran a hand over her face.

"Okay." Keeley got out of the car.

Annabelle met her daughter on the other side of the car, now convinced that honesty was the cure for all that ailed them. "Listen, Keeley, I'm not okay. I'm sad. It's really hard being without your dad and fighting the good fight, you know?"

"I know." Keeley looked away. "I left math class the other day because Nicky Mulroney showed me the front page of the newspaper with Dad's story. I didn't mean to skip, Mom. I really didn't. I just meant to go the bathroom and try not to throw up. But the next thing I knew I was in the car. Then the next day I didn't want to face them again—so I didn't go again. I'm sorry."

Annabelle took her daughter's hand. "Why didn't you tell me?"

"You didn't give me a chance . . . and I hated you and life and Dad and Nicky Mulroney and school and everything."

Annabelle nodded. "We'll get to the other side of this, okay? Let's just not hate each other. It's hard enough without that."

"Deal." Keeley ran up the stairs to the porch. The screen door fell shut behind her.

Annabelle sat on the bottom step. She would stay strong for Keeley. There was more at stake than her own belief and trust in Knox; her daughter was also in danger of losing faith.

TWENTY

SOFIE MILSTEAD

*S*ofie curled her knees to her chest as she sat up in bed, stared across the room toward the easel holding her mother's uncovered artwork. The hospital had only held her for one day, and then released her the night before. After Bedford had tucked her in, bought groceries and made sure she had everything she needed, he'd left her to return to finish his lecture series.

The quilt fell to the floor and Sofie reached for it, wrapped it around her legs. Nothing made any sense. She still could not remember why she'd gone to the boat, why she'd become so confused as to break all the rules of diving.

Her fitful sleep revealed scraps of ragged remembrance: morning light streaked across the bow of the boat; peeling red paint on the hull; the mask too tight across her forehead. Yet in wakefulness, she found that these images did not fit together into one whole.

She curled tighter into herself and willed sleep to come and reveal the truth. She suspected Bedford was telling her only the parts of the day he wanted her to know: how he was there when the coast guard had brought her in, how John had been beside himself with fear, how her scuba tank had been empty and how the shrimp boat's men had seen her floating in the water and dragged her into their boat. Her breathing

273

had been rapid and shallow when they pulled her on board. They had believed she was unconscious from the hit on the head. Her savior had been the buoyancy vest, which left her floating faceup.

There was more to the story; she knew there was. Just like the one time she had asked her mother for the whole story about her father. She'd wanted to know all of it, not just the ending when Knox Murphy saved them. All her life she'd been waiting for the whole story.

Sofie felt the same way now: there was more, so much more to this tale.

And as she had then, she waited.

She didn't know what or whom she waited for until the phone rang. Even before she answered it, she understood that Jake Murphy knew something about that day that would help her. What stopped her from answering the phone was one glistening reality: if he offered her the truth, then she must tell him the truth about his father.

She huddled under the quilt, stared at her mother's canvas and fought the urge to weep when the answering machine picked up the call. "Hi, Sofie," Jake said. "Um . . . I think you're home. I hope I didn't wake you. I have to head back to Marsh Cove, and I just wanted to say . . . goodbye. . . ."

Sofie grabbed the phone from the cradle, whispered, "I'm here." She heard her voice on the answering machine as she spoke. She reached over, shut the machine off.

"I'm downstairs," Jake said. "Can I come up?"

Silence filled the room, filled her mind as Sofie closed her eyes. If she let this man into her condo, she would know what had happened to her that day, but life would shift, maybe so imperceptibly that she or anyone else wouldn't notice at first, but eventually, like a giant ship that made the slightest adjustment in navigation, the direction would change dramatically, the destination altered completely.

"Are you there?" Jake's voice came from a long distance away.

Maybe a change in destination wouldn't be all that horrid, all that fearful. What worse thing could happen now? *He will find you—that's what,* she heard her mother's voice say, as real as the canvas across the room. ***That*** *is the worst that can happen.*

"No," she said out loud, for the first time overriding her mother's objection, "*that* is not the worst thing that can happen." And although she was still not sure what the worst thing would be, it was no longer the fact that her father could find her.

"Sofie?"

"I'm here," she said. "Come on up." She replaced the receiver and rose from the bed. Her jeans hung low on her hips, and she pulled a white linen tunic over her white tank top. She scooped her hair into a ponytail, swiped Carmex on her chapped lips and opened the door to Jake Murphy—and to whatever new direction he would take her.

When Jake entered the room, Sofie fought the urge

to throw her arms around him, let him hold her until she felt well enough to take a deep breath, without the searing pain of her hurt lungs, without the headache from the large bruised lump on her skull where she'd hit the boat. Instead she tried to smile. "Hello." She stepped back.

He reached toward the bruise on her cheek, then withdrew his hand before he touched her. "Are you okay?"

"Tired," she said. "Would you like a cup of tea?" She lifted a hand to her hair. "I know I look a mess, but you surprised me."

"You couldn't look a mess if you tried," he said, walked farther into the room, into her life.

"Good line," she said, moved toward the stove.

"I don't have lines." He laughed, followed her as she placed the kettle on the burner. "So this is where you live."

"Yes, Mother and I lived here together." Sofie turned on the gas, looked over her shoulder at Jake. He glanced around the room, then back at her.

"You both slept in one room all these years?"

"No." She waved toward a door. "There's a small room in the back, which was actually my room until . . ."

"The plane wreck."

Until that moment Sofie had almost forgotten the one thing they truly had in common: they'd each lost a parent in the plane crash. They both carried the irreversible emptiness of a parent gone, love vacated.

She moved toward him with slow steps, almost like

a swimmer against the current. He held out his right hand; she took it. He lifted their hands to his lips, kissed her palm. She closed her eyes to fight the dizziness overcoming her; then she felt him draw her toward him and she fell against his chest.

His heart beat steadily in her ear. His hand ran through her ponytail until tingles trilled along her scalp; his fingers seemed to be healing her bruises. She heard a slight exhale of relief and realized she had made the sound.

She leaned away from him; he touched her cheek. "I don't remember anything from the day I did the dive. Can you tell me what you know?" she asked.

The teakettle whistled and they jumped back, laughed. Sofie filled two mugs, threw in organic green tea bags—her mother's favorite—and handed him a cup. They sat at the round zinc kitchen table for two. "I got there when the ambulance did—I didn't see anything before that."

She sat across from him, placed her hand over his on the table. He wound his fingers through hers. "Tell me what you do know," she said, squeezed his hand.

"Okay," he said, took a sip of tea. "I went to tell you I was leaving town. My mother called and said she was driving home that morning. She needed to get back for my sister, Keeley. I wanted to talk to you before I left."

"Oh." She turned away, attempted to pull her hand from his. "You came to ask me a few questions before you left."

"No," he said, would not release her hand. "I came to see you. When I got to the research center, there was a crowd out on the seawall, and I saw the coast guard boat coming in fast. I asked someone standing there what had happened, and they said you had gotten into some trouble diving, and that the coast guard had you on the boat. Then the ambulance came, and I couldn't get anywhere near you, and no one would answer my questions—which I understand because I was a complete stranger. Then Bedford saw me—that wasn't pretty."

"What did he do?"

Jake shook his head. "Doesn't matter. Anyway, I saw the boat captain."

"John Morris," she said.

"He was standing alone and looked scared as hell. I went over to him, and he told me that you were too upset to dive and he should have seen the signs. That you stayed down too long and got low on oxygen, and then you came up too fast and hit your head on the bottom of a shrimp trawler."

"Miles and miles of empty water, and I come up under a boat and knock myself out. Nice."

Jake smiled and Sofie saw his beauty. "Then he said that the shrimp boat captain said that the only reason they even saw you was because the dolphin pod made such a commotion—squealing, clicking, whistling, kicking up the water, swimming in circles around the boat. They had to lean over and see what was going on. One dolphin was nudging you toward the boat. . . ."

In a rush, tension left Sofie's body and she felt at one with the dolphins again. She remembered the day now in serrated fragments. While she sat there and held Jake Murphy's hand, she remembered: Michael Harley knocking on Bedford's front door and knowing her mother wasn't from Colorado; Michael Harley knowing her mother was on the plane with Knox; her panic; Bedford talking to him even though she'd asked him not to; John taking her out on the boat; and then finally her going too deep and not caring. Most important she heard Delphin calling her name again and again.

"Oh, Jake, I remember." Sofie let go of him, stood and paced the room in her bare feet. "I shouldn't have dived—that's true. It was all my fault, but he called my name. I heard him."

"Who called your name?"

"Delphin called me by the name he has for me. I can't explain the name—I just know it is his name *for* me."

Jake stood and went to her. "What made you so upset in the first place?"

She shook her head. Jake walked toward the window, stared outside. "Why can't you tell me?"

"I just . . ."

He turned and she saw his gaze move toward the canvas; then he took two steps toward the easel. Sofie stepped in front of him. "That was my mother's," she said.

"Did she paint it?" Jake attempted to move around her.

"Yes," Sofie said. "But she never finished it." She leaned down, picked up the fallen muslin and placed it back over the translucent starfish.

"You won't let me see it." Jake's voice took on a hard edge where soft concern had been moments ago.

"It's not mine to show you." Her voice shook.

"Yes, it is."

"Are you here to find out about my mother?" A flood tide of anger rose in the empty places of Sofie's broken heart. "I thought maybe you were here . . . for me."

"I am." He reached for her hand.

She backed away from him. "I'm so tired. Thanks for telling me what John said—I need you to go now."

Jake stared at her, and his face shifted like the surface of the water when a strong breeze blows over it. He walked to the kitchen counter, wrote his phone number and e-mail address on a scrap of paper. "If you need anything, let me know. I'm sorry about what you've been through." He went to the door and placed his hand on the doorknob before he faced her again. "I know you don't trust me. But if you knew me, really knew me, you would. I have no idea what you're so scared of, but it shouldn't be me."

She backed into the wall, lifted her hands to her face so she wouldn't have to watch him leave. The door clicked shut, and she slid down the wall, sat on the hardwood floor and wept for all the things that were true: Delphin had called her name; Jake cared for her; her mother was dead; Knox Murphy was dead; and she held the key to Jake and Annabelle's questions, yet she couldn't let the answers go, couldn't release them into their hands.

When she rose from the floor and moved to the kitchen, the need for knowledge overwhelmed her. Somewhere out in the open sea, her heart had changed beats, and the need to know finally overcame her need to hide. The power her secrets had held over her had never caused her heart to hurt like this new ache that spread through her body. Before, it had been enough that she had Bedford, her dolphins, her town and the water. But now a new world called to her and the only barrier was the never-ending, escalating fear of her father; her old life had to be disassembled so she could create a new one.

Sofie ran to the back bedroom, to the filing cabinet she hadn't touched since her mother's death, and pulled the top drawer wide. After Sofie had sold the art studio, she'd shoved the signed papers in here, ignoring the stacks she glimpsed in her mother's handwriting. They'd lived a simple life, relied on cash for their basic needs. There had been no reason to go through records looking for insurance claims or bonds, for stock options or mutual funds because there were none. Now it was time to find *him*. There was nothing else to be scared of but him. If her mother and her grandmother and Knox were gone, what else remained?

Only one fear: that she would never know her name, that even the dolphins couldn't tell her who she was.

Papers piled across the floor as Sofie went through file folders filled with old report cards, thick papers confirming ownership of the art studio, their condo, their car. Sofie worked her way to the back of the cabinet, finally pulled out the last folder and opened it. Inside was her birth certificate: Sofie Eloise Parker. Mother: Liddy Marie Parker. Father: Unnamed.

Sofie threw the birth certificate across the room.

She dug deeper. The last item was a brittle yellow envelope taped to the inside of the folder. The glue had long since given out. Sofie shook the envelope; a driver's license fell out. The picture on the Ohio license was blurry and cracked, but it was her mother as a young and breathtaking beauty. Sofie leaned closer: her mother's eyes were wide and almost haunted, staring past the camera as though she were looking at someone behind the photographer.

Sofie glanced at the name: Diane Margaret Collins. A shudder ran through Sofie.

She tried it on her tongue: *Sofie Eloise Collins.*

Collins might be her given name, but it was not her real name. Sofie Eloise Parker, then Milstead were the names given as gifts from her mother. A lifesaving name meant to protect and nurture.

Just as she'd told Jake, there was only one of almost everything in this town, and she called the only private investigator: Joseph Martin. She'd gone to high school with him, and he'd once told her that he'd imagined for himself a glamorous life of tracking down criminals and racketeers, maybe even pirates, but mostly he exposed wayward spouses and uncovered insurance fraud.

He answered the phone on the first ring. "Hey, Joseph, this is Sofie Milstead."

"Hey, Sofie. What can I do for you?"

"I know this is a strange request—but I'm looking for a woman named Diane Margaret Collins who once lived in Ohio in the early eighties, and was married. I want to know what happened to her . . . and to her husband."

Silence filled the line.

"Are you there?" Sofie asked.

"Yes," he said, "just writing it down."

"Joseph, of course I'll pay you. I'm not asking for a personal favor."

"Do you know this woman?"

"Yes," Sofie said. "Do you need to know more than that?"

"No . . ."

"Thanks, old friend. Just call me if you find out anything."

She hung up and stared at the canvas across the room. Half-finished, partially known things were cluttering her life: knowledge of her father; her relationship with Bedford; telling the Murphy family the truth; her mother's art; her own research.

She needed and wanted something to be finished, whole and complete. She walked toward her mother's canvas, ripped off the muslin. She stood and stared at the starfish as a fiery wind filled her middle, as her fingers picked up the paintbrushes waiting for her touch.

She opened the paint tubes one at a time, squirted colors onto the palette. When she first touched the brush to the paint, time and space collapsed. Her hands and arms moved of their own accord; the instructions her mother had imparted to her returned in a brilliant remembrance. Sofie recalled what her mother had once taught her about background and foreground, about the play of light and dark, the translucent nature of paint.

Sofie painted methodically, not moving to another part of the painting until one section was complete. Thoughts and memories ran through her head like a rapid-fire slide show. Although her focus was on the minutiae of the painting, her mind wandered to elusive memories in hidden corners of her mind, briefly glimpsed.

Her mother had stood behind her, holding the brush, reaching forward. The sun had come from behind them, falling through the windowpanes onto the canvas, onto their faces. Warmth had spread through Sofie while her mother held her hand and arm. "No, Sofie, stop forcing it. The paint is like truth or love— you cannot make it something it is not. Let it come naturally—let the picture rise from the brush while you surrender to the work."

Then came a memory of Knox, dimly lit. He and her mother were in the kitchen. Sofie was in the bedroom, but could see them through a crack in the door. They thought she was asleep. The next morning, when Knox was gone, her mother would be withdrawn, painting furiously and silently, shutting out Sofie and everyone around them. The days before Knox came were buoyant with happiness, and the days after he left overflowed with misery.

When he prepared to leave, it was worse—her mother stood in the kitchen with her head in her hands, her face contorted with silent sobs. Knox held his hand over her head, touched her while she crumpled into him like a broken figurine. The only words Sofie remembered were her mother's: "Please, please stay. This time please stay." She always begged for that.

When grief from this memory prodded at Sofie's heart, she did what her mother had taught her—she painted with more focus, more determination. Knox and her mother were both gone.

Gone.

Then Jake's face came to her, and dizziness overwhelmed her. She sat down on the round stool in front of the painting, felt the weakness in her arms settle into her shoulders. Knox's son. She'd almost forgotten that before anything else, he was Knox's son.

There had once been bright and brilliant days when she pretended she was Knox's child. He'd come for a visit and take them sailing or cook them dinner while Liddy talked faster and with more animation than usual. And under her breath, Sofie would whisper, "Dad," although she knew he wasn't her father.

Her own father must never know she existed. He did not deserve the title "dad," or so her mother had told her numerous times. To Sofie, he was a man without a face, without a name.

Sofie had hated Jake, despised Keeley, for they had Knox. He was their dad, their steadfast rock, the ones he went home to. How had she forgotten that she hated Jake, hated the Murphy family? Oh, the agony of loving someone you can't have, who cannot stay.

While she painted, she brought forth the hate, let it rise around and above her like an overflowing tide. She allowed her loathing for the Murphy family to become part of her again. Then she kept painting, and the emotion subsided as she recalled Jake's sweet touch, his belief in her ideas about the dolphins.

Sofie allowed all these thoughts and emotions to sweep over her like clouds in time-lapse photography. She noticed them, but didn't try to follow them.

When exhaustion spread over her body, she lay down. When hunger prodded her, she ate. When thirst brought a headache, she drank.

One afternoon a long time ago, it might have even been in Marsh Cove, she'd asked her mother how she knew when a painting was done. Her beautiful mother had stared off into space for such a long time that Sofie thought she hadn't heard her question. When she finally turned to Sofie, she shrugged. "I wish I had a good answer for my little girl, but like love, you just know and you can't fake it."

Now Sofie knew what her mother meant. The

painting was done and she knew it. She didn't love Bedford, and she knew it. This was why her mother painted—it showed her the truth, it revealed the heart—and Sofie felt a thrill and fright at this knowledge, at this powerful connection to her mother's psyche.

Two days had passed, and now the painting was complete.

Sofie walked into the kitchen, made a cup of tea and waited for Bedford. He was due back any minute now—she'd heard the message machine in the distance of her art-induced fog.

Bedford opened the door with his key; Sofie took a sip of tea and backed against the counter. He smiled. She stood still and quiet, cocked her head at him. "Hello, Bedford."

"I've missed my sweet girl." He came to her. "I've been so worried about you. Why haven't you answered your phone for two days?"

"I didn't want to talk to you." Sofie found the truth easy and weightless, so freeing that she smiled when she said it.

He placed his hands on her shoulders. "I can understand you've been exhausted and haven't wanted to talk on the phone. But I sure missed your voice."

She moved his hands off her. "No. You're not listening. It wasn't that I didn't want to talk on the phone—I didn't want to talk to *you*."

He stepped back. "What do you mean?"

"Bedford, it's over between us. It probably never should have started."

He glanced around the room as if he were searching for someone else, a reason she would utter these words, as though someone must be holding a gun to her head. He moved toward the canvas, and then gazed over his shoulder, up and down her jeans and the old T-shirt spattered with paint. "You've been painting."

"Yes."

"It's okay, Sofie. You're having a mild breakdown. It's going to be okay. You've never really processed your mother's death, and you've been alone for three days, embedded in her artistic passion. You don't feel like yourself."

She laughed and the sound rising from her throat felt foreign and sweet. "I am not a chart, a diagram or a psych patient. I am not having a breakdown. I am not embedding myself in my mother's art. I finished a painting." She lifted her hands in the air. "Formulate a hypothesis, observe, analyze, interpret. I can say it in my sleep. You see life through the prism of the scientific method. What about mystery and wonder? What about love and God?"

"You want to believe in fairy tales and talking animals, Sofie. That is your problem—you can't face reality."

Bedford walked around the easel, brushed his hair back from his face. Sofie found the familiar motion irritating. "You play with your hair like a girl," she said.

His head snapped up. "What did you just say?"

"Bedford, please go home."

His clenched his fists at his sides. Control was his North Star, his guiding force, and she had just removed it. She reacted as she did when a shark came near the dolphin pod: remained calm, kept her movements slow. "Bedford, please don't say anything you'll regret."

He laughed. "Regret? I only regret the time I've spent with you. You're a spoiled child whose mother completely warped your sense of self and your notion of real life." His hands gestured wildly. "You live in a fantasy world, Sofie. You will never accomplish anything because you think Prince Charming is going to come in on a white horse and save you. That a dolphin will talk to you. And now you're throwing away the only true and solid thing you have: me."

Sofie stared at him, stunned that his brutal words brought her no pain, that they flew over her without damage. It was like standing in the middle of a swarm of hornets that buzzed around her, but never stung.

"Thank you for the lecture, Bedford. Leave now, please."

"No need to ask. I'm gone. You will so regret this decision."

"Hmmm . . ." Sofie lifted her finger to her cheek in mock thought. "Probably not."

He slammed the door; a small picture of a dolphin painted on a discarded windowpane shattered when it fell from the wall to the floor. Sofie went to the glass splinters, picked them up one by one and remembered when her mother had found the old panes behind a house next door that was being renovated. The wood frame around the window was a pale blue, and Sofie's mother had immediately known what should be painted on it.

This was what Mother had been good at: knowing what art would work in what medium. A sliver of glass sliced Sofie's palm and she dropped the glass, watched the blood leak in a thin line across her flesh: a crimson path across the palm that Jake had held only days ago.

She went to the kitchen, rinsed the cut, swept the glass from the floor and threw it all in the trash. What had her mother left her besides this condo, this one piece of unfinished art, some money in a bank account? Sofie had planned to get her master's degree and then make enough money to live on—nothing more, nothing less.

The ring of the phone caused her to jump. She recognized the caller ID—Joseph Martin. For a minute she couldn't think why this old friend would be phoning her. Then, like a dream that returned in the middle of the afternoon, she remembered her fogged day of going through papers, of calling a private investigator.

"Hey, Joseph," she said in a whisper, as though they were meeting in a secret place.

"Sofie . . ."

"Yes?"

"Do you know this woman Diane?" he asked.

She didn't know how to answer, so she didn't answer at all.

Joseph took a deep breath. "Listen, Sofie. This information was so easy to find, there is no way I can charge you. All you had to do was go back to old Ohio newspapers and search for her name."

"Okay," Sofie said, sat on the hardwood floor and leaned against the footboard of her bed while an old high school friend released her from the ties that had bound her.

When she hung up, she curled into a ball and wept. When the dull throb of shed tears brought a headache, she moved to stare at the finished painting. Now, finally, some things were complete. For the first time her tears were not of grief, but of relief. Joseph had told her who her father was, and what had happened to him. She'd been let loose from his threat. Knowing had set her free.

TWENTY-ONE

ANNABELLE MURPHY

The weeks that followed passed for Annabelle in a succession of days blurred at the corners, sweet as spring headed toward summer. Her body moved with fluid motions as though something had been released inside her.

The jar of remember shells overflowed onto the hall table until Keeley came home from school late one day with an antique apothecary jar she'd bought downtown, stating that they needed a bigger jar for the memories. Annabelle held Keeley's face in her hands, kissed her and waited until her daughter left to let her tears fall in private.

Some shells had cracked under the weight of the others and yet the container remained full and beautiful—brimming over with reminders every time Annabelle felt the tug of doubt and darkness. Sometimes she'd remove a shell and hold it; other times she would walk to the beach and find another shell, another memory.

Jake arrived home with his Tahoe packed to the windows, his trunk half-open and tied with a bungee cord to hold his favorite threadbare lounge chair, which Annabelle absolutely refused to let back into the living room. Jake hauled all his college belongings upstairs to his old room, and once again the house overflowed with activity, conversation and warmth. He told her that Sofie had healed quickly after her diving injury, and when he dropped the subject, so did Annabelle. She basked in this full house as others did a bubble bath or a swim in the warm sea.

She'd gone into the office the day after her return from Newboro, asked Mrs. Thurgood to please allow her to continue in her job. Writing for the newspaper calmed her in a way it never had before. Annabelle read between the lines of the letters asking her advice, searched for more than a surface understanding of what the reader wanted. Mrs. Thurgood was pleased with Annabelle's work, satisfied that she'd returned unbowed and unbent, ready and able to do her job.

The article about Liddy's identity and presence on the plane was, of course, front-page news in most of the local papers in North and South Carolina: *Mystery Woman Identified as Ex-Artist from Newboro*. The fact that Knox was taking the artist to visit her sick mother was also printed. If there was talk of Knox and Liddy having an affair, Annabelle never heard it. She was immersed in her job, her memories, her conviction in Knox's faithfulness.

The book she'd started five years ago began to speak to her in soft tones of seduction. Annabelle wrote a few paragraphs a day—like sneaking a tryst with a lover. She barely allowed herself to think, *I am writing a book,* but when the thought crossed her mind, a thrill ran through her. Soon a few pages gathered inside her Word file and on the side of her desk. She hadn't read through them, only kept adding to them. Sometimes she would fold the laundry or walk through the grocery store and realize that she was done with her tasks, yet the entire time she'd been thinking about the archaeologist or the man she loved in the page she'd last written.

Annabelle began to covet her personal writing time, and her time alone with Jake and Keeley. She didn't question Jake about his future, just enjoyed his presence at home. She ignored her friends in such a sweet and quiet way that they barely noticed she was avoiding them until one night they sent Cooper over to find her. The house was still and warm while Annabelle proofread her advice column about a woman who wanted to know if she should allow her son-in-law to borrow money to buy her daughter a birthday present. The columns had taken on a more honest tone, and Mrs. Thurgood was sending more difficult questions, those involving not simple etiquette but tough choices with far-reaching consequences, questions of honesty and trust, deceit and betrayal, the breaking and mending of family bonds.

A knock disrupted Annabelle's thoughts, and she looked up from her laptop. Cooper walked into the room without waiting for her to open the door. "Annabelle Murphy, get up. We are nothing without you." He grinned, but held his hands behind his back in that nervous way he'd had since childhood.

"Hey, Cooper," she said, closed her laptop and went to kiss his cheek. "How are you?"

"Seriously, Belle, we miss you. The dinner party at our house is going on right now, and they've sent me to get you."

She shook her head. "You're sweet, but really, I don't want to go."

He sat on the couch next to the dented space she'd left. She settled in beside him. He shifted his weight and tilted his head. "Have you cut us out? Have you decided that you can't be around your dearest friends?"

"That's not it. I just want some time alone with Keeley and Jake."

He glanced around the house. "They're not even home, Belle."

"And myself," she said. "I need some time alone with me. I don't want to hear what everyone has to say, and I don't have anything to say to anyone."

"Don't you think that's a bit selfish?"

"Oh, Cooper, I don't mean for it to be. I'm so sorry. I would never, ever want to hurt y'all. I've just been trying to . . . sort through how I feel, get my family's feet back under us. I love all of you." She reached out and took his hand.

"What if we need you and not just the other way around?"

Annabelle rubbed her face with her free hand, remembering that she hadn't put on any makeup that day, that her hair fell free and wild over her shoulders and white shirt. "You all do not need me." She smiled. "I'd like to think that you do, and it's sweet of you to say so, but you don't. You have Christine. Shawn has all of you. Mae has Frank."

"That is ridiculous. We all need all kinds of people, not just one or two."

His words held a truth she couldn't fully see yet, and as though he'd written them on his forehead, she squinted at him. "'We all need all kinds of people,'" she repeated his words, then stood up. "Cooper, I promise I'll be back, but not tonight. Not now."

"Christine thinks you're . . . unavailable because

you think we're hiding something from you."

"No, I don't think that. I might have once, but I don't now."

"We're not. Listen, we're all just as hurt and confused as you are. Everyone is struggling with this . . . not just you."

"I know."

"Shawn quit his job—did you know that? Your friends' lives are still going on."

Annabelle shrank into her seat. "No, I didn't know that. How could he . . . not tell me?"

Cooper raised an eyebrow. "How? Telegraph?"

She attempted a smile. "Okay, I get it. I'll do my very best to get out of this shell because I love every single one of you. And how are *you*?" she asked.

"I'm hurt, Annabelle. Hurt that one of my best friends never told me what he was doing. That he lied about going on a hunting trip alone. I'm sick of the whole thing and want us all to just be the way we were."

"That's the problem. We've all kept secrets. And they've changed us."

Cooper stared at her for a long time. "What secrets are you talking about?"

"We all have them," Annabelle said, and felt a moment when she wanted to release one of them. "Did you know that I was pregnant when Knox and I married?"

"No, but does it matter?"

"It matters because of the motivation. Maybe, just

maybe he wouldn't have married me if I hadn't been carrying his child. Or maybe he would have. Either way—he did marry me, and we never told anyone."

"What do you want me to say, Belle? We're all best friends. We need each other. We need you."

"Thanks, Cooper." She hugged him goodbye, walked him to the door.

He left, but looked over his shoulder as he went down the porch steps. "What are you waiting for?"

She shrugged. "I'm not sure. Thanks for being such a good friend. I promise I'll be part of y'all's life again."

"We love you, Belle," he said.

"I know," she said. "I love all of you, too."

He drove off in his car, and Annabelle said the word again: "Love." It was a word that had once seemed simple in her known world, yet now the definition expanded in its implications, in its possibilities.

TWENTY-TWO

SOFIE MILSTEAD

Sofie focused on her work, spending long hours at the research center as the weeks passed. Every spare moment she swam with Delphin—asking him to speak to her, to tell her what to do now. She felt suspended between two worlds, the past and the future, and she was unable to cross the divide between time and space.

All this time, Jake's e-mails, funny and full of the life she longed for, came across her screen. This was safe, this e-mailing. She wanted to tell him the truth, but she wrestled with how to reveal it, when to tell him, then again whether to tell him at all.

Some things were best left alone. Hadn't her mother always told her that? When she asked about finding her father, or the past, or the future, "Some things are just best left alone," Liddy would say with a kiss and a smile.

Telling Jake the full story was like that—wasn't it? But somehow Jake seemed the person least likely to be "best left alone." Everything in her wanted to do everything with him except leave him alone. Oh, she tried. Sometimes she went three or four days without e-mailing him. Then she'd run in from work and find a message, and her heart would fill to the edges at the sight of his name on the screen.

They played a game: Jake would e-mail her a myth recast in present-day names and circumstances and make her guess what myth it was, what gods and goddesses the stories were about. Sometimes it would take a day or two, but she always figured it out. When she tried this game back at him a couple of times, he always had the answer in less than five minutes.

They communicated about everything and nothing—his search for a new school, her research on the dolphins, the weather, the equinox coming next month. They did not mention Bedford, Liddy or Annabelle or even his sister, Keeley. How long could they go on pretending these people weren't part of the story?

After the FAA had contacted her about her mother's remains, Sofie had taken her mother's ashes to the seawall and said goodbye one last time by scattering them on the waves. This farewell had been more real, more complete than the memorial service two years ago. Somehow her mother felt truly gone now. Her echoing instructions and fabricated life floated away.

News sources were asking questions about her mother, and Sofie told them she'd known her mother was on the plane, yet she'd told them nothing else. The secrets were gradually being exposed.

Once, Bedford came to the house to beg for their reunion, in his own way, which meant telling her how wrong she was and how much she needed him. He could have been a stranger, a talking head on TV, for all the emotion he aroused in her. She smiled at him, and told him that it was funny how he always thought he knew what was best for her, but he'd never really known—not once.

She'd apologized to John, sought him out at the dock and asked his forgiveness for frightening him the day of her botched dive. She promised never to do it again. He'd stared at her for a long time and told her that the demons that had chased her to the bottom of the ocean would never leave her unless she released them. She'd mumbled something about appreciating him and his understanding.

The morning she was summoned to the research

center, she drove to work with a knot in her stomach, the kind that made her think she might be getting sick. She took a seat in Andrew Martin's office. He appeared unusually disheveled, his gray hair mussed, his baby blue buttondown shirt wrinkled, his *Conservation Matters* lapel pin crooked.

"Okay, give it to me. What's happened?" Sofie asked.

"I might as well shoot it to you straight, Sofie. Our funding has been cut."

"What?"

"You'll have to stop the work you've been doing. The center has all they need from your project, and the funding is being channeled elsewhere."

"But . . . we can't stop. We can't make our case unless we understand the dolphin's behavior." Sofie's voice shook.

"Yes," Andrew said. "But we have to let it go. We have to stop the research . . . for now."

"We can't," Sofie said in stuttering words, lifting her chin. "You can just tell the foundation that we aren't done yet. We're almost there . . . but not yet."

"Sofie, we don't have any choice. Funding has been cut everywhere. It's not just our center and it's not just your project. The time and money are better used elsewhere. We can give the National Science Foundation what we've got, still publish the results of the data you already have."

"But I'm not done." Sofie shook her head. "When does this happen?"

"Now," Andrew answered.

"Will you find me another project to work on?" She held out her hands, began to count off the projects. "There's the winter stock structure, the right whale habitat, the sea turtles and fisheries . . . any of them."

"Sofie, I promise we'll try and find more work for you as soon as possible. You can take the summer off, though. When school starts back up, we'll find a place for you if you have time. But we have nowhere to put you right now."

"I'll do anything, Mr. Martin. I'll stay off the boats. I'll log data, clean the tanks. . . ."

He took a deep breath. "You've been working here nonstop since you were fifteen years old, Sofie. Go have fun for the rest of the summer. Please. I don't have a choice. You've recently been in a terrible accident. Take some time off."

"They saved me. Those dolphins saved my life and I have to help save theirs." *They're all I have left,* she thought. *All I have. I can't let them go. . . .*

Andrew rose from the table. "You have helped them, Sofie. You've done research that will make a difference in their lives, in understanding their behavior around nets and boats. But this particular study at this center is over."

Sofie stood then and walked out of the room, her legs carrying her to the seawall before she had a plan, before she knew where she would go in this strange world in which she was free to do whatever she wanted. Her job was gone, her boyfriend dismissed, her mother dead.

Sofie listed the events that had brought her to this point, to this unbound life: one discovery of a woman on a plane, plus one art historian, plus one secret revealed to Jake Murphy. Adding those three events together could not, and did not, equal the number three, but a sum of greater magnitude than could be calculated with simple addition.

Sofie stood on the seawall and willed her dolphins to come. The water blinked in the glory of morning. Along the shoreline, pluff mud lay exposed and dark in the low tide, clumps of spartina sprouting from the rich almost-black mounds. Then the waves rippled, three dorsal fins broke the surface, scattering drops of water like silver confetti.

It took Sofie a moment to understand what the dolphins were doing as they circled a single dolphin in the middle. The pod was surrounding Delphin's mate, Sandy. In protective unity, the dolphins pulled closer. They cried out to one another, danced around the female. Sofie swung her legs over the seawall and peered down; her breath caught with a cry of joy—a just-born dolphin calf swam below Sandy.

Sofie had been taught that dolphins were born tail first as the mother bent in the middle, that newborns were four feet long and weighed about forty pounds, that the calves were usually born between May and July, and that the fetal folds on the skin appeared to be stripes. Yet these facts did not explain the marvel of a newborn dolphin calf swimming next to its mother. Facts could never capture the full wonder of experience.

The mere facts of her life could not fully encompass who she was and whom she was going to become.

Sofie's joy threatened to overflow in tears. Just as she had come to say goodbye, the pod was greeting new life. Delphin rose above the surface, nudged his nose toward Sofie.

Go, she told him in her mind. *Go, take care of your new baby. Thank you for saving me . . . for knowing my name.*

He splashed with his snout and then nudged his new baby toward its mother, where the calf would nurse and then get a free ride in the mother's slipstream. Sofie exhaled with this truth—she had done the same thing: been carried along in her mother's slipstream, living life beneath her mother's fiction and fears. She would not travel that way anymore.

Sofie returned home to tell a story, one that would open the door to letting go. To the truth.

She typed an e-mail with slow, deliberate strokes.

Hey, Jake, so you think you've always got the best story? I've got a great one for you. Ready?

Here's a little intro: The ancients thought names were powerful. The name of an individual was often not the real name at all, as the real name would bring danger or knowledge, yet changing the name changed the destiny. Here is a *naming* story:

One day there was a goddess named Diane.

She was married to a god of money, fame and power who didn't love her, but loved to own her. She ran from him and gave birth to wisdom. The bargain she made with the gods was this—in exchange for this escape she would never find true love or reveal her real name. For the rest of her life, true love evaded her no matter how hard she tried to find it.

Think I finally beat you this time—bet you can't name this one. . . .

With love, Sofie

Then she rose and stared out the window toward the water, toward all she was letting go at this moment. Then the ring of incoming e-mail made her return and sit again.

Hey, Sofie, okay, I'm officially stumped. You have to tell me which one it is. Celtic? Greek? How are the dolphins?
Love, JM

Sofie placed her hand on the screen as if she could touch Jake's face. When she saw his initials like that, with the word "Love" in front of them, her heart ached for something she couldn't label—like a distant land she'd once glimpsed but never reached.

Then she typed what she'd rehearsed over and over in front of the window.

JM, I'm coming to Marsh Cove. I'll leave today and be there day after tomorrow to give you the answer. . . . Love, Sofie

She didn't want to see his reply and learn that maybe he didn't want her to come. She turned the computer off and yanked her suitcase out from under the bed. It was time to tell the story—not a myth, not a tale, but her story and her name.

TWENTY-THREE

ANNABELLE MURPHY

*J*ake sat on the front porch, tilting his laptop for the best reception on the wireless Internet. Afternoon shadows fell across the scuffed white floorboards. Annabelle came up behind him, hugged his neck. "Let's make some decent use of your time—the porch floor needs painting."

He turned to her as her gaze wandered down to his computer screen. He held his hand up in an ineffective effort to cover the words.

Annabelle straightened. "You're e-mailing Sofie?"

Jake rolled his eyes. "Oh, Mom. Yes."

"How long has this been going on?"

"Nothing is 'going on.' We just talk. . . . She tells me about her work. I talk to her about all the stupid, boring things I'm doing while I decide where to go next. . . ."

Annabelle had to ask the question. "Has she told you anything else about her mother?"

Jake shut the laptop, stood up. "We don't talk about it, Mom. Really, we don't. It hasn't come up since I left. I tried. Then I stopped."

"Is she recovered from her hospital stay?"

"Fully," Jake said.

Annabelle had been a scholar of her children's faces since babyhood and understood even now that he was telling the truth. He wasn't hiding anything from her. She stared at him, and then asked, "Is there . . . something between you two?"

"A friendship, Mom. A friendship. We like the same things and it's nice to talk. . . ."

"I wish you'd told me. . . ." She turned her head to the ringing phone inside the house. "You could've told me."

"You've seemed so . . . happy lately, and I didn't want to bring it up again."

She touched his shoulder. "I have to get that—I'm expecting a call from the newspaper."

"Sure," Jake said.

Annabelle saw the relief on his face that this particular conversation was over. She grabbed the phone a half ring before the answering machine came on. "Sorry," she said. "I'm here. . . ."

"Oh . . ." A male voice, one she'd heard somewhere before, came through the line.

"Uh, who's this?" Annabelle sat at her desk chair, turned on her computer to prepare for taking notes during the call.

"This is Michael Harley. I'm looking for Annabelle Murphy."

Annabelle's stomach plummeted. She tried to speak, but her words stopped at the base of her throat.

"Hello?"

"This is Annabelle. Hello, Michael. How are you?"

"I'm fine. . . . You're a hard woman to find. I've been calling for two days."

"You didn't leave a message."

"No . . . I didn't think you'd call me back, so there really was no point." He laughed, but she detected nervousness in it.

"How can I help you?" she asked.

"I'm in town."

Annabelle closed her eyes, leaned back in her chair. The beep of the call waiting indicating an incoming call sounded on the line. "Listen, I have a scheduled call coming in on the other line."

"Can I come see you?"

"No, I'd rather you didn't."

"Will you meet me at the Marsh Cove Art Studio?" he asked.

Annabelle sighed. If she didn't meet him there, he might show up at her house, or continue to call. "I'll meet you there in an hour." Then without saying goodbye, she clicked over to Mrs. Thurgood's voice.

The call was about expanding Annabelle's role at the newspaper and possibly having her write a commentary on Southern life once a month in the living section. Annabelle focused her full attention on the call. When the conversation ended, she promised to think about Mrs. Thurgood's offer.

First she had to meet Michael Harley at the art studio, where Liddy Parker had once lived and worked.

During the past weeks, she'd found comfort in her self-imposed isolation, in the simplicity of being alone. There had always been people depending on her, expectations to meet, obligations to fulfill, and these days of solitude had soothed her. Now she needed to put on some makeup, find an outfit and go out into the world.

Anger at Michael skirted her thoughts—he'd interrupted what should have been a sweet moment: a vote of confidence from the newspaper's publisher. She stood and went to the front of the house and stared into the hall mirror, examining her appearance. "All right," she said out loud, "let's go."

The art studio was situated between the Curiosities gift shop and the Sweet Tooth bakery. A sign lit by tiny white Christmas lights perched above the double wooden doors stated simply MARSH COVE ART STUDIO. There was a two-bedroom loft above the studio— Annabelle had visited there a few times to pick up Jake when he'd gone home to play with Sofie after school. Once, Annabelle had found Jake and Sofie on the floor with a huge piece of butcher-block paper and so many crayons that Annabelle remembered being stunned that Crayola even made that many colors.

Now she stood outside the studio and stared at the double wood doors painted bright blue. If pressed, she wouldn't be able to count how many times she'd been here for cocktail parties, art shows, an afternoon with a girlfriend looking at new work in the gallery. The present owner offered classes and showings on a regular basis.

Annabelle ran her hand through her hair, wiped her palms on her jeans. After Liddy had left this place, Annabelle had wondered for a year or so where she'd gone. Then she'd forgotten about Liddy altogether. But someone hadn't forgotten.

Her heart took a quick skip when she heard someone say her name. She turned, expecting to see Michael, but found Shawn instead. He held a cup of coffee in one hand, a newspaper in the other. He was unshaven, and his white linen shirt hung loose over a pair of khakis. He was tan and appeared calm, so well-rested.

"Hey, girl." He held up his full hands. "I'd hug you if I could."

She smiled at him. "You look well. Guess unemployment is doing you good."

He laughed, then crinkled his eyes. "How'd you know about that?"

"Cooper told me." She lifted her sunglasses, set them atop her head. She didn't know what to say or do because she hadn't seen him since he left her on a bench at the bay after his confession of love and her mute response. Nervousness moved like quick-fire sparks across her skin.

"So you're emerging from your cocoon? Does this mean you might come out of hiding and rejoin the rest of us?"

"I haven't been hiding, Shawn. Just . . ."

"Hiding." He took a sip of his coffee, shoved the paper under his arm and used his free hand to rub his face. "Listen, I didn't mean to freak you out last time with my sudden revelation. I didn't mean to make you hide. I just needed you to know."

"You didn't freak me out."

"Can't we go back to before? Pretend I never said it, okay?"

Annabelle felt a sudden and irresistible urge to mend their friendship, but she didn't know how. "How do we go back to before?" she asked.

"A little at a time. How does that sound?"

"Good, I guess. Good." She stared at him for a moment. "Why'd you quit your job?"

"To start my own company."

"Really? What kind?"

"Guess."

She stared at him, grinned. "Our beach wishes."

They'd been sixteen years old and had drunk too much Tickle Pink at a beach party. Annabelle had never drunk alcohol before, but Shawn had told her it was fizzy lemonade. She'd only half-believed him, stretched back on the sand with him to watch the stars move in the sky, and then said, "Fizzy lemonade, my ass." Shawn laughed so hard he started to hiccup. That night, he told her that he hoped to someday open his own marina and start a sailing team. She wanted to write a novel that would be made into a movie. John Travolta would star in it. Shawn teased her that she'd taken her wish one step too far, and they'd laughed until curfew, knowing those were wild dreams . . . impossible dreams.

Annabelle reached out and touched Shawn's arm. "Maybe dreams told under the stars on a Lowcountry beach are the kind that come true."

"You remember."

"I remember a lot lately."

"Sometimes you have to stop remembering and live."

"I know. You think I don't know that? But I'm not done remembering . . . yet."

He nodded. "I get it."

They smiled at each other, and for Annabelle a single crack in their broken relationship had been mended. She turned to see Michael Harley walking up the sidewalk toward them. She waved.

Shawn gave her a puzzled look. "You know him?"

She nodded. "He's an art historian. I met him in Newboro. . . ."

"In Newboro?" His eyebrows lifted. "I thought you said you let that go. . . ."

"I did. He didn't."

Michael came to them, and Shawn briefly introduced himself, his words clipped; then he walked off.

"Hello, Michael," Annabelle said.

He offered a brief hug. "So good to see you again."

She nodded, returned the embrace. She lifted her hand toward the studio. "Here it is." She tried on a smile that felt like an ill-fitting outfit.

Michael nodded toward the place where Shawn had just stood. "Did he know Liddy?"

Annabelle laughed. "Why, yes, he did."

"Can I talk to him?"

"I'm sure you can. I'll give you his number. I bet he can tell you some things about her that I can't." Annabelle noticed the bite to her words, but she allowed herself to feel the slight jealousy and then laugh. "Okay, come on. I'll introduce you to Kristi."

Michael nodded. "This is a precious town."

"Precious?" Annabelle lifted her eyebrows.

He looked as though he were searching for words, but found none. He pointed at the art studio. "It's bigger than I expected."

"When it first opened, this downtown area was struggling to get back on its feet after Hurricane Hugo. Space went for cheap then . . . not now."

"It still couldn't have been easy for a single woman."

A chill ran through Annabelle: in that moment she knew how Liddy Parker had bought this space in the middle of Marsh Cove in the aftermath of Hurricane Hugo. Knox had paid the down payment. In those days real estate was inexpensive, down payments kept low to encourage businesses to move downtown. In all their years of marriage, she had never questioned Knox on the issue of finances. She had put the family bills on his desk and knew there was a notebook listing their investments. He'd had some family money, which he'd used to start their life together, and he could have written a check for a down payment on cheap space in a hurricane-ravished downtown, and Annabelle wouldn't have ever known.

She turned away from Michael so he wouldn't see the blood rush from her face. She thought she'd killed all doubt in the quiet weeks that had just passed, but this new knowledge watered the seed of distrust still hidden in the farthest corners of her heart.

Michael's voice came from behind her. "Okay, let's go see this place. Nothing better than art I haven't seen." He walked toward the doors, and Annabelle followed with shaky steps.

Kristi sat behind an antique oak desk scarred from years of use and the spilled paint and ink of the studio. She wore her hair loose down her back, a pen stuck behind her ear and reading glasses perched on the end of her nose while she examined a drawing. She looked up when Michael and Annabelle entered.

"Hello there, Annabelle." Kristi got up to hug her. "It is so good to see you. It's been a long while since you've been in. We have so much new art."

"Hi, Kristi," Annabelle said, gestured toward Michael. "This is Michael Harley, and he's interested in some of Liddy Parker's work. Do you still have any?"

Kristi shook her head. "We haven't had any since the year after she left."

Michael shook Kristi's hand. "Nice to meet you. This is a wonderful place. By any chance do you have any pieces by an artist named Ariadne?"

"Oh, yes. I have one left. It arrived about two years or so ago, and I'm surprised no one bought it. It's priced on the high side, but many have remarked on its beauty. It's not as . . . soft as some of the artist's other work, but I like it."

"May I see it?"

"Sure." Kristi gestured toward the far wall. "It's right there."

Annabelle and Michael turned to the back wall, and Annabelle stared at a painting she'd seen many times at gatherings here in the studio. It was an image of the marsh at dusk. Nighthawks flew over the middle of the picture, and a thin moon perched in the upper-right corner. The left side of the canvas showed the setting sun, while the middle of the work remained in shadow.

Michael walked over and touched the frame. "The moon rising, the sun setting, twilight in between. Something coming, something leaving, with dusk and shadow in the middle."

Kristi came to Michael's side, pointed to the price written on a piece of paper. "This artist wants fourteen thousand dollars for it."

"Do you ever hear from Ariadne?" he asked.

"Not in a couple years. I've never met her, only heard her voice. Her work was always shipped here. Then I mailed a money order to a P.O. box in Raleigh,

North Carolina. It's always been very mysterious, but until this painting I didn't care because they always sold. Now I don't know who to contact. I've mailed a letter to the P.O. box to ask if she'd lower the price—but I've received no answer."

"That's because she's dead." At Annabelle's proclamation behind them, Michael and Kristi turned to her.

"Who's dead?" Kristi asked.

"So you agree with me?" Michael asked.

"Yes, I agree with you." She looked at Kristi. "Michael believes that the artist Ariadne was actually Liddy Parker."

Kristi nodded. "Well, that would make sense."

"Why?" Annabelle steadied herself against an exposed wooden pillar.

"Well, Liddy moved without wanting anyone to know where she was going. It would make sense that she wouldn't want anyone to know this was her art."

Michael took a camera out of his satchel. "Do you mind if I take a few photographs?"

Kristi shrugged. "I guess not. But why?"

"I'm an art historian writing an article on artists who hide their identities."

"Will you mention my studio?" Kristi asked, then laughed and posed like she should be in the picture.

"Of course." Michael snapped a picture of Kristi, and then took multiple shots of the artwork. When he finished, he sat on a stool at the desk. "Can I ask you a few more questions?"

"Sure," Kristi said, and sat down next to him.

"Did you buy this studio from Liddy Parker?"

"Yes. Ten years ago. She announced to my art class that she and her little girl, Sofie, would be moving away. She asked if any of us knew of someone who might be interested in buying the place. It took me less than five minutes to decide. This was my dream, and whatever made Liddy leave town helped me to fulfill it. My husband and I paid Liddy in cash, and well . . . I've been here ever since, and never wanted to be anywhere else."

"Did you pay cash because Liddy was willing to sell cheap?"

"It wasn't cheap—but she did ask for cash."

Michael nodded. "Well, did you ever see her again?"

"No, I paid her more than the place was worth, gave her the money and off she went. Who can put a price on a dream?" Kristi shrugged. "She called me once, about six months after she left, but that was before caller ID. I have no idea where she was calling from, and all she wanted was her portion from the last sale of her work here."

Annabelle took two steps forward. "Where did she have you mail that money?"

Kristi looked back and forth between Michael and Annabelle. "I didn't mail it."

"What did you do with it then?" Michael asked.

"It was a long time ago," Kristi said.

Annabelle felt tentacles of suspicion spring from new-grown roots and wrap around her heart. "I know you remember."

Kristi cringed. "I gave the money to Knox and we never talked about it again and she never called again."

Her knees weak, Annabelle sat on the remaining stool and stared at the painting across the room. "Oh."

"It never crossed my mind that the person on the plane was Liddy—I would've said something. That was the only time I was asked to give Knox anything that had to do with her." Kristi shifted papers on her desk.

Annabelle nodded. "Okay." But the tentacles squeezed tighter.

Michael spoke into the quiet. "Annabelle, don't you have a painting of hers?"

"Yes."

"May I see it?"

She squinted at him through the sunlight coming in from the high windows. "You can see it and you can have it."

He shook his head. "That's not what I'm asking."

"No, but it's what I'm telling you."

A group of five children entered through the front door, talking over one another, laughing and pushing to be first to the art table set up in the back of the room. Kristi hollered to the mothers, "Hello, all. I'll be right with you."

She leaned her elbows on the desk, looked from Annabelle to Michael. "I have to teach my kinder-garten budding artists class now. Please excuse me. If there is anything I can do, please feel free to call. I'm sorry I can't tell you more."

Michael stood. "Have you kept a pictorial record of your sales?"

"I sure have," Kristi said. "I'll make a copy of all Liddy's and Ariadne's sold art. But it won't be ready until late tomorrow. I have too much on my plate today."

"No problem," Michael said, glanced at Annabelle. "I don't mind staying in this town one more day."

Annabelle walked to the front door without saying a word. When she slid behind the driver's seat of her car, she realized that she'd left Michael on the sidewalk. He hollered after her, "I don't know where you live."

She poked her head out the window and heard the breathless quality of her voice, as though someone had taken something significant from her words. "Do you have a car?"

He nodded. "But it's back at the inn. I walked here."

"Then get in," she said, reached over and opened the passenger-side door.

Michael slid into the seat, leaned back and rolled down the window. "I hate that I'm making things hard for you. Since the moment I met you, I've wanted to make them easier."

"You're not making things hard for me. Knox did. Or Liddy did. Or . . . hell, maybe I'm making them hard on myself." Annabelle started the car and pulled out onto Broad Street, following the familiar route until she pulled into her driveway and gestured. "My house."

Michael climbed out and followed her up the front walk to the porch, through the front door. Annabelle pointed to the painting over the hall table covered in today's mail, a set of extra keys, and a note from Grace saying she'd stopped by to say hello. Michael didn't look at the paraphernalia on the table, which Annabelle sifted through to avoid staring at the painting.

Michael touched the frame's edge. "How long have you had this?"

"Since we were first married." Annabelle shrugged. "I knew she painted it, but I didn't think anything of it—just that it was beautiful. See how she painted only in gray and white, but you think that there is blue water because the gray is so transparent. . . . I'm sure there's an artistic word for it, but anyway . . ."

Michael nodded. "Art is always personal. If you like it, then it's beautiful."

Annabelle leaned over the hall table, lifted the painting from the hook. The frame slipped in her hand and slid to the left. Michael grabbed the corner. "Whoa . . . what are you doing?"

"Taking it off my wall. Out of my house."

They shimmied sideways together and set the painting on the hardwood floor. A rectangle remained on the wall where the picture had hung, the rose-and-urn-design wallpaper like brand-new where it had been protected by the art.

Michael bent down to study the painting, turned it over and ran his hand along the back of the canvas. On the bottom right-hand corner was a scrawled signature. He knelt on the floor; Annabelle squatted and leaned over his shoulder to stare at it with him.

"This is the same writing as the Ariadne signature. See the way 'A' and 'E' loop across the letter next to them in this Liddy Parker signature—same way as the 'A' and 'E' in Ariadne." He touched the letters.

Annabelle squinted, unsure how he could read what looked like scratches of paint to her. "What does it say above her name?"

Michael fell silent, stood up. "Here's more proof that they were the same person. I still don't know why she would hide her name." He shrugged. "Can't ask her now, can I?"

"A lot of us have theories," Annabelle said. "And no proof. What does it say above her name?" she repeated, although this time the question came in a whisper.

Michael looked away.

"Tell me," she insisted.

"It says, 'I love you always. . . .'" He looked away from Annabelle as he answered.

The familiar hallway, the center of her home, swayed before her, moved beneath her feet. Anger filled her heart to the edges, overflowed inside her body and consumed her with a need to scream, rant the emotion she had fought against all this time. Grief was allowed; sorrow was permissible—anger seemed a betrayal. Until now. Now she let it take over her mind and body. Simultaneously she understood that she must hide this feeling from Keeley and Jake; this rage was hers alone.

"Michael, I have to go. . . . You can take the painting." Annabelle backed up to the front door.

She walked carefully down the porch steps, her flip-flops making rhythmic slaps. Michael's voice called after her, but Annabelle made it to her car, and then to the beach before the ocean's waves overcame the pounding of her heart, and she fell to the sand, curled into a ball at the edge of a sand dune. She wept.

She couldn't stop weeping any more than she could stop the waves pounding one after the other on the shoreline. A seagull swooped down and past her while a wind rose and lifted the scent of ocean and sea life, rattled the sea oats in a sound like beating wings.

Eventually her tears subsided, and Annabelle curled onto her side with a sea grass mound as a pillow, the cushioned sand a mattress. She wanted to leave the anger here in the warm sun, leave the knowledge of Liddy Parker here. When the FAA had come to her the first time, informed her that Knox's plane had crashed and there was no hope, she had thought, *There is nothing worse than this.* Now she knew she'd been wrong—there was worse than that. First death, then disillusionment—a combined burden she wasn't sure she could carry.

She heard her name being called; Shawn was shouting for her. When his voice came louder and fuller, she lifted her head to realize it was not part of a half-dream, but originated a few feet away.

"Here," she said in a whisper.

His footsteps made the sand dune vibrate, and then he was kneeling next to her. "What are you doing, Belle?"

He sat next to her, pulled her close and laid her head on his chest, ran his hand through her hair. His breathing came fast, and then steadied as she leaned against him. She murmured into his chest, "How did you find me?"

"I know you. I knew where you'd run—or I hoped I did. Then I saw your car."

"Why did you . . . come looking for me?"

"Keeley called me, said you'd left and she didn't know where you went. Some guy—that art historian, I think—was there and she didn't know what was going on."

"She loved him."

"Who, Annabelle?"

"Liddy. She loved Knox."

"How can you know this? You can't go off into your imagination . . . making things up, making them worse."

"She wrote it on the back of the painting she gave him all those years ago. Knox is the man she loved all that time."

"Oh." Shawn sank all the way onto the sand with her.

"He must have loved her. . . . He kept that painting and those words . . . in our house for decades. All during our marriage. How could he have allowed it to hang in the hall, in the entrance to our home?"

Shawn was silent and yet she heard his breathing louder than any words he could have said. "Don't you have anything to say?" she asked.

"What do you want me to say, Annabelle? That he didn't love her? That he didn't have an affair with her? That he was always the ever-loving and perfect Knox?"

Annabelle pulled away from him. "Yes, that's what I want you to say."

He shrugged. "Okay, then. He never would have cheated on you or your family. He was perfect. Now do you feel better?"

"No," she said, pushed at him. "Nobody is perfect."

"Exactly. Do I think he cheated on you? Had an affair? No, I don't. Do I think he was perfect? No, on that count also."

"How can you know for sure?"

Shawn laughed and took her hands in his. "How can I know he wasn't perfect? He dropped the pop-up at third base that would have won us the state championship. He threw his clubs once when he made a bad shot in golf. He accidentally released the largest marlin we'd ever caught, after we spent four hours reeling it in. He caused a fender bender with my car in college and blamed it on the other driver. You need more?"

"I meant, how can you be sure he didn't have an affair? I never said he was perfect. Not once."

Shawn shrugged. "Really. I could've sworn you did."

Annabelle sat up. "He's been gone for over two

years now. Isn't that weird? We talk about him like he's at home, waiting for us to confront him about Liddy. He's gone."

Shawn reached for her, ran his right thumb across her cheek. "Sand."

She placed her hand over his and leaned forward, and when he lowered his head to kiss her, she allowed it. His lips fit onto hers the way she remembered, but thought she'd forgotten. She slid easily into his arms and let herself stop the wondering, the doubting, the never-ending spiral of what-if that had consumed her for weeks, even in her solitude when she thought she had been nurturing her faith in Knox.

All of that faded away, and she was only aware of that particular moment, of the way Shawn's hands slid up her back, the way her heart skipped into another rhythm: one she'd never felt before.

They fell backward, slow and steady onto the sand. She forgot why she'd gone to the beach, to this secluded spot. His kiss caused her to dissolve into the sand as though they were part of it. Then he pulled back, sat up.

She looked up at him, reached for him. He touched her face, and wiped away a tear she hadn't realized was there. "Oh, Belle."

He stood now and she stared at him in disbelief. "What . . . Where are you going?"

He took her hand and pulled her to her feet, although she felt as if her legs would not hold her up. Shawn held her against his chest, ran his hand through her hair. "As much as I want you, as much as I want this— it can't be this way. Not while you weep over Knox. Not while you wonder if he was all you thought he was. Not this way."

Their kiss had been her only sweet release in weeks. "No, I wasn't crying about him . . . not that. I didn't even know I was crying. Don't leave." She wished for darkness or at least twilight so the sun wouldn't beat down on them.

"You've been crying for him for two years." He touched her face again. "I'm not telling you that's wrong. He was and is and always will be the one for you. You can't kiss me like this when you don't mean it for me."

"Why didn't you ever say anything before . . . tell me how you felt?"

"When we were sixteen years old and you chose Knox, I made a decision never to say anything about how I felt. You chose Knox and I loved you and I loved Knox, and that ended the questions and what-ifs of us. He was the best friend I ever had. When he came to me and told me that you and he were dating, that he thought he might be in love with you—I let you go. Or at least I thought I let you go. But you've been a part of me ever since. I can't make you feel the same way; I couldn't do it then and I can't do it now. I won't be second-best either. I won't be the comfort and backup plan."

"But I didn't know then. . . . Why didn't you say anything?"

"Would it have mattered? I saw how much you wanted him—how great you two were together. My proclamations wouldn't have made a damn bit of difference, except to ruin two friendships."

His words burst the haze that had come over her while his hand was in her hair, his lips on her neck. She attempted to deny the truth, but only a small cry came from her throat.

"Come on," he said. "I'll take you home. Keeley is worried about you."

Annabelle followed Shawn through the dunes, tripping over plants and driftwood. When they reached the end of the sand, when the road hit her bare feet, she grabbed his arm. He turned to her and she grasped either side of his button-down shirt, yanked him toward her and kissed him as he had her. The wanting seemed more important to her, in that moment, than knowing the truth. She wanted and needed more than anything she had in months, or even years, for him to want her.

He kissed her back, and she felt more than heard the groan in the back of his throat, in his chest. He pulled away, kept his hand on her shoulder. "Belle, you'll regret this and I won't, and it will ruin everything. Please . . ."

She stared at him, sand on her face, in her hair, tears on her face. Afternoon sunlight fell onto them with harsh reality. His eyes were moist, and Annabelle wanted to know if it was from tears or desire, but his set face and hard hand on her shoulder stopped her words.

"Listen to me. I don't want you to choose this because I'm kind, or your friend, or happen to be here at the right time. Get in the car . . . ," he said, walked her to the driver's side.

"Why do you want me to choose this?"

"Out of longing," he said.

"Oh, Shawn." She dropped her head onto his chest. He lifted her face, stepped back and opened her car door. She yanked the car keys out of her pocket. "I'll just . . . drive home now."

"I'll follow you," he said, and climbed into his own car.

After Annabelle pulled into her driveway, she sat in the car to catch her breath. Shawn appeared at the door, opened it for her. Together they walked up the front porch steps, into the front hallway, where the picture was still propped against the wall, the apothecary jar full of shells on the table. Annabelle walked over, balled her hand into a fist and knocked the glass jar to the floor; shells skittered in wind-chime music across the hard wood.

Annabelle had picked up her foot to squash a starfish, crush it beneath her foot, when Keeley came into the hall. "Mom," she whispered.

Annabelle knelt on the floor, began a frantic attempt to gather the shells, hide the evidence of her lost faith.

"Stop it," Keeley said. "I'll get them."

Annabelle looked up at her. "I knocked the jar over."

Keeley nodded and took a shell in her hand, rolled it upside down and handed it to Shawn. "Thanks," she said to him. "I knew you'd find her."

He glanced between them, then hugged Keeley. "I have to go. . . . Do you need anything else?"

In unison, Keeley and Annabelle said, "Stay."

"I can't."

Keeley looked at her mother, then Shawn. "Please?" she said, quiet and still.

Shawn picked up a handful of shells and placed them on the table, tilted the jar, which hadn't broken, and set it upright. "You two can be awfully convincing. I'll go get us all some pizza . . . and be right back. Okay?"

Keeley smiled at him, then at her mother. "Perfect."

Annabelle stood, whispered, "Thank you."

Shawn peered around the hall. "Did that guy leave?"

"Yes. He said he would call you later, Mom."

Annabelle nodded, pointed at the painting. "Shawn, would you mind taking that with you while you run for pizza?"

He picked up the canvas, tucked it under his arm. "Be right back." He opened the front door with his free hand, and bumped into Jake, who came through the door as he came into life: full-blast.

"Hey, man," he said to Shawn, gave a light punch to his shoulder. "What's up?"

Shawn laughed at Jake. "Off to feed your family. Be right back."

The screen door snapped shut, and they all three

turned to watch Shawn walk across the porch, and then down the front steps.

Jake looked over at Keeley and Annabelle, then at the floor. "Oh, what happened?" A shell crunched beneath his flip-flops.

"Mom knocked over the jar." Keeley dropped in a handful of shells.

Jake bent down and picked up a broken one by his foot, dropped it in also. "Yeah, Mom. Keeley told me about this collection—very cool. I even added a few of my own."

Annabelle looked at her son. "You did?"

"Yeah, we're gonna have to get another jar soon. It's weird how when you start to remember on purpose, more and more stuff comes up. You know?"

"I know," Keeley said, stepped toward her brother.

Annabelle attempted a smile for her children. "Okay, I'm going to shower and we'll have pizza in a few. Okay?" They both stared at her without speaking. She repeated herself. "Okay?"

"Mom, are you all right?" Jake squinted at her.

"Sure," she said.

"Why'd you give Shawn that painting?" Keeley pointed at the rectangle of clean wallpaper.

Annabelle shrugged. "I never really liked it."

"It was a piece by Liddy Parker, wasn't it?" Jake asked.

"Yes, it was."

Keeley and Jake looked at each other. Annabelle lifted her chin and took large but careful steps down the hall toward her bedroom. She needed to carry her doubt gingerly so as not to pass her disbelief about their father onto her children.

Annabelle stood beneath the scalding water, let it pound her back, her thighs, her hair. She scrubbed the sand from her face and scalp. Could Knox have wanted Liddy in the same way she had just wanted Shawn, if only for a moment? Could he have loved his wife and wanted Liddy at the same time? On the sand dune, she had both desired Shawn and loved Knox. Was this only possible when someone was dead and gone? These were questions without answers, and Annabelle let them flow over her just as the shower did, let the unanswerables twist down the drain with the sand and sweat.

When she came into the kitchen in a pair of jeans and an oversized cotton button-down shirt, her wet hair dripping down her back, her face scrubbed clean, Shawn, Keeley and Jake were lifting the top of the pizza box. Hunger rose like a sleeping force, and Annabelle accepted a slice with sun-dried tomatoes, feta and sausage—her favorite. She took a bite, closed her eyes. "Yummm," she said.

Jake laughed. "Hungry, Mom?" He held four plates in his hand.

She glanced at each of them, one by one. "I love you guys," she said. "Really, I do."

Keeley groaned. "Geez, Mom. Just eat."

Shawn turned away, pulled four glasses from the cupboard and set them next to a pitcher of ice water.

"You knew my favorite pizza," Annabelle said.

"Of course," he answered, poured a glass of water and handed it to her.

They all stood around the kitchen bar and devoured the pizza without speaking until Annabelle set down the remains of her final slice. "Wow, you'd think I'd starved y'all."

"Long day," Jake said.

Annabelle seated herself on the bar stool. "Tell me."

Jake took a stool across from her. "You're not gonna like this."

Annabelle shrugged. "Go ahead anyway." A drop of water from her hair plopped onto the floor.

"Sofie is coming to visit."

"Oh." Annabelle looked down at the wet drops from her hair.

Shawn came around the island bar, put his hand on Jake's shoulder. "She's coming to see you?"

"Yeah."

Annabelle looked up now, faked a smile. "Isn't that nice?"

"No," Keeley said. "Not so much. Why in the hell is she coming to see you?" She walked toward her brother. "Please don't tell me you have something going on with her. That is way gross."

Jake shook his head. "We're friends."

Keeley rolled her eyes. "Yeah, that's what Joe told me right before he started dating Jessica. Friends, ha!"

"Keeley," Annabelle said, "it's okay. Really." She looked at Jake. "When is she coming?"

He scrunched up his face. "Tomorrow."

"Oh, I'm not sure how I feel about this. . . ."

"Geez, Mom." Keeley slammed her slice onto the plate. "You sound like you're on drugs."

Annabelle leaned onto the counter to stare at Jake. "Why is she coming? The truth, Jake."

He took in a long breath. "She said she wants to tell us her story."

"What does that mean?" Keeley asked. "Her story? Like we care one minute about her story. How weird is she?"

Jake looked at Keeley. "She is not weird."

"Whatever." Keeley threw her half-eaten slice into the garbage, and then bounded up the back stairs. Jake, Annabelle and Shawn looked at one another in silence until the echo of her slammed door reached the kitchen.

"I think she's lost it." Jake picked up the last piece of pizza.

"I think I want this story to be over," Annabelle said, kissed her son's cheek. "When tomorrow will she arrive?"

"Evening," he said.

"Okay," Annabelle said. "Okay then."

Shawn closed the pizza box. "I've got to go." He lifted his hand in a wave goodbye, moved toward the front hallway.

Annabelle walked with him to the front door. "Call us tomorrow?"

"Why don't you call me if you want to talk?"

She took his hand when they were away from the kitchen, away from Jake's eyes. "Shawn."

He freed her hand, put his forefinger over her lips. "Please don't say anything, but do know this—I have always loved you. Always. Tonight wasn't just about seeing you alone and sad. You have always been in the center of my heart. You are the emptiness in me, and at the same time, you are something complete in me."

He paused, then spoke with a steady, sure voice. "Sounds goofy, doesn't it? It's the only way I know to describe how I feel, but I'll never bring it up again, I promise. Tomorrow just listen to what Sofie has to say . . . and move on. Beyond Knox. Beyond me. Past all this mess."

Annabelle closed her eyes, felt dizzy. "I don't know what is beyond us. . . ."

"You will," he said, kissed her on the forehead. "You will."

She watched him walk across the porch, down the stairs. The light seemed to follow him.

TWENTY-FOUR

SOFIE MILSTEAD

*T*he long drive caused Sofie to feel as though sandpaper were embedded under her eyelids. She had thought adrenaline would carry her all the way into Marsh Cove, but fatigue caught up with her as though it had been chasing her Volvo down the highway.

She entered Marsh Cove and wove her car down the forgotten streets of her young life. She moved past Marsh Cove Elementary, the tabby-and-stucco library and courthouse, then into downtown. She parked in front of the art studio and stared at the front doors, at the people coming and going. She tested herself. Had she really lived here? For so long, her mother had trained her to say she'd lived in Colorado, she had almost come to believe it.

How many lies, she thought, *do we tell others and ourselves before we believe them, and the made-up life becomes more real than reality?*

She rested her head on the steering wheel. When the car's air conditioner threatened to quit, she pulled from the curb and drove to the Murphys' home.

Sofie parked in the bay's paid parking lot, shoved quarters into the slender silver meter and walked the half block to Jake's house. Late-afternoon sun headed toward the horizon to bring twilight to the day: her favorite time. In twilight she believed in possibility.

A bird crowed from a magnolia tree in the yard, dove down to pick something off the lawn, then flew back to a branch. Sofie remembered the tree now, remembered this house and street. As though driving here had opened a dam of water-drenched memories, remembrances of Marsh Cove's streets and houses poured in.

Sofie took a step, then hesitated. She'd called Jake's cell phone, told him she'd stop by around this time, but the house looked empty. Maybe they'd all left to avoid her. She took a breath and one step, then another, and then stood at the foot of the porch steps and realized she'd held her breath the entire way across the street. She breathed in the fresh air, and then startled as a teenage girl opened the screen door. She filled the doorway with her height and presence although she was small, thin and quiet. Wavy brown hair fell past her shoulders, and she wore a pair of rolled-up denim shorts and a boy's white tank top. Her arms were tanned and muscular, her legs long and spread in a stance of defiance.

The girl closed the door, stepped out onto the porch. "Are you Sofie?"

Sofie lost her words, nodded. Coming here was a huge, monstrous, outrageous mistake. How could she have let a few friendly e-mails trick her into doing something so foolish?

The girl looked behind her, then back at Sofie. "You can leave now. We don't want to hear your story." She shook her head a few times as if for emphasis.

Sofie backed a few steps from the house, tripped on a tree root that had forced its way through the brick sidewalk. She caught her balance, grabbed on to a branch and stood her ground. "Is Jake home?"

The girl walked across the porch, down the front stairs to come face-to-face with her. "Why are you here? Hasn't your family caused enough hurt for a lifetime? What makes you think you can come here, ask for my brother, my mother?"

"Keeley?" Sofie asked. "Are you Keeley?"

"Yes, I am. And you're leaving, aren't you?"

Sofie astounded herself with her answer, with her strength. "No, I'm not."

Keeley stamped her foot; tears rose in her eyes. "Get out of here. I hate you. I hate your mother. I hate her art. I hate . . . this entire thing. Get out of here."

Sofie felt an odd urge to hug this girl, to save her from the revulsion that crept over her features. She tried with words. "It's okay, Keeley. I understand. I'm here to take away the pain, not make it worse."

"What is that supposed to mean?"

"Please, just give me a chance to explain. Then you never have to talk to me again."

The two girls were staring at each other, Keeley standing with her arms crossed, Sofie with her hands spread wide, when Jake hollered from the porch, "Hey."

Sofie and Keeley both turned; Jake bounded down the front steps. He hugged Sofie before she could put her hands down. "You made it here safely. Great. You remember Keeley?" He stood with his arm over her shoulder. "Of course she was just a toddler when you lived here."

Warmth spread from Jake's arm, across Sofie's shoulder, through her body, to her heart. "We just had the pleasure of meeting," Sofie said.

Keeley glared at her brother. "You're a disgusting traitor."

"Keeley," he said, the single word a sharp stab.

She spun around, ran toward the house, wrenched

open the screen door, then the wooden door while Sofie and Jake watched her.

"Well," Jake said, tousled Sofie's hair, "welcome to the Murphy home."

"Maybe I shouldn't have come," Sofie said. "I didn't even wait for your response. I just came. Stupid." She banged her hand on her forehead.

"If you'd waited for my e-mail, you'd know I told you to hurry up. I couldn't wait to see you. . . . I'm . . . really glad you're here. Forgive my sister."

"Let's go somewhere else. I was a fool for thinking they'd want to hear my story. I'll just . . . tell you."

Jake turned her to face him. "Sofie, let me ask you this. Does this story have anything to do with my father?"

"Yes," she said, averted her eyes.

"Then it is for all of us to hear. Okay?"

She nodded. Jake took her hand and led her toward the house. They entered the foyer and Jake called for his mother and sister. Sofie glanced around the entranceway. So this was how a real family lived. This was where a real family fought and loved and cried and ate. Tears welled up behind her eyes, gathered in the corners.

Annabelle came from somewhere in the back of the house. Sofie stared at her; she'd always wanted to imagine Annabelle as an ugly woman, an almost-witch, who kept Knox Murphy from them. But here was a beautiful woman with a son, a daughter, and a dead husband. Sofie's heart hurt. She placed a hand over her chest. "Hello, Mrs. Murphy," she said.

"Hello, Sofie." Annabelle nodded once, then gestured into the house. "Why don't we all sit down in the sunroom and have some sweet tea?"

"Sounds nice," Sofie said. "It was a long drive. . . ."

"A long, boring drive," Annabelle said in simple words of solidarity.

"Yes."

"Jake?" Annabelle touched her son's arm. "Will you please tell Keeley to come down?"

"Yes, ma'am." He took the front stairs two at a time, and Sofie watched him until he rounded the top of the banister. He hollered for Keeley.

Sofie followed Annabelle into the kitchen, a large room painted a pale blue-gray—the color of the water in Newboro. Black-and-white photos of the land and sea were arranged on the walls along with photos of Keeley and Jake at various ages. A large framed photo of Jake and Keeley with Knox on the bow of a boat sat on the kitchen desk. Sofie walked over, picked it up. Jake's hair had been lighter then, tousled and wet. Keeley was smiling up at her father. Sofie spoke without thinking. "He was a good father."

"Is that a question or a comment?" Annabelle's voice came from behind her.

Sofie placed the frame back down and turned to her. "A comment. Not because I would know, but because Jake is a good man and that couldn't have happened if he hadn't had a great dad."

Annabelle nodded, handed Sofie a tall glass of iced

tea. "Here, let's sit." She gestured toward the sunroom off the kitchen.

The two women faced each other across an antique trunk painted bright green with small lanterns arranged on the surface. The iced tea glass was slippery with the sweat of the ice cubes. Sofie leaned back on the striped cushions and tried to control her shaking hand as she took a sip.

Keeley and Jake entered the room, and Keeley sat on the couch farthest from Sofie.

"I guess you're probably wondering why I came here," Sofie said.

"I don't care why," Keeley said, folded her arms across her chest.

"Keeley," Annabelle said, "Sofie is our guest. Be polite."

"Go ahead," Jake said, leaned forward and patted her leg.

"I'm here"—Sofie took in a long breath—"to tell you my story. To tell you my mother's story."

Cicadas and frogs began their evening song in the backyard as twilight descended, as possibilities opened wide.

"My mother told me this story ever since I can remember. It is a true story, although I didn't know that until later in life. She told it to me so many times when I was young that I thought it was a fairy tale. I knew it by heart. I don't recall exactly when I realized it was true, that it was my story. I think that sometimes . . . sometimes we don't always know things right away—just slowly. And that's how the truth of this story was for me. . . ."

"Can we move this along?" Keeley said.

"Not another word, young lady," Annabelle said, looked over at Sofie. "Go on."

"My mother was always one to tell stories, use them as another would use Vicks VapoRub on a sick child. She told fairy tales, myths and stories of running and being saved. My mother told me that my name was always Sofie. She said that when she was pregnant with me, she understood from the very beginning that I was a girl and I would fill her with wisdom, which had escaped her in her earlier years."

Jake spread his hands like an offering. "That's what you meant by the woman who gave birth to wisdom."

Annabelle shifted in her chair. "What are you talking about?"

Jake looked at Sofie. "Nothing. I'm sorry. Just go on."

"You're right," she said. "The name Sophia means wisdom and was one of the first words in the Bible for God's wisdom."

"Ridiculous," Keeley said.

Sofie ignored her and continued, feeling the strength of the story swelling. "Mother said the story was about a man with no wisdom. He was a man bent on control. A powerful man who wore a mask of gentility that fooled her into believing that what she saw was real. She'd say to me, always, 'Remember this, my Sofie: what you see is rarely the full truth; things are not what they seem—except in maybe art and nature and even then be careful, be wise.'

"She told me that my father was cruel with his words and with his hands. He hurt her. Badly. But she had no one to turn to for help. She'd come from the poorer section of her city, and this man took care of my mother and moved her mother, my grandmother, to a beautiful resort in Colorado. My mother didn't understand, until later, that he did this to gain complete control over her. In this man, my mother thought she saw a chance to escape from poverty.

"What she didn't know was that sometimes we can escape into something even worse. He married her when she was eighteen. When she was twenty years old, he brought her to Charleston, said he wanted her to have a little vacation while he was on a business trip. She was pregnant with me, but hadn't told him. She didn't want to travel, but she went out of fear and a learned obedience.

"When they arrived in Charleston, she felt as though she had come home. In every piece of her being, she felt as if she'd once been torn from there, although she knew she'd never been there before. Her husband was busy with his work while she wandered the streets of the city that captured her heart. In their preoccupation, they didn't watch the news, didn't pay attention to the incoming hurricane until the hotel personnel informed them that they had to evacuate. My mother felt she could never leave that place, that land. The thought of leaving broke her heart more than it had been broken in those months of fear and abuse."

Fatigue spread through Sofie's body, as though the trapped story took her energy with it as she released it to the Murphy family. She wanted more iced tea, but she didn't ask for it.

"This man was confident in all his ways and didn't believe they needed to evacuate. My mother stood on the deck of their hotel room, the opulence surrounding her like a thick, smothering blanket. She watched a man and woman below her balcony. The man touched the woman's face, moved her hair off her cheek and gazed at her, and my mother knew she'd never experience anything like this with her husband.

"When Mother got to this part of the story, she always placed her palm over the place where my ribs met in a V, and told me, 'There is a sacred place inside you that will always tell you when you see or meet something that is yours, that is for your heart.' She said that when she saw that couple, she understood that this kind of feeling waited for her in this land. She also knew, despite what her husband told her, that the hurricane was coming. She saw it in the wind, the rain, and she also knew I was growing inside her. She decided right then to run with the storm."

Sofie stopped, looked at the Murphy family. Annabelle planted her elbows on her knees, leaned over. "The hurricane was Hurricane Hugo."

"Yes," Sofie said.

"Your mother ran into Hurricane Hugo."

Sofie nodded.

Annabelle looked between her children, seemed to bite back words, then sat back, closed her eyes. "Finish, please."

"Mother said it mustn't look like she ran on purpose, only out of fear of the wind and rain that she actually welcomed. The man—my father—was in the bar, drinking and laughing with other men, joking that anyone should be scared of a little storm. They knew nothing of nature's fury."

"Whoa." Keeley held up her hand. "You keep calling him 'the man.' Who calls their father 'the man'? That's totally weird, don't you think, Jake?"

Sofie pulled her feet under her, curled her spine into the back of the chair. "It's because my mother never told me his name . . . ," she said.

"Oh." Keeley looked around the room. "Oh."

"Anyway, Mother took very little from their hotel room: some cash and all her jewelry—which would not seem odd to a man who liked to see his wife decked in finery to prove his own worth. She left a note saying she didn't want to bother him in the bar with his friends, but she had to go to the drugstore for some things she'd forgotten.

"The note must not raise his suspicions about where she'd gone. She took the rental car and drove as far and fast as she could—past the city limits. She knew she had to make it look as if she'd died in the storm, that she was irretrievably lost.

"The police flagged her down, told her she would not be allowed over the bridge toward the coast, only traffic going inland was permitted. She drove the car down a side road and wound through the streets. She made it as far as the Ben Sawyer Bridge and stopped, stared into the rushing water below. There she saw her answer: clear and running, moving and shaping her life. The traffic was clogged. She drove to the far end of the street that ended where a guardrail remained shattered from a previous accident—a providential one that allowed her to take advantage of another's misfortune. She found a large rock, placed it on the gas pedal, stood outside the car and jammed the gearshift into drive.

"Mother said the car took off like a lightning bolt, throwing her arm backward against her body, ripping a tear in her forearm where the side of the door caught her flesh. She had that scar the rest of her life. . . . Anyway, then she fell and watched the car enter the river without a sound. The fury of the storm and honking cars, of nature's chaos, shrouded the sound of a single car entering the raging river. She stepped back and watched the car move toward the opposite shore, sent up a prayer that it would not wash out to sea. If he was to think she was dead, the car must be found.

"Then she started to walk. And walk. She was scared for me, knew she needed to conserve her strength, find food and water. She walked through the storm, and when night fell and the storm hit its climax, she'd made it to Marsh Cove, where she saw a farmhouse on a small hill.

"There was no strength left in her by then. She

didn't care if the storm took us both—at least we were free of him. She opened the wide red doors of the barn—thick with paint and solid as though they'd been left there for her. The hayloft was warm, dry, and there were no animals. She found out later they'd been moved the day before to a safe place inland. She crawled into the hay, and slept through the storm. Looking back, she didn't see how this was possible— that she slept through the devastation that caused so many deaths, destroyed towns and families and farms.

"Finally hunger woke her—and a panic that she'd threatened my well-being, not just her own. Hungry now, she tried to figure out what to do next, even as she wept with relief—she'd broken free of his chains, ones she thought would bind her forever."

Sofie rubbed her face; this was the part of the story where she could not tell them *every* emotion her mother had shared with her. Only the facts here.

"What happened then?" Keeley had scooted to the edge of her seat. "Is this really true?"

"Yes," Sofie said. "And this is where your father comes in. He came into the barn just then."

Annabelle spoke. "It was Knox's family barn."

"I guess so," Sofie said, closed her eyes and heard her mother's words, remembered how her mother's face would fill with joy when she told the part of the story Sofie would not say aloud now—how her mother would stare into a far-off place as she described the moment she saw Knox Murphy, how she believed she had been made for him and he for her. He threw open the barn doors, sunlight creating a halo around him. He looked to her like heaven.

His face was rugged and covered in stubble, his dark hair tousled by the wind. His eyebrows were dark, like his hair, his eyes a warm brown. His jaw was rounded, but then squared off as it met his ears, and his hair was long, curled at the ends and toward the back. His voice was gravelly and deep when he called out, "Bootsie, are you in here?" He was looking for his cat.

He squinted into the barn and Liddy could see that he was young, her age, but he looked older when he did this, as if certain wisdom were already evident in his features. She held her breath for fear that if he saw her, his features would change, and like a myth, this beautiful creature would turn into something ugly or deformed.

The hay beneath her rustled, and he looked up at her, saw her and stepped back. She wanted to tell him not to be afraid, not to go away. But she couldn't find the words. And, as he did from that day forward, he seemed to know what she wanted to say without her having to speak. He stepped forward, climbed the ladder to the loft and came to her.

Liddy told Knox Murphy her entire story, about how she was pregnant, how she had run and faked her own death to escape an abusive husband. She told Sofie that she never remembered the exact words they had said to each other and part of her believed they'd had this conversation without ever talking. Knox left to get food and water and first aid for the jagged cut on her forearm; he returned to take care of her.

Sometimes he slept there with her, yet never touched her beyond offering the comfort of holding her when fear overcame her. Together, they devised a future for her. They found a solution, and although they never once talked of what existed between them in that hayloft, she thought she and Knox had time, a lifetime, for words unsaid, touches not yet given.

But Sofie did not tell all of this to the Murphy family. She only said, "He came in looking for his cat and found my mother in the hayloft. He helped her through the bad days after the storm and then found a small studio and loft in town, and offered the down payment. She opened the Marsh Cove Art Studio beneath the loft. . . ."

Sofie stopped now, slumped back on the chair. "That's the story you never knew. Knox Murphy saved my mother and helped her start a new life. He helped her get a new name, find a new home. That is what he did."

"How?" Keeley whispered, as if the story had stolen her anger.

"He took an old birth certificate from a flooded and ravaged courthouse closer to Charleston. When the town of Marsh Cove met her, her name was Liddy Parker and she was an artist come there to open the town's first art studio."

Sofie closed her eyes for a moment, remembered what her mother had told her about the flat above the art studio. Knox had the flat painted all in white—

white walls, white furniture, white bed with a white quilt. It was as though he had washed her clean of the past. He told her she could add the color, she could choose her new life. But in the end, she could not choose him.

"Were they . . . a couple?" Keeley's breath caught inside her question.

Sofie looked across the room at Knox's daughter. "No. He told her he was engaged to his high school girlfriend. He only helped her."

"Why did you leave Marsh Cove all those years later?" Annabelle asked.

"The way Mom told it, a man from Ohio came and bought a piece of her art. This man took the piece home, and my father saw it in a display at a party, then called the art studio looking for the artist, since he thought it looked just like something his dead wife might have done. Mother was terrified he would find us. So we had to move. Knox helped us choose a new place, and helped Mom change our name from Parker to Milstead."

This also Sofie did not tell the Murphy family—that when she was in high school and her boyfriend broke off their relationship, Sofie was so brokenhearted that her mother confided in her as she never had before. She told Sofie that their secret life would have its casualties. That her own heart was still broken for Knox. She'd thought that being gone from him would cure her of wanting him, but it hadn't. This desperate desire for Knox Murphy never left Sofie's mother.

"We didn't see Knox much through the years. He came when Mother was in a bad situation." Sofie avoided eye contact. "When she ran out of money, or needed to see her own mother. He came about once every two years. He was so good to us. I don't think I can make clear to you how he saved us, how he . . . made sure we were okay."

"That last time he was taking her to see her mother?" Jake's voice filled the silence.

"Mother wouldn't fly commercial airlines since she constantly feared she would be caught with her fake ID. Yes, Knox was taking her to see my dying grandmother, but they never arrived. That day, that terrible day, I lost my mother and . . . a dear friend. Then two weeks later, I lost my grandmother."

Sofie glanced around the room cast in soft light from the setting sun. Annabelle was silent; Keeley had placed her hands over her face; Jake sat back on his chair. Finally Annabelle spoke. "Why did you keep this a secret? Why couldn't you have told us?"

"I didn't want my father to find me. Michael Harley and all of you were suddenly asking about a woman who was dead and never wanted to be found. She taught me to make sure I never, ever told anyone who we were—or he would come after us. After me. She knew he would kill us both. Mother told me this fact all my life. I have never spoken a word about him, or what happened. Fear has held me tight. Mother didn't tell me the most terrible parts until I was older. When I was a child, she only told me he was bad, that he mustn't find us, like a real live boogeyman. It wasn't until I was in high school that she told me how he beat her, how he . . ." Sofie hesitated. "I have hidden my identity for fear of this man. I'm sorry for any pain it has caused you."

Jake stood, came to her. "He can't touch you, Sofie. He doesn't know you exist."

"He would have if Mother's name and story came out sooner. But you know what? Here is the craziest part—it doesn't matter anymore."

"Why not?" Keeley asked. "Why would it matter all this time and not now?"

"A few weeks ago, I dug through our old papers, and found my mother's Ohio driver's license and original name. I called an . . . investigator and asked him to find out everything he could about my mother. He called back within a day to say that the information was so easy to find he wouldn't even charge me."

"What information?"

Embarrassment overwhelmed Sofie, and she turned away to speak these words. "I've been hiding from a man who has been in jail for five years."

"What?" Keeley spoke first.

Annabelle stood, came to Sofie's side. "You're telling us that my husband helped you and your mother hide from a criminal who has been locked up for years?"

Sofie turned. "I don't think she knew it. She never sought him out. She was so scared of him that she had become accustomed to hiding. The investigator found the newspaper articles about my mother's supposed death in Charleston, then about how my father—a man named Brayden Collins—was convicted of killing a man in a bar fight five years ago."

"Damn," Jake said.

"This is ridiculous. My dad died protecting your mother . . . and she didn't even need it?" Keeley asked.

Annabelle placed her hand on Sofie's shoulder. "We can only act on what we know. All we can live with is the part we do understand."

Sofie spoke over her shoulder. "I should have . . . tried to find out sooner. I should have. . . . I don't know why my mother didn't try and find out . . . or tell me."

"Maybe she liked her life exactly the way it was," Annabelle said in a quiet voice. "We all get used to things the way they are, and we can't imagine them any other way."

Sofie looked at Annabelle. "All his power over my life . . ."

"What power?" Jake asked.

"The power of making us afraid. My mother perfected the art of keeping secrets: from me, from Knox, from your family. But it's over now."

Jake touched her elbow. "Thank you," he said.

"That's why I came. The one thing I feared—my father discovering my name—is also the one thing I've craved, that this secret would no longer hold any power over my life." She looked at each of them in turn and thought of the turmoil that could have been avoided, the hurt and pain that should never have existed.

"Are you okay?" Annabelle asked.

Sofie nodded as a terrible thought crossed her mind: *Maybe Mother needed Knox more than she needed the truth.*

There would be many more thoughts and emotions to examine and try to understand. Revealing the story to the Murphy family ended one chapter and began another. "I'll show myself out," Sofie said, turned and walked from the room. She followed the long hall to the front door and out into the evening. She didn't hear Jake come up behind her until he clasped her elbow. "Oh," she said, stumbled.

"You are a brave woman," he said, and placed his hands on both her shoulders, pulled her close and kissed her.

For the first time in her life, she understood what her mother had meant when she said that just being with the right person can fill the empty places.

Jake ran his hand up her back, into her hair, and then released her.

"Jake," she whispered, "these past few weeks, I've had to let go of so many things, and I'm glad I did. But there is one thing I don't want to let go of."

"What is that?"

"You," she whispered into the twilight.

TWENTY-FIVE

ANNABELLE MURPHY

*A*nnabelle and Keeley stared at each other across the sunroom. Mosquitoes buzzed outside the screen door; the condensation from the iced tea glasses formed puddles on the side tables.

"Okay then," Keeley said.

"Are you really okay?" Annabelle moved to sit next to her daughter on the couch, pulled her onto her shoulder and ran her fingers through her hair.

"I'm not sure, Mom. I mean, if all that stuff is true— then we didn't know everything about Dad."

"I'm not sure you can ever know everything about anyone, even someone you love."

"Her mother loved Dad. She didn't say it, but I can tell."

"Liddy Parker might have loved your father, but you can't make someone love you back if their heart belongs somewhere else."

Keeley sat up. "You really believe that?"

"Yes, I do," Annabelle said. "Just like I can't make myself stop loving him just because he's gone."

Keeley nodded. "I know."

"Love isn't something you can make happen at will, or because it's convenient."

"Why didn't he tell us?"

"He made a promise to help her, protect her . . . or at

least that's my best guess. If he told anyone, he risked jeopardizing her safety. He didn't anticipate that the secret would one day bring all this pain to us. He thought he was doing something . . . good."

"He was." Keeley rubbed her face. "He was doing something good, wasn't he?"

"Yes." Annabelle nodded. "But it sure didn't look like it for a while, did it?"

"Guess we can't always judge things by how they look."

"Guess not." Annabelle laughed, smoothed her daughter's hair.

"But on his last trip to help her, she didn't even need it."

"He didn't know that."

Keeley stood. "I hate this."

Annabelle stood to face her daughter. "I do, too."

"I'm going to Laura's house. She's having a few people over tonight. Can I have the car?"

"You have two more days until you get the car keys back."

Keeley exhaled through pursed lips. "I'll walk."

Annabelle went into the kitchen, grabbed the car keys off the hook on the wall and threw them to her daughter. "Be careful."

Keeley brightened. "Always," she said.

Annabelle stood alone in the kitchen and tried to remember where she had been on the exact date of the hurricane—sometime between September twenty-first and twenty-second. She'd been at Aunt Barbara's with the knowledge of a child growing inside her. Knox had been helping a stranded, abused and pregnant woman in his family's barn. It didn't seem possible that these two events could have happened simultaneously, that those two moments had existed within the same universe and then branched off into separate lives in which Knox Murphy played a central role in both.

Annabelle went to her desk, flicked the computer on, and typed in bold letters at the top of the page: TO BELIEVE. Then she began to write of the need to believe when doubt seemed larger and more powerful.

When she was done, she leaned back in her chair and stared at her first article for Mrs. Thurgood's living section. Then she e-mailed it for her boss to see first thing in the morning. She walked down the hall and passed the jar of shells; she plucked one out, took it to place on her bedside table.

Liddy Parker might have had a talent for creating beautiful canvases and for keeping elaborate secrets, but those were not the most important forms of art. Believing when all the facts seemed to point to disbelief, keeping the faith when the circumstances fostered doubt—those were the true art forms.

Annabelle woke the next morning and knew that it was more than a new day; it was the start of a new life. Keeley and Jake were asleep in their beds; Sofie was in a hotel across town that Annabelle had arranged for her. And Annabelle didn't need to know what would happen next. She just needed to kiss her children and take another step forward. After a jog on the beach, a shower and a strong cup of coffee, she responded to Mrs. Thurgood's earlier "Come now" barked into her phone machine, headed to the *Marsh Cove Gazette* offices.

The room full of reporters buzzed as though mosquitoes had been released inside the building. There was a developing story about a car accident downtown involving the mayor and an open bottle of bourbon. Annabelle laughed as she wove her way among the desks. Her and Knox's story was old news. No one cared now how it had ended, how Knox Murphy had protected and cared for a woman he had found in a hurricane.

Annabelle knocked on Mrs. Thurgood's door, then entered in response to a raspy "Come in."

Mrs. Thurgood motioned to the chair in front of her desk. "Sit," she said.

Annabelle remained standing. "No, thank you. You called, asked to see me."

Mrs. Thurgood laughed. "I just wanted to talk to you about the piece you sent."

Annabelle nodded. "Go ahead."

"It is the best piece of work you've ever done for the paper. You know I don't particularly like to give compliments—it breeds laziness. But this is good, quite good. I want you to start that new column we discussed and address your observations about life from the perspective of the Southern Belle."

Annabelle sat down. "I can't write what I was writing for the Southern Belle column. I can't give you that good-girl Belle anymore. I wish I could, but I see things a little differently now. I'm not sure that perfect advice is always the best advice. For me, things aren't as black-and-white, or as neat, as they used to be."

Mrs. Thurgood stood up. "That is exactly what I want to hear. We will now have a brand-new column from the new and improved Southern Belle. It will be fresh, it will be original and it will be witty and sharp and funny."

"Whoa." Annabelle held up her hand. "I don't know if I can be all those things."

"You, my dear, already are." Mrs. Thurgood winked. "Now get out and do your job. I have an up-to-the-minute scandal to report today."

Annabelle laughed, stood up. "Yes, ma'am," she said, and walked out of the offices with her next article already brewing in the back of her mind: *Belle Wakes Up.*

Annabelle pulled her car in front of the art studio, shoved a quarter in the meter and entered the room as the bell over the door announced her arrival. Kristi hollered from the back room, "I'll be right with you."

"Okay," Annabelle replied. To avoid Ariadne's painting on the far-right wall, Annabelle walked to the shelves of pottery and picked up a mug with a palm tree etched into the side. Mumbled voices came from the back room. Her head snapped up; she heard her son's voice.

"Jake?" Annabelle called out as she headed toward the back.

He poked his head around the corner. "Hey, Mom. Come in here."

It took several seconds for Annabelle to register the scene before her: Sofie holding up a painting of a starfish, Jake's hand on her back, Kristi with a magnifying glass raised to the left corner.

"What are you doing?" Annabelle asked.

Jake took his hand off Sofie's back. "Sofie is selling this painting to Kristi. Her mother started it, but Sofie finished it. Isn't it beautiful?"

Annabelle forced herself to look at the painting. "Yes, it is." She turned to Sofie. "Why are you selling it?"

"This"—Sofie pointed to the art—"was my mother's life. This painting and all the secrets that were part of it were hers, not mine. I don't want them."

"Kristi," Annabelle said, "you should call Michael Harley. He'll want this piece. I know he will. Or he'll at least want to see it."

Jake squinted at his mother. "Who's Michael Harley?"

Sofie answered, "The art historian who came to Newboro."

"Oh," Jake said. "Mom? What are you doing here anyway?"

"I actually came to ask Kristi if she'd take the canvas I had in my house . . . on commission."

Kristi looked around the room. "Shawn already dropped it off. He said you'd probably come here about it."

Annabelle laughed. "He knows me a bit too well, doesn't he?"

Sofie walked toward Annabelle, stood in front of her and then hugged her. Annabelle took a moment to overcome her surprise, and then she reached her arms around this lost child and returned the hug. When she glanced over her shoulder, she swore there were tears in her son's eyes.

When, later, they all paused outside the art studio, Jake pulled his mother aside. "Can Sofie stay with us until she figures out what she's gonna do?"

She shook her head. "No, but I'm sure we can find her a place to stay. Mae has the apartment over her barn, or—"

"Hey, that's a great idea." Jake grabbed the cell phone from his back pocket. "Thanks, Mom," he called over his shoulder as he returned to Sofie's side, and they moved down the sidewalk together.

Now Annabelle could stop thinking about Liddy Parker's life and concentrate on her own. Tonight she could return to the friends she had avoided.

Annabelle stood outside Cooper and Christine's house, thought of that bottle of Tickle Pink she'd shared with Shawn, of the ties that had bound them together through so many wonderful, troubled and imperfect times. She entered the house without knocking. Cooper, Christine, Mae, Frank and Shawn stood in the living room holding wineglasses and talking. They all turned as she came in.

"Annabelle." Shawn said her name with a smile, took the dish of peach cobbler from her hands.

Christine came over, pecked her cheek. "What a fantastic surprise. I thought you'd given up on us."

"Never," Annabelle said. "You don't ever give up on best friends, do you?"

In minutes the dance of their friendships resumed with a only few missteps. Frank told very bad jokes; Shawn imitated the mayor being arrested; Christine bustled around the house, and Cooper cornered Annabelle in the hallway. "Are you okay?" he asked.

"Yes, I am now," she said.

"We've really missed you."

"I've missed y'all, too," she said. "I found out why . . . or at least part of why Knox was on that plane with Liddy Parker. I'll tell everyone over dinner."

Cooper smiled, kissed her cheek. "You are amazing."

"Aw, shucks," she said. "You've just had one too many martinis."

Cooper threw his head back and laughed so loud that Shawn came into the hallway. "What's up?"

Cooper slapped Shawn's back. "What would we ever do without Belle?"

Shawn looked at Annabelle, then quickly averted his

gaze. "I don't know, Cooper, but if you figure it out, let me know."

Cooper didn't answer since he'd already moved down the hall to holler for everyone to come to the table, dinner was served.

When the night had wound down, when the wine bottles were empty and the peach cobbler gone, Annabelle told her best friends the story of Knox and Liddy and Sofie. Afterward, silence filled the room until Mae spoke.

"How could we have never known any of this?"

Christine looked at Cooper. "Did you know?"

"No," he said, touched his wife's arm. "Obviously no one did."

Christine gestured toward Annabelle. "You okay about all this?"

Annabelle nodded. "Yes."

"You don't care that he kept this secret from you all during your marriage?" Christine asked.

Mae spoke in Annabelle's silence. "Whether we know everything about the people we love or not, we know we love them," Mae said and kissed her husband.

Cooper lifted his wineglass as if to make a toast, then set it down. "You know, we all need to keep pieces of ourselves that are ours alone."

The table fell silent. Annabelle imagined each person thinking of the one or many secrets they kept to themselves, things they didn't share even with those they loved most. How hard it must have been for

Shawn to share one of the secrets he'd carried for years; in her heart she reached out toward him across the table. She caught his eye and smiled at him; he gave her a nod and half-smile in return.

Annabelle was ready to go home. "Thanks for a great night, Cooper and Christine. I'll get my dish tomorrow. I'm more tired than I realized. The party is at my house next time." They all agreed, and she offered hugs to her friends before she walked out the front door.

Shawn met her outside. "Hey, I know you walked here. Come on, I'll give you a ride."

"Thanks," she said. "I'm so tired all of a sudden."

He opened the passenger door. She climbed in, looked at him. "How's the new business going?"

He slid behind the wheel, started the car. "Good. It should be off the ground by next month."

"Great." Annabelle leaned back on the seat, and they drove in companionable silence until he parked across the street from her house. She looked over at him. "Thanks, Shawn. No need to walk me in."

He nodded. "I'll wait until you're safely inside."

She left the car, then leaned into the window, stared at him for a moment. "We're okay, aren't we? You mean so much to me. . . ."

He opened the driver's-side door and got out; she stood and looked at him over the top of the car while he spoke. "I can't change the way I feel, but neither can you. We're fine. Always have been. Always will be."

Annabelle nodded. "Good night, dear friend."

She walked across the street, and stopped on the sidewalk in front of her house. Two figures sat under the porch light, where a blue hue from the painted ceiling fell onto their faces. Jake and Sofie.

Jake's laugh echoed across the night; his fingers touched Sofie's cheek and she leaned into his palm, answered his laugh with hers.

After Shawn had revealed his love, Annabelle had told him that his confession broke life into pieces she couldn't put back together.

She'd been wrong.

Jake and Sofie—imperfect, rough-edged and broken pieces—were coming together to make something beautiful.

She glanced to where Shawn stood waiting for her to enter the house safely. She knew he couldn't see her; she walked across the street, startled him when she came to his side and spoke. "I once told you that our lives were broken into pieces I couldn't put back together."

"I know, Belle. I remember." He leaned on the car door.

"Well, maybe broken things can't be fixed, but maybe they can come together to make something that is a little imperfect, rough around the edges, but entirely new." She took his hand, wound her fingers through his.

His smile showed in the dark before he whispered, "Entirely new." He lifted their entwined hands to his lips.

Behind Shawn, a full moon trembled on the very edge of a horizon into which Annabelle had once wished she could disappear. Now she wanted to stay exactly where she was, until a new day lighted the thin edge of beauty where water met sky.

QUESTIONS
FOR DISCUSSION

1. Did you enjoy *The Art of Keeping Secrets*? What parts did you like best? Least? What do you consider the strongest aspects of the novel? The weakest?

2. Annabelle struggles to believe in her husband's love, but he's not there to talk to. Are there people in your life, dead or merely gone, with whom you wish you could discuss their true feelings about some past event?

3. Like Annabelle, have you ever faced a situation in which something fundamental about your life suddenly seemed uncertain? Were you able to keep on believing? Why or why not?

4. Do you think most married women worry and wonder whether their husbands have remained faithful? If so, why do you think that is? Do men worry about their wives in the same way?

5. How does Patti Callahan Henry use the gathering of shells in this novel? Do you have a ritual in your own life that has helped you through a hard time?

6. Annabelle and her best friends come to the conclusion that "we all have our secrets." Do you agree? Do

you think we keep secret parts of ourselves from even those we love most? Do you think Knox should have told Annabelle about Liddy and Sofie?

7. Have you lost someone and then discovered something eye-opening—even shocking—about them after they were gone?

8. Mrs. Thurgood tells Annabelle that it's not about what the reader *needs* to hear, but what the reader *wants* to hear. Do you think people who ask for advice want the truth, or to hear their own preconceptions reaffirmed?

9. Liddy and Shawn both talk about the agony of loving someone who doesn't return the feeling. Have you ever loved someone who didn't love you back? How did you handle it?

10. If you were Sofie, would you tell Annabelle and Jake *everything* as soon as they arrive in Newboro? Is Sofie justified in keeping her secrets for as long as she does?

11. Why do you think Sofie was attracted to Bedford? Why does she stay with him?

12. Which is your favorite novel by Patti Callahan Henry, and why?